ORIGINALS

NEW WRITING FROM
BRITAIN'S OLDEST PUBLISHER

This is the fourth year of JM Originals,
a list from John Murray.
It is a home for fresh and distinctive new writing;
for books that provoke and entertain.

A Kind

of Freedom

Margaret Wilkerson Sexton

JM ORIGINALS

First published in the US in 2017 by Counterpoint

First published in Great Britain in 2018 by JM Originals
An imprint of John Murray (Publishers)
An Hachette UK Company

1

A CIP catalogue record for this title is available from the British Library

ISBN 978-1-47367-959-7
Ebook ISBN 978-1-47367-960-3

Printed and bound by CPI Group (UK) Ltd, Croydon, CR0 4YY

John Murray policy is to use papers that are natural, renewable and recyclable
products and made from wood grown in sustainable forests. The logging and
manufacturing processes are expected to conform to the environmental
regulations of the country of origin.

John Murray (Publishers)
Carmelite House
50 Victoria Embankment
London EC4Y 0DZ

www.johnmurray.co.uk

For my mother, who also cheered

Still running with bare feet, I ain't got nothing but my soul. Freedom is the ultimate goal. Life and death is small on the whole, in many ways. I'm awfully bitter these days 'cause the only parents God gave me, they were slaves, and it crippled me.

—TALIB KWELI, "Four Women"

They were the children of once-upon-a-time slaves, born into a kind of freedom, but they had traveled down through the wombs with what all their kind had been born with—the knowledge that God had promised next week to everyone but themselves.

—EDWARD P. JONES, *All Aunt Hagar's Children*

Evelyn

Winter 1944

Later, Evelyn would look back and remember that she wasn't the one who noticed Renard first. No, it was her sister, Ruby, who caught the too-short right hem of his suit pants in her side view. Ruby was thicker than Evelyn, not fat by a long shot, but thick in a way that prevented her from ever feeling comfortable eating. Her favorite food was red beans and rice, and Monday was hard on her. Their mother would boil a big pot and feel relieved, two pounds plenty to feed the family for at least three days, but Ruby felt taunted by the surplus. She'd cut in and out of the kitchen the beginning of the week, sneaking deep bowls of rice and applying as little gravy as she could to maintain the flavor but not alert her family to her excess. Then on Thursday, she'd examine the consequences. It would start in the morning on the way in to school. Ruby attended vocational school and Evelyn attended Dillard University, but their campuses were only a few blocks apart, and they walked the majority of the way together.

"My thighs are touching," Ruby would say, as if they just started touching the minute before.

"You can't see it though," Evelyn would assure her, her own legs so far apart another leg could fit between them.

"Who are you fooling with 'you can't see it'? Anybody with eyes could see it. You don't even need to have eyes; you just need ears, and you could hear my thighs swishing together."

"You can't hear anything so soft," Evelyn would go on, and she'd spend the rest of the day wading through that topic. Just when she'd think she got to flat land, Ruby would pull her back into the murk with a question about her behind. Matters would improve a little on Friday, but Ruby would maintain an edge around her even then, and everyone near her felt the prick. Today was a Friday.

"His pants legs are uneven," Ruby said about the new boy standing on North Claiborne and Esplanade wearing a brown wool suit, a grey V-neck sweater beneath the jacket. He stood next to Andrew, whom all the girls fawned over at the debutante ball last season. Evelyn's own escort had been second in charm; he had even silenced her nerves by pointing out his friends' waltzing mishaps, but despite her mother's urgings, she hadn't accepted his visit, and a week later when his interest subsided, she couldn't help but sigh.

She looked up now, exhaled the smoke of the cigarette dangling from her fingers. It was still early February, and the winter air hadn't lost its chill. Still all the Seventh Ward girls congregated after school outside Dufon's Oyster Shop, the best Negro-owned restaurant in the city, and smoked. Evelyn had come to relish the anticipation of the first, slight inhale—she was a lady—and the long release afterward. She would never have referred to herself as an anxious person—Ruby had claimed that role in the family—but any nerves that jingled inside her settled at just the thought of a drag. She blew the smoke out of the side of her mouth so as not to hit her sister and smiled at the thought of the uneven hem. "Maybe he was in a rush."

"Even still," Ruby said, breathing in so sharply she almost made herself choke. "He might have found time to even out his pants' hems," she laughed. "Cute though. Too brown for most people, but it is a nice shade of brown."

Evelyn nodded. Cute he was.

Men and women rushed past them, bustling in and out of offices and stores, the Boot Seed and Feed, Queen of the South Coffee, Miller Funeral Home, Meriwether's Photography, Bejoie Cut-Rate Pharmacy, the Sweet Tooth Ice Cream Parlor, and Fine Time Billiard Hall. The outdoor market where Evelyn's mother made groceries was just a block away at St. Bernard Avenue, and Evelyn could smell the Cajun spices simmering. The butcher let out a high-pitched call. "Veal to roast, and cabbage and green beans."

Ruby raised her voice to combat the new noise, "And his hair lays so flat, and that's not a conk either."

The uneven man looked over at the girls then, and Evelyn held his gaze for less than a second, so quick if he doubted it had happened, he could convince himself it hadn't.

She shook her head back at her sister. "No, much more natural looking than a conk."

"All that, but he couldn't hem the pants evenly."

"I wouldn't have ever noticed those pants if you hadn't hit me over the head with it, Ruby," Evelyn said, though it wasn't true. It was clear that despite his pressed suit and neat tie, the uneven man didn't belong among the *passé blancs* he stood with, no, not with their damn near-white skin, straight black hair and even straighter nose, their moustaches like silk against their lips, and she didn't know what possessed her to declare otherwise. She liked what she'd said though, not only that, but the fact that she said it, and for the rest of the day whenever she thought of the uneven man, she thought of the weight of her voice when it came out firm.

Since that day was a Friday, she had to go the whole weekend without seeing him again. That was fine because she had memorized him. Evelyn was in her second year of nursing school at Dillard University, and for a Negro woman to even consider such a rigorous field, she had to be up on her memorization. Because of it, she didn't need to see a face more than once to imagine it fully, and she spent the weekend doing just that. She remembered details she hadn't even known she'd seen in the first place: that the shorter hem of his pants revealed a faded grey sock. That he was the color of ginger cookies her mother might bake then sprinkle sugar over, that that similarity made his skin seem like something she might taste, that he was tall, taller than her daddy even who was six three, that he was skinny, but not breakable, that he had small slivered eyes that when she caught them seemed to be breaking through their lids with something vital to say. When she thought on him longer, she realized he had been holding a biochemistry textbook, probably studying to be a doctor. Just like Daddy. Maybe he could help her with amino acids. In all her memorization, she couldn't get the codes straight.

The following Monday, Evelyn led the way from her house on Miro Street to St. Bernard Avenue then North Claiborne, her sister swishing behind her, and looked for a cigarette, feeling steadied by it even as she reached through her pocketbook. Sure enough, the uneven man walked up halfway through her smoke. He was with Andrew again, a boy with an even hem, but something lacking, and maybe it was an uneven hem, which she'd grown used to associating with comfort.

"That ol' *passé blanc* has a smug look on his face," Ruby said about Andrew. "He must think he's too much."

"He's cute," Evelyn said, smiling while she talked in case the uneven man looked over.

"Not so cute he can't look at a woman decently," Ruby said. "Besides, not as cute as Langston." Langston was her last boyfriend, and he had been cute all right, so cute Ruby had heard from a senior at vocational school that he was carrying around phone numbers for every girl in the Seventh Ward with hair past her bra strap. Ruby had taken that hard, which meant their mother cooked her favorite food all week, and every sentence Evelyn directed at her was presented like a question that had no business being asked. When Ruby had gotten over it, she had sworn off the light brights, but here she was again.

"I could do better," Ruby said, "and I have done better, but he's over there looking like he's the best I could do in the state of Louisiana. Not so," Ruby added.

"He's not so bad, just putting on a show," Evelyn said. The uneven man looked up at her again. He leaned, whispered something to his friend, and both men walked over. Ruby's man was leading the way, which confused Evelyn but didn't deter her. When the men reached the girls, Ruby's stood in the front right beside Ruby, and the uneven man lingered in the back watching his shoes. They were okay shoes, Evelyn noticed. One-tone lace-up oxfords that had been shined too many times. She hadn't seen them the day before in all the fuss about the hem, and they were okay, but certainly no competition for the rose blush she had applied to her soft nearly white face, or for the long hair Mother had straightened the night before and which Evelyn had rolled into a coil at the base of her head. She stared at him, holding her head high and still, feeling as if she was pushing her chin forward to coax him into talking.

"How do you do there, young lady?" Ruby's man asked.

Ruby was most confident Monday afternoon. They hadn't gotten back to Mother's yet, and those beans were still at the top of the pot.

"Not as good as I was when it was just me and my sister," Ruby answered.

"So that's your sister, huh?"

"That's what I said, isn't it? You're not too quick on your feet, are you?"

"Y'all are some pretty sisters. Your mama must be pretty too, huh?"

"Why are you asking about my mama?" Ruby wasn't even fooling this time; she was fierce when it came to their mother.

"Aw, I was just making conversation, lil' girl. Don't get ya panties all up in a knot."

"You certainly don't need to know a thing about my panties," Ruby said, trying to maintain her frown, but it was hard on her pretending to be so uninterested. She had a weakness for red beans and red boys. And then that talk about her panties.

Evelyn couldn't take it anymore; she could feel her face heating. The uneven man was lost in his shoes, and she was just standing there, being ignored, as if she weren't the one Daddy twirled around the parlor for their extended family when he drank more than one glass of Sazerac after Christmas dinner.

Evelyn moved her books around in her hands to get his attention. The uneven man looked up, but when he saw her, he looked down again. Evelyn hadn't noticed the color of his eyes the other day either. They weren't so brown they were black like most people's his color. They were an actual brown, the way the color came out in the crayon box. He had long eyelashes, and their tips might have touched the top of his cheeks when he blinked. He looked up again.

"You two are sisters?" he asked, stammering over the word *sisters*, and as he spoke he lifted his grey felt fedora and pressed it into his chest.

"We are," Evelyn said, nearly sighing she was so relieved.

"Are you the oldest?"

"How'd you know that? Everyone always thinks she's the oldest 'cause she's—" Evelyn almost said the word *vocal* but didn't want to sound resentful.

"I could just tell." He looked down again.

"How many brothers and sisters do you have?" Evelyn asked, partly to keep the conversation flowing and partly because she was interested.

"Twelve living, two dead," he said.

"Are you the oldest too?"

"No ma'am, the baby. My mama died having me."

Evelyn's heart was beating fast, and she was feeling powerful emotions she didn't know how to read. It wasn't what he was saying, but the way he was parceling out his story, like a mother would cut meat for a child, that made Evelyn's heart feel fragile. She moved forward a little and hoped Ruby wouldn't see her do it.

"Where do you live?" she asked.

"Amelia Street, Twelfth Ward, two blocks from Flint-Goodrich Hospital."

Evelyn was surprised to hear that. Though she knew he wasn't one of them, she didn't think he was that far off. She looked down at his books again, large hardbacks, biology and organic chemistry. She'd been right; he would have had to be premed to be studying subjects like those, but there weren't any well-off Negro people uptown. She considered his hem again. She never cared about status the way Mother and Ruby did; it was more how unaccustomed she was to being wrong.

"Where do you live?" he asked. His stammer was back this time on the first word, *where*.

Evelyn smiled again. She told him, and he raised his eyebrows. The Seventh Ward—it was a mostly Creole area of rich and poor and everything in between, but he looked at her as if he could envision her massive bungalow, as if he knew her daddy had birthed every one of the babies on the block except the white family's across the street.

Ruby and her man seemed to be finishing up their talk. The uneven man looked over at them, then back to Evelyn.

"What's your name?" he asked.

"All that talking, and you still don't have the name?" Ruby cut in.

Evelyn wanted to shush her, but that wouldn't be polite. She smiled even wider. "Evelyn," she said, addressing the uneven man as if her sister had said nothing.

"I'm Renard," he said. "Renard August Williams." He turned away as soon as he said that.

Evelyn wanted to reach out, spin him around, and get him to commit to something further as soon as could be, but she stayed in her spot and mouthed the word *good-bye*. His friend followed him off, glancing at Ruby over his shoulder.

Evelyn's cigarette had dwindled to a stump and almost burned her fingers. She startled and threw it down, stamping her foot on it harder than necessary.

"You're excited, huh, girl?" Ruby asked. She started walking toward home, and Evelyn followed her. Ruby didn't wait for her to answer.

"Those damn near-white boys are all the same, think they're too cute to ask you on a proper date."

"He didn't ask you out either?"

"Are you crazy? He did, but I could tell he didn't think he had to. I had to lead him over to it."

"Oh." Evelyn paused. "When is it?"

"This weekend. He wants to take me to Dufon's, says he knows the owner. That's another thing about them. They always have to boast, but Mama says, if you have, you have, and you don't have to talk too much about it. Not that I think he doesn't have. His daddy helped found Valena C. Jones Elementary."

"Yes, chairman of the library committee," Evelyn mumbled.

Ruby didn't seem to hear her. "And Daddy says his daddy's real active in the Seventh Ward Civic League," she went on. "I may play it cool before I let him know I'm the one he's been looking for." She paused as if she suddenly realized she wasn't onstage. "What about you, Evelyn? When is he taking you? Maybe we can go together, for the first part at least."

"We're not," Evelyn said. She couldn't bring her head up, but she didn't let it drag either. It was more level than anything. She looked ahead. Ruby wasn't as pretty as Evelyn, not as smart either, and Evelyn had tried to muffle herself her whole life to even them out. Here they were though, Evelyn pushing twenty-two and Ruby only twenty, and it was Evelyn who hadn't gotten a number.

"What, Evelyn? You didn't even get him to ask you on a date? Haven't I learned you anything?" Ruby studied the air in front of her own face, as if the key to Evelyn's incompetence might spring out of it. Then clarity came on her hard and fast. "You're too nice to these boys, that's what I've been telling you. They're only good for two things, marriage and babies, and you're trying to make friends with them. I'm your friend, you only need one. Next time you see him, make him work for it, and watch." Then she laughed, tipped her head back as she turned, skipping beneath the sprawling oaks. Her pleated silk skirt waved behind her in the wind. Evelyn's was the same material and color, but Ruby had asked their mother to take her hem in higher. Now Evelyn walked faster to keep up with her sister even as she felt the straps of her cork-soled shoes pressing into her ankles. When they neared their house, the grandest on the block, Ruby stopped, leveled her expression, reverted to her normal pace. Even still, she might not eat a single bean this evening, no matter how long the pickled meat had been soaking in the pot.

That Friday night, Evelyn lay down in bed listening to Ruby get ready, plowing through the hallways, turning the bathroom faucet to its highest setting. As big as the house appeared on the outside, it was compact inside. Evelyn and Ruby shared a room, and their baby brother's bedroom was so adjacent to theirs, they could hear his bedsprings creak when he shifted at night. There was the parlor, but Mother didn't like them to sit there; it was where she met each week with the Ladies of Equal Justice and the Seventh Ward Educational League. There were guest rooms upstairs next to their parents' bedroom, but that was where Mother stored her summer drapes, her winter rugs, and, more than that, where she rested when the weight of the world hunched her shoulders.

So, Evelyn had long since learned she was stuck. Ruby had scared most of her friends off by elementary school, and the ones who lingered were gone by the end of Evelyn's freshman year at McDonogh 35. She would never forget the time Ruby told Evelyn's school friend in front of company that Ruby had heard the girl's mama had run off to pass in Mississippi. That had been the one friend Evelyn still thought of sometimes. She couldn't remember a single thing the girl said, but she did remember that they'd practice elocution and debating in the Hi Smile print shop; that during breaks they'd walk up and down South Rampart Street, peer through the windows at the shoe and jewelry stores. Sometimes they'd stop at Peter's Famous Creole Kitchen for an oyster sandwich and watch the neighborhood folk walking by. There was a feeling Evelyn could access then that she hadn't had since that girl ran off; it was a different kind of comfort than she had with her sister. It wasn't as deep, but Evelyn felt it more deeply because to her it seemed earned. That girl hadn't had to love her; she could have been in anyone's company, but she chose Evelyn's, and Evelyn missed that.

Ruby bounced into the room then.

"Are you just going to sit up here all night with Brother?" she asked, nodding at the only boy, the baby of the family who stood in their doorway.

"I ain't staying in this house." Brother dashed through their room just then for the front door.

"*Am not staying*, Brother," Evelyn corrected, "and where are you going?"

"Ain't none of your concern." Just as he spoke, they heard the neighborhood boys outside screaming for him to hurry before the bakery closed and they missed the brokers, scraps of cookies and cakes the owner distributed after dark. Brother screamed back.

Their mother's voice rang out close behind.

"Don't you raise your voice like that, Nelson Jr. You better act like you're from the Seventh Ward."

Ruby smirked. "And you better be back before Mama turns that parlor light out," she added.

Evelyn started to chime in with another admonition, but Ruby stopped her.

"And what about you? You're all worried about Brother. What are you going to do?"

"I'll figure something out," Evelyn said, though they both knew there was nothing to figure out. Sometimes she would join Miss Georgia across the street to help her knit the winter gloves and scarves she sewed year-round. There were other girls at Dillard who went out on the weekends, mostly to movies at the Circle Theater, and she'd hear them on Monday raving about Humphrey Bogart or Ingrid Bergman. Those mornings, she'd wonder if maybe there was something wrong with her in the social department. She'd heard people were sometimes born with certain deficiencies, like Brother read backward, and maybe hers was in the area of people, organizing interactions with them, what she would do, what she wouldn't do fogging over into an unthinkable plot of her mind, and that was why she was stuck at home on a Friday night when even her twelve year-old brother had plans to do something mystical.

The kicker came when Evelyn's mother strutted up to Evelyn's bedroom door in a rabbit fur. Evelyn's daddy eased up behind his wife. He placed his hand on the bottom of her stomach, and his thin gold wedding band shone from across the room.

"Where are you going, Daddy?" Evelyn asked.

"Aw, just to Uncle Franklin's."

In all Evelyn's folding and unfolding of her memories of Renard, she had forgotten it was February, and every first Friday of February, Uncle Franklin and his wife, Katherine, threw a pre–Mardi Gras soirée.

"Oh. Well, have fun," Evelyn said just above a whisper.

"What's that, baby?" Daddy walked over.

Her mother excused herself. "I'll be in the parlor when you're ready, Nelson."

"All right, Josephine," her daddy called back, then he eased over to the edge of Evelyn's bed, sat down, and combed his fingers through her hair. The two couldn't look any more different. Evelyn had a sharp, narrow nose, her eyes were light brown, not so brown they looked black like most other Negroes'; her lips were thin and pink, and like her mother and sister, she was the color of a Spanish woman more than a Negro one. Her daddy on the other hand was a black man. Born of freed Senegalese people who never mixed, his color was so notable in the Seventh Ward that it was the first thing people said about him when they wanted to reference him but not give him too much shine. "That big black doctor that think real high of himself," they'd whisper. His lips were thin, but everything else about him screamed Africa: his broad nose and wide nostrils and his hair, which he slapped pomade in but which reclaimed it-self by afternoon, shooting out in rough bunches.

"What's wrong?" he asked.

"Oh nothing, Daddy."

"Don't tell me 'nothing.' Daddy can tell when his Evie is pain-ing inside."

Evelyn just sighed and brought her arm over her face.

"Don't tell me you're still too scared to stay alone. I can run Ruby's man off, and she can stay with you."

"No, Daddy," Evelyn said forcefully so she wouldn't have to re-peat it. Ruby would never let her hear the end of it if that happened. "I just wished I had something to do tonight is all."

"Play with your brother, then. You're not too old for that, are you?"

"Brother's not even here. He's out with the twins."

"You want me to call him inside?" Evelyn's daddy leaned to-ward the window, preparing to shout.

"No, Daddy. We don't play together anymore anyway. I'm too old to play any games he'd be interested in."

Her daddy sighed and propped on his elbow on the bed beside her. "Baby girl, you want me and your mama to stay in with you tonight?"

Evelyn wanted to say yes—there was something about the silence of that house tonight that seemed formidable—but she thought of her mother in the kitchen. She could hear her clanging pots and glasses that were already clean, fussing in Creole so the kids couldn't understand her.

"Cofaire to pas laisse moin tranquille?"

Mother thought Daddy was too easy with their oldest daugh-ter; she often said Evelyn's head was in the sky, and instead of root-ing her, Daddy propped it up there as if the clouds were a row of pillows. She thought Evelyn should be seeing boys, on the verge of courtship, but her daddy would raise his voice at any intimation of the sort.

"She's got plenty of time for that," Evelyn had heard him shout.

"Does she? Seems like the good men are already getting snatched."

"Not the ones that have the sense to wait." He'd pause. "She's going to be more than somebody's wife, Jo," he'd say, and her mother would clam up, fry Evelyn's eggs too long the next morning.

"No, Daddy," Evelyn said. "I'll be all right." She paused. "I'll read some. And then I could always study."

He lit up at that. He had hoped for a sharp and disciplined mind from his son, but he'd soon learned that was like expecting corn from a pumpkin seed. He'd be lucky if Brother graduated from Valena C. Jones Elementary on time, he often joked. But Evelyn being a nurse, now that was something even his own grandfather, the first Negro doctor in the state of Louisiana, would be proud of.

"Go on now, Daddy," she said. "And don't get so drunk you get Mother upset."

"What are you going to tell me about behaving? Like I'm the one was birthed by you." He smiled.

Mother cleared her throat from the other room, and he tipped his hat at Evelyn and clicked the door behind him.

Evelyn turned over and stared at her ceiling. She returned to imagining Renard again, but as she settled on a memory of his hands, she began to wonder at the point. He was somewhere doing something interesting, and she was at home lying under sheets and blankets that might as well have been chains.

She dozed off. When she came back to, she didn't know where she was for a while. She never slept outside the confines of her nightly slumber, and she didn't understand why Ruby wasn't in the bed next to hers, why the lights were on, and why the doorbell was ringing. After a few seconds she sat up. It was probably Miss Georgia. She came by sometimes for company. Her only son was away at the war, and her husband had died before he could give her more children. Evelyn could relate to her loneliness though she'd been surrounded by people her whole life. When she'd explained that to her mother once, the woman grabbed her by the wrist and looked her dead in the eye: "If you forget everything I tell you, remember this: You can't ever be friends with somebody who wants what you have."

Evelyn only nodded and said, "Yes, ma'am," but she'd folded and unfolded the statement around in her mind several times since and still couldn't find an angle in which it held meaning.

She walked through her bedroom, through the kitchen, then the parlor, and peeked through the small curtain guarding the window on the side of the front door. Lord Jesus, it was not Miss Georgia, it was the uneven man. She turned to the mirror on the wall nearest the entrance. The right side of her face was red from where she'd fallen asleep on her hand. Her hair was tousled on that same side, and though she licked the palm of her hand and dabbed it down best she could, some still stuck out in every direction. She tucked her blouse back into her skirt, which had ridden up, and cinched each of her breasts out of her bra, then plopped them back in, seated a tad higher this time. The doorbell rang again, and she almost shrieked. She wondered if she could pretend to be out, but he must have seen the curtain on the window move. Her heart was beating enough to sustain ten men, and it was too much for her, thoughts flooding her mind, her hands shaking when they should have been still, her whole body paralyzed by its doubled intentions.

The doorbell rang one more time. She heard Ruby's voice in her ear. *You didn't even get him to ask you on a date?* How tickled would she be when she came back to see Evelyn had found something to do all right. Evelyn settled her hand on the knob. A note slipped through the door, and she almost bent down to read it, but she stopped herself and inched the door open.

Renard had started walking down the steps and turned around. "I hope I didn't bother you, miss," he said, stammering on the last word only and calling her *miss*, not *ma'am*, which Evelyn thought was a good sign.

"No, no, I was just in the back room sewing a dress." Evelyn didn't know where the lie came from; in fact, one of her expressions that Ruby mocked most was that lying didn't get enough emphasis in the Ten Commandments, but here she was. Maybe next Friday she'd be off at Circle Food stealing glazed meat.

"You sew? That's mighty nice." A pause. "You sewed what you're wearing right now?"

Evelyn looked down. Mother had sewn this in fact, but should she say she had to lend her previous lie more credibility? Or was what she was wearing so drab that the new lie would detract from her intent? "Whether you did or you didn't," Renard went on, "it's mighty nice on you. I reckon this is what an angel on earth looks like." He stammered all over that last sentence, every single word but *an*, but that was because he was nervous saying what he meant, and their nervousness together was like two negatives multiplied. She felt herself quieting inside. With her head a little clearer, she considered her options: There was absolutely no way she could invite him inside. Her parents wouldn't be home for three or four hours at least, but Brother could come in any minute, and she'd have to shine his shoes for the rest of the year to get him to forget a man had been in the parlor. If she sat outside though, Miss Georgia would certainly peek out at least once during their visit. She might even walk across the street and embarrass Evelyn. That was a risk Evelyn would have to take. She cleared her throat.

"My parents aren't here, or I'd invite you in," she said.

"That's all right, I'd best be going anyhow."

He didn't move though, which gave Evelyn the courage to state her mind. "I can come out and join you if you want to stay a spell."

Renard's face lit up. "I'd love that, miss."

She reached into the hall closet for her trench coat and cinched the belt around her waist. They sat on the swing her daddy had built when she turned five, pushing themselves back and forth with their knees bending and straightening at the same rhythm. Evelyn thought about the house from Renard's perspective, its wood frame with sky-blue trim, the baskets of fresh watered ferns adorning its porch, the pansies and petunias on either side of the long, winding driveway. A large palm tree guarded the corner of their property, and in the summer she and Ruby would sneak under it with books and frozen cups, sugar water iced until it was solid. Evelyn thought to share that memory but realized how extravagant it all might seem. The night air had cooled, and when Renard saw her shiver, he inched over. Even through their coats, she felt grown with his arm so close to hers. She wanted to reach for his hand, but there was Miss Georgia to consider.

They didn't say anything for a while, and finally Evelyn thought to ask, "How'd you remember where I lived?"

"I made myself memorize it when you said it," he said. "I went over it in my head the whole walk home so I wouldn't forget."

"So you knew all this time you were coming by to see me?"

"I didn't know but I suspected." He grinned. "I wasn't sure I had the courage, but I knew I wanted to."

"How did it happen?"

"How'd what happen?"

"How'd you get the courage?"

"I don't know. I work for Todd's Restaurant, over in the Quarter, and I spent the afternoon there, packing and loading boxes, thinking about you. At first I tried to make up excuses. I told myself you probably wouldn't even be in, and your sister would answer and make me feel like a fool, but when I got home, something surged in my body, and I stood up from my seat and dressed. I don't know where it came from. Nothing like that has ever happened to me before."

"Me neither," Evelyn said, but she understood it because it was happening now. Her body was being cooled down when just the thought of the two of them sitting anywhere together with an open night laid out in front of them and no schedule on how it should go would have made her frantic just minutes earlier.

"I'm glad you came," she said.

"Me too." Renard looked back toward the house. "Where's the rest of your family?" he asked.

"My mother and daddy are at a Mardi Gras party by my uncle's. My brother's out playing. You can hear him if you listen closely."

"And your mean old sister?"

Evelyn laughed though she was normally protective of Ruby. "She's out with your friend. He didn't tell you?"

Renard laughed. "No, he didn't tell me, but I should have known." He paused. "We don't talk about stuff like that."

"He's your friend though?" Evelyn proceeded carefully, not knowing much about friends herself.

"Yeah, we grew up together."

"I haven't seen you around much."

"No, I suppose not. My mother used to work for his family and they took me in when she died. I eat supper over his place every night, and they paid for me to go to school, but we never really traveled in the same circles outside. Now that we're both studying medicine, it's just easier to walk together."

He delivered so much sadness with such a casual tongue, Evelyn wanted to tell him she was sorry, but she wasn't sure what she was sorry for, or if he would mistake her care for pity.

All of a sudden he straightened his back and said, "But don't worry, miss. That's why I'm going to be a doctor. I always wanted to be one, and I'm so close now nothing can stop me. And then I'm never going to have to ask for anything that doesn't rightfully belong to me. Me, nor my family."

"That's mighty inspiring," Evelyn said. "You'll make a mighty fine doctor." She wrapped her fingers around his hand. Miss Georgia could tell the world for all she cared. When her skin met his, he looked over at her with the gratitude of a man who had never felt a woman's touch. They stared in each other's eyes in silence, breaking out into grins from time to time when the heat of the connection felt as if it would snuff them out if they didn't do something to drain it.

Evelyn wanted to get closer, but she remembered herself and asked for the time.

"It's a quarter after ten. Maybe I best be going," he said. "I have to get up early tomorrow for work." He stood.

"At the store?"

"No, tomorrow's my day killing chickens. The market sells them live but people pay good money for them already plucked. It's awful work, but . . ." He trailed off as if he wasn't sure if he was going to say the next thing. "The government's hiring plenty for all the ships and tanks and guns they need." He shook his head, and his face darkened for the first time. "Those jobs aren't for us though, so I'm killing chickens."

Evelyn stood, her heart burning with compassion. She didn't know how to respond. "Well, it was so nice of you to stop by," she said finally. "Maybe you'll do it another time."

"I most definitely will." He took a step toward the porch. "I have church on Sunday but maybe after that."

Evelyn nodded. "Me too," she said. "Where do you attend?"

"Holy Ghost. What about you?"

"St. Augustine," she said. "My daddy won't step foot in there, says he won't go to a church that seats Negroes in the back, but Mother says that's just his excuse, he wouldn't go to any church, even one that let them sit on the altar next to the priest himself."

They both laughed.

"I wonder how my sister and your friend are doing," Evelyn smirked, still trying to stretch their time. "They're out some late."

"Going to be much later with my friend," Renard laughed.

Evelyn didn't join in. Ruby wasn't as conservative as she was, not by a long shot, but Evelyn wouldn't stand for her being ridiculed.

"Oh, I didn't mean anything by it, miss." His face scrunched up with regret. "I'm sure he's treating her real respectable. He's a respectable sort of guy, but he's a night owl, that's all, and he loves to talk. They're probably just seeing a movie, and you know how that goes, it takes so long to exit from the Negro balcony, that's all I meant."

Evelyn nodded.

"I meant it, miss. I won't suffer anybody talking ill about a lady. He wouldn't try it, but even if he did, I'd make sure it was the last word he said about your sister."

Evelyn smiled. "And what about you? How do you speak about ladies?"

He smiled. "I haven't had much reason to speak about them before," he said, his stutter gone. "But if I saw Andrew today, I might tell him I made a new friend."

"Just a friend, huh?" Evelyn didn't know where her boldness had been lurking.

"A special friend," Renard finished. "Real special," he repeated, walking backward now, down the porch steps and then the sidewalk until he was out of sight.

Evelyn revived the night in her mind once he was gone; so thoroughly was she coiled inside the retelling she didn't hear her sister until Ruby reached their bedroom.

Usually when Ruby went out and Evelyn stayed home, she had the decency to be quiet, as quiet as she could, but this time she slammed her nightgown drawer shut, she kicked off her shoes. She stomped to the bathroom, made a to-do of splashing water over her face. Once she was back in the room, Evelyn had no choice but to sit up and ask what had gone wrong.

"Everything." Ruby was close to tears.

Evelyn had seen her like this only one other time when word had gotten back about Langston, and Ruby had considered transferring to secretarial school in Baton Rouge.

"It started off all right I suppose. He held my hand, he took me to Dufon's, he told me to order anything I liked. But we hadn't been seated for more than five minutes when another girl walked up to the table. I think she's one of the Chapitals; I've seen her around your campus. Surprised I remembered her, not much to look at, really, Evelyn, I could outmatch her on my worst day, but he sat there and held a conversation with her for five minutes before he turned back to me. He didn't even introduce me. I've never been so embarrassed in my life."

"Oh, Ruby." Evelyn didn't know what to say. Normally her sister's moods infiltrated her own, and Evelyn was certain something tangible would befall her as a direct result of them, but this time she felt insulated in a world of her own creation. "Oh, Ruby," she repeated, not sure how long she had stalled since the first time she said it. "I'm sure he didn't mean anything by it. I'm sure he was just being polite." She almost slipped and said Renard had mentioned that his friend was an outgoing fellow, but she couldn't reference Renard, not at a time like this.

Ruby shook her head, huffing. "The blind leading the blind," she said. "I should have known not to ask you your opinion."

Evelyn smarted at that and was tempted to correct her, but she held back. If she introduced Renard now, he would forever be a wedge between them; it was early, but Evelyn already knew that she would see him again.

"Anyway, I've already decided," Ruby went on, "I'm never seeing him again. There's no way. He's the type to think too high of himself, and let me tell you his hair is not as straight as it looked the other day, he puts some sort of oil in there, and he's not as light as we thought either. I still can't get a read on his family, what they did before his daddy lucked up on that teaching gig, and anyway if Brother's grades are any indication of the kind of educating they're doing at Valena C. Jones, that whole family is in a world of trouble."

Evelyn could tell her part in the performance was over, and she turned to the wall and made like she was sleeping. Ruby kept going for another hour though: The man hadn't ordered his food the way Daddy would; she could tell he wasn't used to eating at such fine establishments by the way he asked rather than told the waiter what he was going to have; he talked about the war like he wanted to be a part of it, when everyone knew you didn't discuss such gruesome matters in front of a lady. Not only that, when they walked home, a white man passed, and Andrew lowered his head and nearly pushed her to the side of the street.

"Daddy never would have done it that way," Ruby whispered. "He wouldn't have gotten himself killed, this is Louisiana, but he would have found a way to protect us and maintain his dignity. That's the kind of man I'm looking for, and that Andrew, he was nowhere close. Let me tell you, Evelyn, you ought to count your blessings that his friend didn't ask you out. You know what they say about birds of a feather. If Andrew was no count, then that old uneven-hem man must be the bottom of the barrel."

The next morning, Evelyn slept in, though she heard the eggs cackling, smelled the bacon smoking on the fire. She was so tired she even tarried in bed past the doorbell ringing, then Miss Georgia's shrill voice and high laughter. Finally she heard her own name.

She shot up, stuck her ear to the door, but couldn't make out the conversation, just a few smatterings of words here and there, "nice looking," and "about an hour," and "I kept an eye out to make sure." Evelyn couldn't hear any of her mother's responses, but it didn't matter. As she dressed, her late-night excitement faded into the dull certainty that whatever magic had been sparked on that swing had been snuffed out in her mother's sitting room this morning. Her father hadn't been home, but he would be in a matter of minutes, and there was no question her mother would repeat what she'd heard, her father would storm in her room and forbid her from even thinking about Renard again, and she'd go on attending classes at Dillard, coming home at night, and barely fending off her loneliness, which was rising above her head.

Still, she didn't feel sad, just settled in her new understanding that this was life, and she had been foolish to expect much else. As she was about to head to the kitchen for any scraps Ruby had left behind, her sister walked in their room with a sneaky smirk on her face and two biscuits in her hand.

"So"—she plopped on her made-up bed and threw a pillow at Evelyn's chest—"you didn't tell me you had a visitor last night," and as she said the word *night*, the pillow bounced off Evelyn and hit the floor. "You're keeping secrets now, huh? Or trying to? You know Ruby always finds out in the end." She sang the last part of the sentence. "This time it only took twelve hours."

Evelyn smiled back, but she was afraid. She lowered her voice. "You had a bad time last night. I didn't want to pour salt on the wound."

Ruby didn't answer for a little while. She just played with a thread hanging from the end of her apple-red skirt. Sometimes when she was in a bad mood, Evelyn would volunteer to sew any of her clothes that needed mending. Evelyn wondered if in an hour she'd be weaving a needle through that bright cloth.

Ruby looked up. "Evelyn, don't be stupid, I'm your sister, your joy is my joy." She stared at her, her eyes wide and intense. "Anyway, I'm the one who introduced you to this man. What's his name? Raymond? I should at least reap the rewards of my efforts through you." She had inched her voice up a notch from its regular octave in an attempt to sound happy, but there was something in her face's plain affect that made Evelyn certain her sister's anger was near.

Evelyn sat down next to her to get it all over with. "How'd you find out?" she asked.

"How do you think? Miss Georgia's loud mouth. Lord Jesus, I can't change my girdle without her getting word. Let that be a note to you, girl. Don't do anything in front of this house that you don't want Daddy to know about because lucky for you Mama happened to be home this morning. If it had been Daddy who answered the door, we already know Ray would be a page in your memory book." She paused. "And you'd be off at the Sisters of the Holy Family convent by now." She cackled.

Evelyn shrugged. "Mother's going to tell him anyway; that's over now."

Ruby gripped Evelyn's wrist and locked eyes with her in a rare show of emotion. "She won't," she said. "She would never. That time I got caught holding hands with Langston at the St. Bernard Market, she yelled about my reputation and threatened to lock me in my room, but she never breathed a word."

Evelyn sighed. "That's because it was you; it's different." She caught Ruby grinning then, the first genuine smile the girl had had all morning.

Evelyn didn't leave the house the rest of the day; she just waited for Daddy to get word, act on it, but it never happened. Even before dinner when it was just the two of them in the kitchen, and she gathered the silverware to set the table, and he prepared a whiskey straight, he just went on about the patient he'd seen. "Miss Sylvia still hasn't dropped that baby. I told her husband to walk her up and down Napoleon. That little thing would be out by the morning, but these women don't listen. You'd think they were the ones who spent the eight years in school. I should take off my stethoscope when I walk in their houses, pass it over, let them listen to my heart beat. I told her, if she goes any longer, she's going to be delivering at Charity, and she'd have better luck giving birth in a manger than in the Negro ward of a hospital."

Evelyn nodded and smiled, waiting for him to approach the real transgression. Halfway through dinner, when he and Mother had gone on and on about Mardi Gras preparations, the debutante receptions, soprano recitals, and whist parties; when Ruby pontificated over who would be riding with Zulu this year, how early she'd need to reach North Claiborne to catch the Indians, why the Skeleton Men frightened her; when Mother added that the Million-Dollar Baby dolls were scandalous and Daddy smirked and noted they were just costumes after all, Evelyn realized he didn't know. And she stared at her mother as if just noticing a subtle feature in the older woman's face that had transformed her into a different person altogether.

Without her daddy's interference, Evelyn and Renard spent their free days together. They'd meet at the Sweet Tooth for ice cream and giggle at the owner of the store, who would scoop the ice cream up, toss it in the air, then catch it with a cone. After paying, they'd drift outside to walk, past the women haggling with the butchers over turkey necks and kids gaping at the posters outside the Circle Theater. They didn't speak at first—the bustling environment seemed to grant permission to their silence—but finally after a few days of the same, Renard's voice inched out in a cracked whisper.

"How was your treat?"

"Delicious," Evelyn said, so eager to engage with him the word shot out. She actually hadn't gone inside the Sweet Tooth before, though she'd stood on that street for years because it tempted Ruby to see someone eating something she wanted but couldn't have. He nodded at her answer and put his head back down.

"How was yours?" Evelyn asked as sweet as her double chocolate malt ball shake.

"The best I ever had. Andrew's mama makes shakes all the time. Don't tell Andrew, but I think this one was better."

The rest of their conversation seemed to pour out—first about their studies, then about what time they would head to the parades, and finally about the disparate versions of the stories Andrew and Ruby had relayed about their first date.

"I heard they didn't have the best time. Don't tell him I told you, but I guess they ran into another woman, and my sister felt like he talked to her too long."

Renard chuckled. "Yeah, that's my friend for you. He knows just about everybody in the city. Man or woman. And he doesn't just leave it at a simple hello, he wants to know how their mama is, how their mama's mama is, their brothers and sisters. He gets a full report on each one. That girl was probably from a big family, that's all."

"That's what I told her, that he didn't mean any disrespect."

"No, he's the kindest man I know. He wouldn't hurt a fly. All his people are like that. When my mama passed, they didn't have to take me in. They certainly didn't have to pay my way. Andrew's mama lost two of her sons; she has her own grief to tend to."

"To the war?"

"No, tuberculosis; there aren't too many Negroes fighting in the war."

"But Miss Georgia's son is there."

"He may be there, but odds are he's not holding a gun."

Evelyn lowered her eyes. "Oh." She wanted to change the subject; the war was tragic in the way slavery was; it hadn't affected her, and she thought talking about it might invite it in. "Well, at least Andrew's mama still has him," she said.

He nodded, then went on. "My mama was just as sweet as Andrew's, you know. I never met her, but they tell me that. They tell me she was beautiful. She was a twin." He looked up in the sky, talking out of the side of his mouth. "Jet-black hair down her back, they say. Beautiful woman." Then he jerked back into the conversation as if he were coming to. "What about yours?"

"My—?" Evelyn asked, confused.

"Your mama?"

She shrugged. "She's stunning," she said. "She's the classiest woman I ever met."

"What's it like, having her? That probably sounds crazy, but I always wondered . . ."

Evelyn didn't know what to say. She didn't want to sound ungrateful. She knew her mother loved her—there had been the time Ruby convinced Evelyn to swallow a dollar piece to make it multiply, and Evelyn had been rushed to Flint-Goodrich for the night. Her mother couldn't be comforted, sobbing beside her bedside. Evelyn had heard her as she came to, and in those seconds she thought maybe there was a blessing inside that dollar, some voodoo magic that might open her mother's heart, bind her to her, but after Evelyn was discharged, it was more of the same. Nothing Evelyn said came out right; nothing she did could warrant the woman's approval.

"We're not so close," she said. "I guess I'm more of a daddy's girl."

"That's too bad," Renard said.

"It's not so bad," Evelyn said. "I shouldn't complain about it. You lost your mama, and I'm complaining about one who corrects me too much," she tried to laugh.

"Naw." Renard shook his head. "Don't say that. There's all different types of ways to leave somebody. Maybe it's sadder that she's there, and she just feels far away."

From then on, Evelyn woke up each day with a renewed tolerance for the world; the feeling she'd been searching for her whole life had been missing because she hadn't met Renard, and now that he was here, she could grasp the higher octave of joy her solitude precluded.

Still, she made him say good-bye to her two blocks from their house and bribed Brother, who had caught them snuggling, with all the hog head cheese he could stomach.

One morning Daddy walked into the kitchen while she whistled.

"You've been in a mighty good mood lately, Evie."

She turned to him, startled into silence. "I have?" she asked finally. "I didn't mean to be."

"No? What's causing you to be so happy beyond your control?" He sat down, perched one leg atop the other, and smiled.

Brother walked in just then, and she hurried to dish his snack before he could answer Daddy for her.

"Extra mayonnaise," Brother grinned.

Her daddy glanced from Brother to her, his eyes narrowing. "I'll take a sandwich too," Daddy said.

"Yes, sir." Evelyn spread twice as much meat on the Wonder Bread as normal and added an extra teaspoon of mayonnaise too. She served her daddy first and shot Brother a pleading look to compensate for it. Mother had made lemonade, and she poured each of them a tall cool glass.

"You don't want one?" Daddy asked, a dollop of the soft meat on his lip.

She shook her head, standing at the edge of the counter, waiting.

When Daddy finished, he let out a huge belch he would have never delivered if Mother were there and finished off his lemonade. He pulled a toothpick from a jar in the center of the table and plucked the fat from between his teeth.

"Why don't you bring the boy by then, since you don't want to talk about him?" he asked finally.

Evelyn gasped, jerked her head toward Brother.

"I didn't say nothing. I swear I didn't."

"I didn't need a little bird to tell me. You think I don't know when a gal is in love?" Her daddy let out a bellow of a laugh.

Evelyn could feel her face heating on the inside. Renard had told her on one of their dates that he had never seen a Negro woman blush before. Then she had blushed again and smiled.

Now, Daddy got up from where he was seated, shuffled to the parlor and out the door, and Brother followed him. Before Brother left the room, he turned back, "Do that mean no more sandwiches?"

Now that Daddy knew about Renard, Evelyn let him walk her all the way to her porch before he kissed her hand each evening. Renard had settled matters between Ruby and Andrew, and since then, Andrew would walk Ruby to the porch too, only later, and Ruby would allow him more than a kiss on the hand. Ruby had tried to discuss the details with Evelyn, but Evelyn had yawned one night just a few moments in, and Ruby took the hint and began whispering with Mother instead. Evelyn heard them sometimes.

"First of all, you've got to see his car, a black 1937 Chevrolet. Just sitting inside it would have been plenty to me, but then he took me up to his house and introduced me to all his family, and friends too, called me his lady out there in front of everyone. Then we drove around, you know; finally we parked somewhere and just talked. I would have stayed out there all night, but it was his idea to come on back. He said he didn't want to leave a bad taste in my daddy's mouth. And look at this—" Evelyn didn't need to be present to know Ruby was referencing the silver-toned rhinestone brooch she'd seen on her sister's lapel that morning.

"Be careful," her mother would interrupt. "You're old enough to know what can happen when you're not."

"Oh, it's not all that serious, Mother," Ruby would giggle, and after a few seconds Evelyn would hear her mother giggling too.

Daddy sulked around the house, only partly feigning sadness.

"Both of my girls are leaving me," he'd pout. But one night after a dinner of smothered pork chops and rice, after he set his toothpick down on the rim of his plate, he said it was time for him to meet these boys—no, men, he corrected—these men who'd zeroed in on his daughters' hands.

Evelyn couldn't wait to tell Renard the news the next day. It was Mardi Gras, and though Evelyn would normally be dashing between the St. Bernard Market for seafood for the good gumbo or finishing last-minute hems on the ball gowns, she had never enjoyed those rituals. Renard agreed that there was too much made of the festivities each year, so they decided to attend just Zulu, the highlight of the season. Evelyn woke up early to help her mother fry calas, then after she had eaten a few fritters, she joined Renard and the thousands of others crowding the streets at the head of the New Basin Canal. Once the three floats had passed, the black-faced riders had tossed out all their coconuts, and the bands of music had faded, Evelyn and Renard headed back to Dufon's and shared an oyster loaf between them. As they ate, she told him about her daddy's offer to meet him. She thought he'd be as relieved as she was, but he only picked at his portion of the sandwich. Eventually he tried to smile, but it came out more like a grimace.

"Andrew will be there too," Evelyn added.

"I know," he said, not looking up.

"Isn't that better? You'll have less to worry about with your old friend there."

"Sure," he said, and he started to say something else, but he stopped himself. "You're right," he said, "it will be great. I've been wanting to meet your parents. It had to happen sooner or later."

She tried to console him. "They'll love you," she said, "especially my mother. I think she thought I would stay in the house forever. And my daddy loves the idea of having a doctor for a son-in-law, and you should see how he's been grinning. He's sad his little girls are all grown up, but he's proud too, I can tell."

Renard smiled a little wider, but it was still forced.

Later, after he dropped her off, his mood began to affect hers. She thought about all the ways Ruby or her mother might ruin her night. Her sister would probably monopolize conversation, steer it toward Andrew and his glory so Daddy might think she'd gotten the better catch. Or Ruby might goad Renard into saying something improper to her. That had never happened, and Evelyn couldn't imagine Renard actually giving in to Ruby's taunts, but in the light of Evelyn's dismal talk with Renard it seemed likely. Evelyn's mother had been saying she was excited, and she'd even taken Evelyn aside one night after dinner to tell her she was proud of her for becoming a lady, but who knew what she'd say when she actually saw Renard, when she was actually in the presence of another man who adored her daughter as much as Daddy did? Mother wasn't a devil; she wanted to be happy for her child, Evelyn knew that, but something about the moments in which Evelyn commanded love turned Josephine against her firstborn every time.

The morning of the dinner, Evelyn and Renard agreed to meet at the Sweet Tooth. Renard was waiting for her as she walked up, pacing.

"What's wrong, baby?" she asked when she reached him.

He pulled her to him. "I don't think I have it in me to meet your father today," he said.

"What do you mean?" Evelyn stroked his back the way she'd seen her mother rub her daddy's, up and down, up and down, then in a full circle.

"I'm not like Andrew and the other boys. Andrew could hold a conversation with President Roosevelt if he needed to. I ain't had to talk to nobody but my sisters for most of my life. What yo daddy gon' think of me?" He looked down at his shoes and motioned toward them. "I tried to polish 'em today, but wasn't no use. Only so much you can shine shit."

Evelyn had never heard him speak in anything but the King's English, and she had to stop herself from portraying her alarm. "Don't say that, baby," she said, still rubbing his back, and she said it again when she could think of nothing else to follow it. "It will be a privilege for my daddy to meet someone like you." She thought to slacken her tongue to even them out a little. "At the end of the day, ain't we all just Negroes?"

"But he did something with hisself. He live over there in that fancy house. And he got him a nice high yellow wife. That's something." He held his head up suddenly from where it had been dangling. "That's something."

"And you're going do the same thing, baby."

"If you'll have me." He seemed to be calming.

"I wouldn't have anybody else." They kissed there for the first time. He pulled her closer to him, and she felt him stretching toward her beneath his pants, needing her. She had a primal urge to take him to the alley behind one of the stores and pull him inside her. She didn't know what it all entailed, but she would figure it out. Instead they started walking. They didn't say a word; still, she seemed to feel better with each step as if the anticipation of the night was wafting off of her as she moved. She felt Renard relax too. Before she knew it they had reached the end of Esplanade Avenue and were staring up at the broad magnolia trees of City Park. Evelyn was hot as a layer of hell from the walk, and the large trees beyond the park entrance taunted her with their shade. Of course she didn't dare go in. She wiped the perspiration from her forehead with a handkerchief and caught her breath.

"One day we'll be able to walk in there," Renard whispered. "Sit under the magnolias, climb up the steps of the museum." He pointed to the end of the park where tall columns marked the entrance to the Delgado Museum of Art.

"Of course," she said, to assuage him. She didn't know whether that day would come in her lifetime, nor was she so eager to pass into territory people blocked her from. Her life was all right.

But Renard stepped forward. She held his hand beside her, parked where she stood, but he kept walking, gazed in at the winding paths and sparkling lake as though something he'd longed for his whole life lay before him. He let go of her hand, and she called for him. Just before he turned his back, she heard a voice behind her.

"Get back, nigger, you know you're not supposed to be in there."

Renard stopped where he stood. Evelyn turned to see a red-faced officer clutching the baton at the side of his waist.

"He wasn't going in, Officer. He knows the law," Evelyn called out. It was second nature for her to plead like a little girl in front of whites, and she didn't notice that she did it now, only that the officer took his hand off the club at his side.

She felt him sizing her up, but she looked down before he could get any ideas.

"Well, all right, just get on then," he said after a minute, and he waited for them to leave.

Evelyn hustled over to Renard and grabbed his hand. She was prepared to run all the way back down Esplanade, but she had to pull Renard behind her.

She assumed the day was over after that. They walked back home in silence of a different sort than the one that had led them in—this one seemed to weigh on them, leave them heavier with each step. Evelyn didn't know what to expect by the time they reached Miro Street. She was certain he wouldn't make it to dinner now, and she didn't even hold it against him. Something about brushing up against their limitations made her understand the sense of weakness he'd been referencing earlier, and she understood too that it might show up and announce itself in front of a man like her father. But he turned to her, smiled even, said, "I'll see you tonight," and it came out so sturdy she might have thought she had imagined his anxiety an hour earlier.

"Oh, Renard," she squealed. "I wasn't sure what you would do, after what just happened."

He shook his head. "I wouldn't let anything like that shoo me away. If anything, it only confirmed it. We're all we have. Like you said, we're all Negroes anyway."

Back home, Evelyn tended to the normal Saturday chores: dusting her bedroom, bleaching the toilets, scrubbing the hard wood with vinegar until it shined. Ruby had sometimes helped her in the past, but since Andrew had come into her life, Ruby's time tending to anything but him was long gone. Once Evelyn finished, she ventured out into the kitchen for a cool glass of lemonade. As she was setting the pitcher back, her mother cornered her between the icebox and the stove. She hunched over so close Evelyn could smell the late-afternoon coffee on her breath.

"Does Renard like veal?" her mother whispered, picking at the hair that had strayed from her loose bun.

Evelyn was relieved by the question's minor nature. "I'm sure. He's not picky, Mother."

"Yes, but that's not what I asked you. Does he like it?"

Evelyn nodded. "I think I remember him saying he loved the taste of a nice veal," she lied.

Mother jerked her head toward her. "Well, I was planning to roast it with some celery and onions and bell peppers. And then I would bake a pan of macaroni and cheese with the long spaghetti noodles and a tomato salad. I don't suppose he would have an issue with that. I would have made fish but we've been eating it every Friday."

Evelyn shook her head. "Whatever you make will be delicious, Mother."

It was only when her mother had ushered her out into the dining room and Evelyn was alone with the place settings and the cloth napkins that she wondered what had come over the woman. Evelyn had never seen her doubt herself in the kitchen or otherwise; Mother threw receptions and parties nearly every month of the year, and guests never left without complimenting her gumbo or sweet potato pie or just the careful way she organized the flowers, linens, and centerpiece just so. Evelyn wondered too if Mother had been just as eager to please Andrew, if she had the same conversation with Ruby; Evelyn hadn't heard anything, but if not, why? Why would Mother be more nervous about Renard?

A little while later, Ruby burst into the parlor carrying a bunch of tulips.

"Is that for dinner?" her mother asked.

"No, indeed. They're from Andrew, for me." Ruby held her head high and back; the pink blossoms had started to wilt, but they might as well have been an engagement ring.

"Hmph, well, go get changed and help me in this kitchen," Mother snapped.

Ruby took her sweet time anyway and managed to come out only once Evelyn and Mother had completed all the tasks.

"What a coincidence. Just in time to taste the veal," their mother huffed.

"It's perfect," Evelyn said, wiping the gravy from her mouth, piling the compliments on so her mother might relax.

"Real good, Mama, a little salty though," Ruby added.

At that, Evelyn pinched her sister, Ruby swiped her back with a wet towel, and their mother smacked them both on the bottoms with the palm of her hand.

"What did I do?" Evelyn screamed. "Ruby's the rude one."

Mother just glared back, unaccustomed to managing the conflict. It wasn't that Ruby hadn't tried to antagonize Evelyn for years, it was just that Evelyn had always preempted the attacks by catering to her sister's needs before Ruby even knew she had them. If Evelyn sensed Ruby was on the rag, she'd make her a sugar sandwich; if it was a Monday and a boy hadn't asked Ruby out, Evelyn would compliment her on her figure. *Oh, I wish I had your breasts*, she might say. *Even Brother's are bigger than mine*, and Ruby would laugh Evelyn into a net of safety. But since Renard had come along there had been a great change in Evelyn. Who was Ruby to criticize their mother's cooking when Mother had spent the morning straining her nerves into a jumble? Who was she to waltz in twenty minutes before a dinner party with flowers in her hair? Evelyn was tired of her sister's whims, her privilege, her moods, and her authority in thinking the whole house needed to be privy to them.

Their mother just shooed them into their bedroom, and the sisters sat in silence there until the doorbell rang. When Evelyn walked out, her parents were standing at the front door whispering.

"Let's not make them wait, Nelson," her mother said, still grim faced.

And even when Renard and Andrew walked in with flowers, Mother didn't adopt her normal state of ease. Evelyn was concerned. She found that with her mother on edge, she couldn't relax either. She fulfilled the expected duties: She ushered her man into the house and introduced him; she set the flowers he brought in a vase on the kitchen counter; she spoke in an educated manner about the riot in Detroit. But the ease she had hoped to feel introducing her new family to her old one escaped her.

Renard, on the other hand, soared. When Daddy remarked that Negroes expecting Roosevelt to address the violence against blacks were going to die waiting, Renard agreed, adding that it was educated folk like Thurgood Marshall who were changing things in this country. He remarked with a genuine air that their mother could have been their sister. He ate every morsel of food on his plate and asked for seconds. He raved with Brother about Satchel Paige's three scoreless innings at the last East-West All-Star Game. Evelyn had worried that Renard and Andrew would compete with each other, but neither man took over the table, and instead they yielded it to each other. Renard went on about Andrew's father's intelligence. And Andrew gushed over Renard's work ethic, said that he would surely be a doctor one day, and that anyone who was treated by him would be lucky. Even Ruby praised Evelyn's bread pudding.

"I don't like raisins," she said, "and you usually overdo it with them, but the way you plopped them so scarce in here, you can barely taste them, Evelyn."

After dinner, Evelyn helped her mother with the dishes, and the men snuck off to the parlor for cigars and whiskey.

When Evelyn was done, she joined them. Both men were seated on the sofa, Daddy in between them. Andrew was shouting.

"Have you read the *Courier*? All I know is we have a duty to give our all to the war effort, and maybe when we exercise our duty this country will start to exercise theirs."

Daddy scoffed. "Don't hold your breath waiting. Anyway, remember, son, the likelihood is you won't be flying planes or healing the sick over there. You're going to be serving meals, cleaning quarters, digging graves."

Andrew shrugged. "Maybe in the beginning. But after a while

when things heat up, they're going to need more of us. And that's when it will all be worth it, when we'll be able to prove ourselves."

"Prove yourself how? By getting killed? Or better yet, you'll be like that Simmons boy in Tremé, heard of him?"

The boys shook their heads.

Daddy smirked as he spoke. "He was a mail clerk in France. Got sent home after he lost his leg, came back to an opening at the post office down on Loyola. He rode over there and took the test, thought he was a shoo-in. Veterans were supposed to have first preference after all, and he made the highest mark of anybody, but you think they hired him?" Daddy repeated, "You think they hired him?"

Neither boy answered.

Finally Daddy turned to Renard. "What do you think about all this, son?" he asked, shaking his head.

Renard looked at Evelyn before he spoke. He cleared his throat and took a sip of his water. Evelyn whispered a little prayer.

"Well, I think we're living in a state of hypocrisy bigger than any this country has ever seen," he started.

"Amen," Daddy shot in, seeming surprised by his own agreement.

"And something has to be done so that we don't sacrifice our lives just to come back still not quite American. Let's say we are victorious overseas, what's going to come of the next generation of Negroes here? I mean, before I defend this great nation with my life, I'd want to know that we as a people would be guaranteed full citizenship rights upon our return."

"Exactly, exactly, now this brother has some sense. I'm going to call you Ernest Wright from now on, set you up out there on Shakespeare Park." Daddy smiled at Renard, but it was Andrew whom he slapped on the thigh.

Renard looked up at Evelyn again, this time with gratitude. And she was proud of him; she'd expected half his speech to come out in stammers, and none of it had, and from what she could understand, it was profound; even her daddy had said so. Still she couldn't internalize his joy; her mother's mood alarmed her.

Evelyn knew because of Mother's concern over Renard's preferences that she wasn't being malicious. No, she had assessed the situation and determined there was cause for concern somewhere, but Evelyn couldn't locate it, and that was what spooked her worst of all.

Evelyn walked Renard out that night, fighting herself to be as happy as he was.

"Did you hear it when your daddy called me son?" he asked. "He did, Evelyn, he did. I never heard that word come out like that before."

"I knew he would like you," Evelyn said.

"I know. I should have believed you, but I was so nervous. Imagine if he hadn't. You're the most important person to me. I couldn't live if I couldn't have your hand." He kissed her in front of the house the way she'd always wanted, but Evelyn pulled away, feeling someone somewhere was watching her.

Once he was gone, she walked back up the porch steps. She could hear her parents arguing from the door.

"But did you see his shoes? And did you hear what he said about where he lived? Twelve brothers and sisters. Can you imagine? For our daughter? And in a house on Amelia Street the size of a shack? He's a low-class man, Josephine. Not middle, middle I could take, I could do something with it, but low."

Then her mother's long silence, its heaviness breaking: "I thought that was endearing to tell you the truth. *Piti a piti, zozo fait son nid.* Don't tell me we're up so high we can't reach our hand out to someone below us."

"It's not that I won't reach my hand out, don't you say that. You know I do more to lift our people than most. The New Orleans Urban League, the Black Savings and Loan Association, you know how many free medical exams I gave out last year alone? Do you?" As his voice lifted, her mother's seemed to cower.

"I'm not saying you don't."

"I just don't want to waste all our effort, and on what, an unlikely prospect. Think about your daddy. What would he say?"

"He would say to give a young Negro man a chance." She paused. Then, "Not everybody gave you a warm welcome either, you know."

"I was a doctor."

"You were becoming a doctor just like this boy."

He raised his voice now. "I was from a good family, you were lucky to end up with me. And I've done well for you and the kids."

"That's what I believed too." She seemed to walk over to him then. "But I'm just saying everyone didn't agree with my assessment."

"Josephine, if I didn't know you better, I'd think you just wanted her out of the house, that you didn't care who she ended up with, as long as she was gone from here."

Mother didn't say anything.

"Or maybe it's more than that. Maybe you don't want to see Evelyn come out with a better match than Ruby."

Evelyn heard the scrape of a wood chair against linoleum, and her mother's house shoes batting against the floor.

"You say what you want, Nelson."

"You know I will."

"You say what you want," her mother repeated. "You think you know everything, but one thing you can't know is how much I love that child. You didn't carry her, nor did you push her out. You're a mighty good provider, but you didn't learn her how to eat with a spoon and tie her shoes and write her first word, and for those reasons alone you can't know." Her voice broke. "My love for her took over when I had her. There's no room for anything else."

Evelyn's daddy's sharper heels tapped, then stopped.

"Well, I love her too, and I won't have her fighting her way through this life. It's already hard enough. I won't make it harder, I can't. I promised myself that."

Jackie

Fall 1986

Jackie didn't blame Terry for leaving her; mostly she just worried she would get a call one morning that he had been arrested inside some crack den, or outside it, stealing to support the habit. He was by no means a thief, but Jackie had learned the hard way that life could drag disgrace out of you.

No, she didn't blame him, but on her bad days resentment jabbed her from the inside. Today was a bad day, she knew, because she hadn't even turned on her Chaka Khan when she got into the car. Instead, she stared outside as she jerked her beat-up Camry out of Stately Grove. She had to keep her windows down because her air conditioner had broken a few months before in the dead of summer, and she could reach out and touch the soiled mattresses beside the dumpster if she tried. No, there was nothing stately about this apartment complex, this neighborhood. Still, she studied her surroundings while she drove in to work, forced her body to feel the potholes, let her eyes linger on the boarded-up houses, liquor stores, and bail bondsmen. Billboards dotted every corner: Nancy Reagan leaning into a black child's face, bold white letters above her head. JUST SAY NO.

At the light, Jackie even peered through her rearview at the housing projects behind her, covered in graffiti and littered with trash. There were at least ten police cars parked in the vicinity already, and residents who should have been at work seemed to guard the overgrown grass, the slumped brown brick towers. In her old neighborhood, her lawn was as fresh as first-day-of-school haircuts, and she could have slept on her sparkling green grass all night without being bothered if she wanted to. But that had been a house in New Orleans East, with patio furniture in the yard, even room for a pool once T.C. got older, and things were different now.

She felt herself exhale as she pulled onto I-10 east, reached the exit for Chef Menteur Highway, slid into the version of heaven where she and Terry had built their first home. The East had been the promised land for the black middle class. It was swampland until the '60s when developers drained it to make room for homes. Black lawyers, doctors, bankers, and even teachers settled in the small pockets of colored housing. Then in the '70s the white neighborhoods became fair game. It was the lawyers and doctors who integrated first, but just ten years later, her middle-class parents secured enough of a down payment to pluck the corner house on Lake Forest. It wasn't long before she and Terry moved a few blocks away.

Now she drove down Chef, which bustled with schools and shops, beauty salons, clothing stores, Bessie's Dog Boarding, Inez's Beauty Supply. She turned onto Lane Avenue, a residential street with new brick houses, iron lions guarding its fronts. The neighborhood was quiet by this time, carports emptied, curtains drawn; most everybody worked, except the occasional mothers who stayed home to walk their children to school.

Jackie parked in front of the house on the corner with the baby-blue trim. She stepped out of the car, lifted T.C. She strained under his weight, though it made her proud that at six months, he was more than twenty-five pounds. It was only eight thirty in the morning, but she could hear the infants and toddlers shrieking before she reached the sign: ACTION ACADEMY in bold red letters above the front door. She walked inside, sidestepped the babies upright in high chairs, grits dribbling down their chins. Once she dropped T.C. with her Aunt Ruby, she climbed upstairs to the Dwarfs Room, the toddler class she'd named after "Snow White." She had wanted to keep her baby with her, but her daddy had said it wouldn't be good for business, that the customers would think she was favoring her own child and start to look for signals of it, unchanged diapers, dirty faces.

"But you know I wouldn't favor T.C. over anybody. I treat them all like they're my own."

"I know that. But you know how these new mothers are, any excuse they can think of to complain. They're mad they can't mind their own children, so everything becomes our fault."

Jackie had argued with him a little longer, but he'd had the final word because he was probably right; he always was, wasn't he? Anyway, what was she going to do? Quit with a newborn, no child support, and rent due? She hadn't gone to law school like her sister, Sybil, and, yeah, she graduated from Xavier, but she'd applied for seven jobs after college and never got past the interview phases. She'd come home excited after each one, told Terry they went great, and he'd massage her with excuses each time they didn't work out: *They probably went with someone they knew*, or *They might have been racist*. Finally, after seeing her hurt so many nights, he suggested she stay home. That had been before his layoff, before the drugs, back when he made enough to take care of them both.

Upstairs, the kids in her class attached themselves to every inch of her body as she walked through the door, syrup from biscuits on their hands and now her skirt. They almost made her forget her chronic grief, the guilt that tugged at her heart because despite everything Terry put her through, who knew what trouble he was in right that minute? Maybe she should have fought harder for him to stay.

She knelt beside the table where the kids ate. The talkers had already started, an avalanche of words that wouldn't let up until nap time, and that was what she loved most about her job, how it swept her so thoroughly out of her real life, how the freshness of each moment kept her wrapped inside it. Even now, a boy named Carter was reciting the ABCs; then, without stopping, pulling her face to his, he said, "Puff was sad."

"Puff?" Jackie answered.

"Puff, the magic dragon, he was a little sad. When his friend left. He was a little sad."

"Oh," Jackie said. She had read the book yesterday. "That's right, but didn't he feel better when his new friend came along?"

"I'm a little sad," the boy said this time.

"Oh, no." Jackie moved to hug him, though she could see the poster of emotions in her periphery. They'd gone over them earlier this week, and since then her toddlers would pick a feeling without warning, cling to it the whole day, clutching anger or sadness, and she'd think, *You don't know what sadness is.*

"His friend came back; his friend came back!" the boy exclaimed suddenly. "Now Puff's a little happy." He kissed her on the cheek.

During naptime, she went for T.C., carried him back upstairs to nurse. There was a TV in the back room and Jackie had snuck an extra helping of her mama's butter beans up from the main floor. Sometimes Mama would join her in here and they'd watch *The Phil Donahue Show.* Jackie turned it on today, but she barely glanced up—one woman from the audience said she would sacrifice getting married and having babies for a thriving career. Sybil said things like that too, but Jackie knew she didn't mean it.

She lifted T.C., slipped her full breast in his mouth, pressed him up against her, inhaled his newborn freshness from the top of his head. She loved watching him nurse. These days most women preferred the formula. *Breastfeeding makes your boobs sag,* Sybil had warned her. *You trying to get a new man, right?* But Jackie couldn't imagine herself with someone new. In the beginning when Terry would show up still seeming like himself, all showered and shaven and good-hearted, only a fraction short of the pharmacist she married, she would cater to him as if he were still her husband. But now, she never let him in her bed, just tossed a blanket on the sofa. Sometimes she stood in the hallway and watched him. Once he was so paranoid he paced the room for hours, but another time he just slept for almost a full day. When he woke up that time, he asked her to bring him a po'boy from We Never Close. She drove all the way to Chef, stood in the line and everything, but by the time she got back, he was gone.

The last part of the day at the nursery always seemed to rush by. Once the children woke up from their naps, Jackie and the other teachers marched them around the neighborhood; while they were gone, Mama prepared their snack, usually Cheerios or pretzels. Then they'd congregate in a circle and read *Green Eggs and Ham* or sing rhymes Jackie and her sister had danced to as children:

> *Down, down, baby, down, down, the roller coaster*
> *Sweet, sweet, baby, I'll never let you go*

Afterward the teachers cleaned up, urging the kids to stack the books in the shelves themselves and pick up their own Legos. When the last child was gone, Mama and Aunt Ruby would change into their nylon tracksuits that swished when they walked and collapse at the kitchen table.

"That lil' Jennifer seemed to be doing better, don't you think?" Mama asked now.

"Umhmm," Jackie nodded, though she thought the child whined more than normal. She flipped through *Ebony* for pictures of Whitney Houston. People had told her she looked like a light-skinned version of that woman, and Jackie had come to agree.

"I think it's 'cause her mama's putting her to bed earlier," Mama went on. "That's important, you know. With you girls I kept you on a schedule."

"It was too much," Aunt Ruby interrupted, shaking her head. "I couldn't get Evelyn to do a thing unless I went to *her* house and sat up on *her* porch. She couldn't go shop, she couldn't eat out. All that and she only had two kids. What did she need to schedule them for? You blink and you forget they're even there. Now, me, I didn't keep a schedule but I still had my seven under strict control."

"No, I guess I didn't need to," Mama cut in. "Jackie and Sybil were nine years apart; by the time Jackie came along, Sybil had been in school for years, could run the house by herself if I needed her to, but children need structure, and if you don't give it to them, they act a fool seeking it elsewhere. Then before you know it, there's a crazy boyfriend in the picture, or worse, drugs . . ." She trailed off.

Jackie knew she hadn't meant to use that example.

Then Mama turned to Jackie as if she were seeing her for the first time that day. "What's the matter, Jackie Marie? You seem a little down."

Jackie shook her head. "Nothing, Mama." She plastered a smile on her face. "I'm just tired, that's all."

"The baby kept you up?" Mama asked. "Well, that's normal for his age," she answered before Jackie could. "But in a few months he'll be sleeping through the night, you watch. Both my kids did by nine months."

"My jokers still don't sleep through the night, and the oldest will be twenty-nine tomorrow." Aunt Ruby cut her head back and laughed, a shrill tinkly number.

Jackie and Mama just smiled.

"Well, you'd have them out all hours, then wonder why the feel of their mattress didn't put them in the mind for rest," Mama said.

"Well, I had to work." Aunt Ruby's voice began to rise. "I had to provide a steady home. Must be nice to have a—"

"Chasing men," Mama muttered.

"What?" Aunt Ruby jerked her head up.

Jackie didn't even look up from her magazine. When it came to her sister, Mama couldn't be without her, but she couldn't say a positive thing about her either. Times like these it was best for Jackie to just nod.

Her daddy walked in the room then, wearing the same track-suit as Mama, only its stripes were blue instead of pale green. Sometimes her parents were so in sync it made her sick. He squeezed Jackie's arm. "You okay, princess? You seem a little down."

"I said the same thing, Renard, but it's just that she's tired. You didn't get up with those babies, so you don't remember, but I remember. Oh, I remember," Mama added.

Then they began to bicker in their sweet way about who got up when, and Jackie shut out their sounds, asked herself the same questions they had. What was it that had come over her, a darkness of some manner? Of course she'd been this way when Terry first left, but she'd been steadily improving, and she didn't know what it was about the day that made her feel like every evenness she'd regained was being snatched back, that she was doomed to a certain and dark fate, that that fate was upon her even now and she could barely walk through it, it clung to her so thickly.

The door to the nursery opened, and Jackie heard her sister's heels clacking against the hardwood floor, smelled her Armani perfume before she saw her. Since Jackie had started working at the nursery a few months earlier, she and her parents and sometimes Aunt Ruby ate dinner together every night. Nothing fancy, whatever Mama had prepared for the kids' lunch, spaghetti with sausage and meatballs, red beans, beef stew or cabbage and rice. Jackie had dreaded those meals at first. Her depression wanted to extend itself, wanted to strap her to her couch at home eating TV dinners in front of *Murder, She Wrote*, but it was those meals with her parents that had brought her back to her own. They didn't talk about much: layoffs, what the Saints might do next season, but it was more the chemistry of them together, the soft rhythm of it that reminded her so thoroughly of her time as a child that she could convince herself her biggest problem was whether she'd learn to fishtail her doll baby's hair before her playdate with Lucita McConduit.

Now her sister was here with her waxed eyebrows, red blush, and pink lipstick, her shoulders pushing through the top of her business suit, and her pumps making such a racket Jackie was certain she'd wake the baby. Jackie looked down at her own washed-out sweatshirt and faded jeans. She was still looking down when Sybil kissed her on the cheek, which in itself felt condescending. They didn't do that with each other. It was likely something she learned from one of her law school friends, and it was all well and good when Jackie had her man beside her, certain Sybil would study herself into a lonely oblivion, but now they were both alone, and Sybil's alligator bag probably cost Jackie's rent.

"Where's my baby?" Sybil scanned the room looking for T.C. and Mama had to shush her. "He just went down. Let Jackie Marie have a break."

"He'll be up after dinner, wanting to eat what I eat," Jackie chuckled, and Sybil wrinkled her nose as if Jackie had told a tasteless joke, or farted.

"What a nice surprise." Daddy walked back in from washing up and hugged his oldest daughter.

Sybil's face lit up when she saw him. "I got off early and knew you'd be here," she said.

"Good. You deserve a break. Well, stay for dinner, darling. Mama made some butter beans and salad, didn't you, Mother?"

Mama just nodded. She had already laid the plates out in the kitchen and added another setting before they said a quick grace. By the time Jackie was halfway through her meal, Sybil still hadn't spoken, and Jackie prayed the rest of the dinner would pass that way. She knew Mama had made Jackie's favorite that morning, bread pudding, but she was willing to forego it to skip out on a conversation with her sister.

Sybil cleared her throat. "I have some news."

"Oh, Lord, are you pregnant?" Aunt Ruby asked.

"God, no, Aunt Ruby." Sybil shook her head.

"Well, is there a man at least?" Aunt Ruby went on.

"Let her say it, Ruby," Daddy said, his mouth full.

Mama and Jackie glanced at each other, then looked away. Neither felt up to Sybil since she graduated law school ten years earlier. It wasn't the accomplishment itself. Jackie loved visiting Sybil's office, looping around Lee Circle past the streetcars ambling onto Poydras, peering up at the Superdome scaling the sky. Her sister had always said she wanted to be a lawyer, but given she didn't start law school until she hit thirty, everybody believed she'd talk her dream out until it was drained of all its power. Still, she had done it, and Jackie felt a vicarious surge in her own confidence when Sybil passed the bar. No, it wasn't the accomplishment itself that made Jackie dread her sister's presence. It was the way Sybil tried to make her feel about it.

Daddy though was proud on all accounts. It was as if Sybil's achievement had brought them closer. Jackie had been his favorite growing up. He had fawned over her when she was a girl, enraptured by her descriptions of her best friends' Uptown houses: their wide-open pools and terraced decks. The two drifted apart some when Daddy opened Action Academy. Jackie was in high school, and she had her own life, cheerleading practices and Terry's football games, and it was Sybil who had helped Daddy most days, bleaching the changing tables, folding spare clothes, and driving to the discount warehouse every week for boxes and boxes of baby wipes. Then Jackie got married, and Sybil went on to law school, and now Daddy sat with his mouth gaping as his oldest daughter went on about her cases. If she paused for even a second, Daddy would jump in with yet another question: How she'd decide whether to settle or go to trial, whether she had considered advertising like that fellow Morris Bart. If so, he had thought of a slogan: *No Need to Retort, I'll See You in Court.*

"Well, you know that contract I was trying to snag with Taco Bell, Daddy," Sybil went on now. "I think it's going to work out this time. They called me in twice for an interview. I met with the regional manager."

"The regional manager. Isn't that Jack Jackson? He used to try to talk to me back in the day," Jackie said to have something to say, but Sybil snapped back in that tone she'd used since childhood, "Jack Jackson manages the Taco Bell in the East of New Orleans. I'm talking about the manager of the Taco Bells all over Southeastern Louisiana."

Jackie didn't say anything to that, just kept her head down, scooped out some more rice.

"That's great, baby, that's really something," Daddy said again, his mouth wide enough to fit the table through it.

Sybil was beaming too. "I know, Daddy. It's been a long time coming. I can't do criminal law anymore. It's starting to eat at me, all these black men on the street."

Daddy nodded. "Not to mention how dangerous it is."

It was as if it were a conversation between the two of them and Aunt Ruby, Jackie and Mama were just some fixtures to navigate around, a table leg that dangled, a chair that creaked when you applied too much weight. Jackie suddenly tried to fumble through her past for fodder, which high-end Creole boy had asked her out, her playdates with the Haydels and Davieliers, but it was no use. She was thrilled to hear T.C.'s wails, but Sybil stood up the same time she did, as if she had as much right to the room where the baby slept.

"Let me see him, Jackie, it's been so long."

Jackie nodded, smoothed her hands down the front of her work pants, which were already covered in dried paint.

"Just wash up first," she added, but Sybil was already out of the room.

Sybil pranced back in with the baby on her shoulder, who to Jackie's dismay didn't cry. He'd stare up at Sybil, then jerk his head back in his mother's direction.

"He's trying to figure out who has him," Mama said.

"He's confused by the resemblance," Daddy said at the same time, though the truth was Jackie and Sybil didn't resemble each other in the least. Sybil had come out more like their father, with his bunched-up nose and lips; her skin was lighter than his, but not by much, and her hair wouldn't lay flat if you dared it. Jackie on the other hand was tall and skinny with a size C cup and skin like the inside of an almond. Her hair fell down her back, and she some-times spiral-rolled it and wore it curly, but mostly she let her mama straighten it, and that was when it reached her behind.

The baby seemed to soften Sybil. Expressions and words Jackie would never associate with her sister sprang out of her now.

"You're so handsome, yes, you are, just as ooey gooey as a shmooey wooey."

Jackie and her mama burst out laughing. Soon the whole room was in stitches and that ease that sprang from the mirth smoothed Jackie on the inside as she loaded the dishwasher, wiped down the counters.

Sybil's comment was more jarring because it was unexpected. "Have you heard from Terry?"

Mama, Daddy, and Aunt Ruby had been cooing over T.C., but after Sybil's question the room went silent. The thing was, everyone knew not to bring that up.

Jackie shook her head instead of answering, almost as if she didn't trust her own voice.

"Good, the farther away he stays from you, the better. You and that precious angel."

Jackie tended to feel the same way, and if anyone but Sybil had said it, she would have stressed her own agreement, might have added that even though she sometimes let him in the house, she had closed off any part of herself that was vulnerable to him: She spoke in one-word sentences, she didn't look in his eyes, and she never went over their past, how being with him in the beginning reminded her of the stories her daddy had told her about courting Mama. She had really believed their love was as full.

But Sybil spoke so authoritatively about matters she hadn't earned the right to dominate. Jackie had let her have the edge on almost every subject: the work, the money, the house, the car. And now she was trying to edge her way into a part of life she didn't understand, and Jackie had had enough.

"You don't get it," she snapped.

Sybil smirked, paused for a minute as if she was considering whether or not to speak. "What exactly don't I get?" she asked finally.

"I mean to say," Jackie stammered, "that it's a complicated situation, not one you can sum up with one sentence the way you just tried to."

Mama stepped in. "You want the rest of this milk for the baby?" She held up a bottle, shook it in Jackie's face to get her attention.

Even Aunt Ruby tried: "You better be careful, Sybil. Every shut eye isn't asleep."

Sybil just ignored them. "Nothing complicated about crack," she went on. "He's either on it or he's not, and chances are he is. So he needs to be gone."

The thing was, Sybil had never even had a serious boyfriend. She had ideas about what she would do in Jackie's situation: call the police on him, or burn all his things. Sometimes she'd ask Jackie questions she already knew the answer to just to get her riled up.

Did he even call you on your birthday, Jackie? What kind of man can't remember to celebrate his own wife's thirty-second? And you're the one stuck with the baby while he's out doing God knows what.

But her commentary didn't work. It was true that Jackie felt overwhelmed—reading to the baby at night, making sure she stared at him while she spoke so he could see her lips moving, choosing the stroller, the car seat, the pediatrician. Making every goddamn single decision alone sucked every drop of energy out of her core. But Jackie knew Terry couldn't help that crack had eaten up his mind, that if he had been himself, he would have sent her favorite flowers, petunias, just like old times, or taken her to dinner at Dooky Chase's, and maybe a part of her was slumped in on itself, pricked free of air, but she couldn't transfer that feeling into full-fledged anger.

In fact, standing here now beside her sister who had never laid beside a man in bed, listened to his dreams, then saw them dashed at every turn, who had never become so entwined with someone it was impossible to kick him out without feeling like a part of herself had been rejected, she had a sudden urge to defend Terry. Jackie wanted to tell her sister that she'd run into Terry's white coworker a few months earlier, the same one who'd started Terry using, and the man had bragged to her that he'd been promoted. She might tell her too that both of Terry's grandfathers had been alcoholics, that Terry's daddy was one too, but he had abandoned Terry when Terry told him he was going to rehab, told Terry a real man would be able to stop on his own; she wanted to explain that Terry had been captain of the football team, president of their class, valedictorian of his pharmacy college, and though she hated his new track, she understood his sudden need to just breathe.

She didn't say a word though, just turned the water off, reached for the baby, kissed her parents, and walked out.

The closer she got to her apartment, the stronger her anger grew. In the car, other instances of Sybil's audacity sprang up for recognition, examination. Sybil had been the one to tell Jackie Terry was on crack in the first place. It was an absurd accusation. Terry had been valedictorian of St. Augustine and Xavier. Then with three offers in his hand, he'd accepted a job at the VA. He fell right in with his coworkers, the white boys from Brother Martin, who'd all gotten the job through connections. Jackie didn't mind that he went out every other night with them. It was part of acclimating, he'd said, but even if he hadn't said it, Jackie liked her alone time. As many friends as she had, there was something intoxicating about not having to rehearse every word before it left her mouth, revisit them once they drifted out. Then Reagan got elected with his tax cuts and spending bans, and it wasn't long before everybody she knew knew somebody who was standing in the unemployment line. Right after Thanksgiving, it was the VA's turn, and by Christmas, Terry was out.

Jackie didn't think it was a big deal—he'd had so many offers he could just go back to one of the pharmacies he'd rejected. *But that's not the way it works, Jackie,* Terry had snapped in a tone that was not of him, not of their relationship. He started staying out every night. Those same friends from work had kept their jobs and they were schooling Terry in how to get another one, he'd said. Still she noticed that his lips were cracked when they kissed, that he was never home, and when he was, he was sleeping, that his jeans sagged around the crotch, and that Sewerage and Water Board called her to say their bill was two months late. She just chalked it up to the new pressure of unemployment, even suggested she try to get work again. But he'd snapped at her then too. It wasn't until Sybil came over for dinner. Terry had burst in their house, all jabber and quick moves, and after he left, Sybil turned to Jackie, said in a pitying tone that she'd seen the same signs in some of her clients, the emaciation, the restlessness. Jackie asked her to leave, threatened to call the cops when she wouldn't budge. Even though she didn't believe Sybil, Jackie confronted Terry when he got home. He cried, told her he had a problem, he wanted help, but didn't know how to get it. He admitted that he started with the friends at work. First pills, then cocaine, and now he was running their savings dry chasing after crack. She vowed to stay with him. She didn't understand the drug then. He went to rehab in Northwest Louisiana for two months and he came back with a light in his eyes and a calm about him. But it was still a tight market and nobody was hiring.

After the first relapse, her parents urged her to kick him out, but it was impossible to leave the man she had become an adult with, the captain of the football team who had chosen her for reasons she couldn't explain. She waited it out for a few years, tossed between his bouts of renewed sturdiness and his collapses. She was ready to defer to her parents until she found out she was pregnant. She told him, hoping the child would be the motivation he needed, and he was clean for the first few months. Terry came home every night, he was the father she'd always imagined he'd be, then one day without warning, he left for coffee she had in her own pot on the counter and didn't come back.

With him gone, she didn't think about the hollow ghost who'd occupied her house the last few years, just the way her sixteen-year-old self would lean into the phone receiver for hours, twiddling the cord around her thumb, the way he'd press his hand into her back and lead her into a room, the way he'd soothe her when someone talked down to her, *If they don't see you as who are you, that says more about them than you, Jackie Marie*, and even now she'd repeat that to herself when she needed strength. But it seemed as though she still couldn't regain her footing. His addiction had blindsided her, and she'd been looking down at the ground while she walked since then, on the verge of falling off a cliff that she wasn't sure existed.

She pulled up to Stately Grove, got out the car, lifted the baby. The elevator wasn't working, so she braced herself for the walk. She opened her apartment door, walked inside, shut it, and slumped against it; she could hear her neighbors upstairs fussing already.

"You been calling bitches? Answer me, mothafucka, you been calling bitches?"

It started like this around dinner, low-grade rumbling that escalated by bedtime, and last night Jackie had almost called the police until she remembered she was stuck at Stately Grove—the last thing she needed was an indefinite enemy. The man yelling just now carried a gun; she knew because she'd glimpsed it creeping out of his peeling brown belt one morning, and then there was the woman downstairs with the gold jewelry and bright red lipstick whom Jackie had heard might be a lady of the night.

Jackie passed by her bedroom window, which she hadn't bothered to drape; police cars framed the block like trees lined her old neighborhood, like potted plants had guarded the fresh lawns. Maybe she could just run downstairs and report the noise, which was steady building; she'd be upstairs before anyone could see her. Then again, the streets had eyes sometimes; the last thing she needed was somebody retaliating, calling the police on Terry one night.

The nightly wail of sirens started as she ran T.C.'s bathwater. But she put them out of her mind as she fell into her evening routine, bathing him, toweling him clean, especially the rolls around his neck where milk tended to gather, greasing his belly and legs with Vaseline, plucking a clean onesie from the hamper, then settling him down beside her. She used to fold clothes; hell, she used to wash dishes and mop floors too, but that was over now. No, she'd nurse him one more time, then they'd sleep until five.

"You're blessed," her mama had said one night. "You didn't sleep through the night until you were nine months old. Sybil neither."

Jackie appreciated compliments like those, but she didn't need any reminders that her son was an angel. After Terry left, she wouldn't have made it without him.

The noise from the couple upstairs picked up along with music from a boombox outside. Rap music, she guessed. *I came in the door, I said it before. I never let the mic magnetize me no more but it's biting me.*

"You mothafucka low-life piece of shit, I nearly died for you and you threw me away for that bimbo." This from upstairs. Jackie wondered what the man had done to rile the woman up so. She wanted to go and ask her about it, tell her nobody was worth her dignity, but she reminded herself not to get involved. She'd hoped initially that she was just at Stately Grove temporarily but she was saving only $500 a month and Terry was sick as ever—it was starting to look as if she might be walking her son to school from this broken-down parking lot, the sign in its center leaning and chipped. Her daddy had offered to put a down payment on a place in the East.

"I have more than enough, darling,"

And he did. He hadn't finished college but he'd hustled through the rest of his life. His ease had been slow coming—there was a package liquor store that went bankrupt, a cleaners that got held up, and years of selling old cars in crooked lots—but Jackie and Sybil always wore winter coats from Maison Blanche, and when Jackie won homecoming queen, her daddy bought her a Lincoln. Still she refused him. Her whole life she had been dependent on a man. She met Terry in high school and grew up beside him. And it was only after he was gone and the garbage needed to go out and the bills needed to be paid by a certain date that she realized she was only halfway grown, like the little girls she saw downstairs some mornings, mismatched foundation caking their face, half shirts revealing their too-taut bellies.

Jackie settled the baby on his stomach as her mama had taught her. He'd slept in her bed the last few months. She told her mama it was him, that he didn't get a good night's rest in his crib. But the truth was, she'd lay awake all night if her son wasn't beside her, the wail of police sirens winding like a snake inside her brain. Without tying her hair or changing out of her daytime clothes, she turned on the television, switched out the light, prayed her eyes would soon close. There was a special on the news about drugs, and while she faded she heard snippets: *crisis, hands on horror, a threat to every suburb in America.* She didn't need to open her eyes to know blacks were being handcuffed, carted into cop cars. Funny, the way they were describing it, when she'd seen protesters up and down South Claiborne last week crying out, *The War on Drugs is a War on Us.*

Jackie didn't know whose side she was on. She was still teetering between her narrow options when she heard the knock.

Nobody ever came by unannounced, especially not at this hour, so she stayed where she was; it was probably some residual noise from upstairs. She didn't think the man beat the woman, but she sometimes heard bangs and crashes indicating something had been thrown. Another knock, louder this time.

She knelt slowly, felt around in the dark for the baseball bat she kept under her bed, held it up to her shoulder, tiptoed to the door, afraid to breathe for fear the person on the other side would hear her. She still wasn't sure what she would do when she arrived.

Just then a man's voice rang out. "It's me, baby."

Jackie opened the door, stepped backward, and watched Terry ease into the living room like butter pouring. He was all brown skin and height: There hadn't been many boys in high school who stood taller than Jackie, but he was one of them, even at fourteen, and her head only reached his shoulder in their wedding photos.

"It's me, baby," he repeated, with his fresh fade and shaved face, which was full again as though he'd been eating.

"What the fuck are you doing here?" she forced the edge into her voice. It might have been there on its own had he shown up yesterday, but after her talk with Sybil she'd developed tenderness toward him.

He started to explain. "I've been staying by my mama," he said. "I went to rehab again. I guess I hit bottom, I don't even remember, but"—he shook his head—"there's nothing like a mother's love, let me tell you. I got myself together. I've been out a month. I wanted to come and see you and the baby right away, but Mama held me back, said don't go in there unless you're prepared to stay. So I did. I'm sorry to scare you," he said. "I just got so excited. I went to my meeting and they gave me this." He held out a green chip. "I know it's not much, I know two months is not that long, but for me, I never thought I would hit a week, you know, so it feels like something. It feels like something. You're the first person I wanted to share the news with. Guess I just got caught up thinking about my own excitement. I can leave if you want."

Jackie thought about what Sybil would say. It was what her father had told her to do in high school if she was having trouble deciding whether to accept the drink at a house party or stay out an hour later because the music at a concert had gotten good. And it had been good advice, the answer always came to her so clearly, but it was following it that had been the problem. She didn't answer right away, just sat down. Not asking him to leave seemed to be response enough, and he sat too, not next to her but on the opposite sofa, on the only patch not covered by unfolded laundry. She noticed a cereal bowl of dried milk on a television tray in front of him and she waited for him to say something about the apartment, which looked like Hurricane Betsy had blown through it. Her family had long since started to comment.

Girl, is there a free inch of carpet in this house? That from her mother the week Jackie paid a mover to place her bed in her living room—her fear of intruders seemed to subside the closer she slept to the front door.

Or, *You ever thought about hiring a housekeeper?* That from her sister the week Jackie cooked a pot of gumbo, a whole roast, potato salad, and rice and gravy but never got around to the dishes.

The questions haunted Jackie even weeks after they'd been

asked, because after everything with Terry, she was still the same woman at heart, the one who, though she nearly always came up short, aimed to please, the one who used to paint her nails and scrub her baseboards and shave and douche her honey pot, and every week she was on a diet, like the one where she ate the same food as everybody else but dished it out on a saucer instead of a real plate.

But he didn't seem to notice. He only turned to her and asked, "Baby asleep?"

She nodded.

"That's good. That's good. You need a break."

"I'm so tired, Terry," she said, but she hadn't meant to. It was what he called out of her, the truth, when she had been so comfortable covering it for everybody else, her mother, her father, her sister; she had learned to smile first thing when people saw her so they wouldn't have the burden of joining her in her despair. She had learned to stretch her cheeks out for thirty seconds, not that she was counting; to answer their questions according to what they might want to hear, not what she was really thinking. *I'm good*, she'd say, but it had to be with the proper lilt, with the last word stretching up so that it tinkled out like a wind chime. The only one she hadn't had to fake with all this time was her baby: It seemed like the soft coos, the warm embraces, and the patience to get up and grab him even when she'd just gotten to sleep herself came to her through a sort of grace. But his father was here now and she was so, so tired.

Terry walked closer, sat down next to her, holding his head down, seeming to know he had caused this pain. He reached out and held her. And for the while that she cried, really sobbed into his chest, she didn't care if Sybil was right, if this was just another temporary lull—and of course it was, she wasn't stupid—she was just glad that he was there now, because she'd needed this release more than she could have known.

When she was done, she wasn't embarrassed. She wiped her face with her shirt, and he got up to get some tissues from the bathroom.

"Excuse the mess," she said when he returned.

"Please, you got enough on your plate to be worrying about housekeeping."

She shrugged. "I always kept a good house," she said, sniffling again. "It was what I was known for. Remember, people would come over for some of my gumbo and pound cake? It didn't matter what time of day it was, I always had something to offer them, gumbo or biscuits or sweet potato pie, something. Now I'd be embarrassed to let somebody in here, much less serve them something out of that God-awful kitchen." She nodded to the back of her apartment, where she hadn't done dishes in days. The refrigerator was empty as a ghost, and even if she tried, the cracks between the linoleum would never be free of that grime.

He sighed, shook his head, held his hand out. Jackie had small hands, and his were nearly twice her size. Often they'd press them against each other to marvel at the discrepancy. She had an urge to do that now.

"Don't take that on as your fault, baby," he said. "It's me, I know it's all me, but I'm—" he stopped himself. "I was going to say, I'm going to do better, but I won't make any promises. That's what my sponsor always says, that there's another side to promises, like a coin, and it's called disappointment, and well, they tell us just to take one day at a time, one moment really, moment by moment, and that's been working for me."

Jackie sat with that for a while. She had heard most of his lines a million times before, but this one was new. No promises. Moment by moment. That's what she didn't want, uncertainty—that's what made her feel so out of control, so desperate. She'd do her best to manufacture conviction during times like those. Last time she had sworn to her parents that it was different, she had bragged to her friends that any minute they'd be back in their house on Rosalia Drive, and if not that one, something better. She'd believed herself when she spoke like that, but when she thought about it now, that belief never led anywhere, did it?

The baby fussed, and she stood to see about him. She beckoned for Terry to follow her, but when they arrived at the bedroom, T.C. had already quieted. Jackie collapsed at the head of the bed, her cheek on her pillow. She hadn't made it up that morning and Terry had to move a twisted sheet to the side to find a clear space on the edge. Jackie closed her eyes, just for a minute. She knew she wouldn't do anything with him tonight. He looked good. She'd had a chance to study him when he walked to the bathroom, and she'd seen the months with his mama had not only fattened him up, but reacquainted him with his normal stride, settled his mind so his words came out steady. Still he had broken her heart too many times for her to manage anything but talk.

The last year was off-limits for them both, so they traveled backward. High school for one: Did she remember their first date, when he brought her home ten minutes after curfew, and he'd moved the time back on his car and pretended he thought they were five minutes early?

She laughed. Of course she remembered. "I stayed up all night that night, reliving the date, driving to the daiquiri shop, then stopping at St. Claude Seafood for crawfish."

"Eating it at the Lakefront on top of our car," he joined in.

"I didn't even brush my teeth or take my makeup off," Jackie went on. "It was like I was too high to follow the regimen of the regular world." She regretted that word after she used it, *high*, but he didn't seem to notice. "It was like if I did something ordinary, I'd fall back down."

"That's right, I sure did take you to the daiquiri shop," he said. "I had to pat myself on the back for that one. That was pretty good right? For a seventeen-year-old? You and them tight shorts and pink pumps. Them rollers in your head."

"It was awright," she said, smiling though. "Not like Commander's for my birthday." She still smiled.

"Oh, well, yeah, that was later when I got a little dough."

"Those were the good days," she said.

He nodded. "Real good."

"Remember when we took Sybil to Dooky Chase's for the first time?" Jackie asked to stoke the glee of nostalgia. "She ordered so much food and after the waiter left you asked her, 'Sybil, were you ordering or reading the menu?'"

They laughed. Sybil had been a broke law student then, and as kids, Mama would cook fancy meals, but they didn't go out much.

"You should see her now, Terry. She thinks her shit don't stink, walking around in her Brooks Brothers suits."

He nodded, shrugged. "Yeah, I'm not surprised, I guess. You could see something like that was coming her way." There was a pile of clothes in a basket beside the bed, and he reached down and started folding them, laying them down on the part of the bottom sheet he had smoothed. "Think about it, she was always second to you growing up. Imagine what that's like, being the older sister but people looked past her for you. You have always been a bright light, Jackie Marie."

She would have fallen into the compliment, she needed it today more than ever, but the sirens interrupted him, louder than she'd ever heard them, like the police car had pulled right up to her door. Jackie thought she saw Terry's eyes water. She felt a need to comfort him, let him know she didn't blame him for the way things had turned out.

"You would think I would feel safer knowing they're here all night." She forced herself to chuckle, rolled her eyes.

He set the shirt he was folding down and leaned in and squeezed her. She didn't fight him off, but she didn't relax into him either. He seemed to sense her discomfort and eased off but not before adding, "I'm going to get you out of here."

She smirked. "I thought you said no promises."

"That's not a promise, that's a fact." He paused, then started again. "When I was gone all that time, it wasn't 'cause I didn't love you. I know you know that, but I feel like I gotta say it. My love for you, for T.C., was the only thing that brought me back, the only thing. Remember that."

T.C.

Summer 2010

T.C. didn't remember meeting his father. But the old man's name was Terry, Terry Cleveland Lewis, and although T.C. wasn't quite a *Junior*—his mother believed in saint names and snuck *Gabriel* in where *Cleveland* should have been—people had called him T.C. since he was born. So even now as he stood six feet seven inches, so tall he had to duck to get in and out of his jail cell, the other inmates yelled, *Watch your head, T.C.* The COs of course called him Lewis. Sometimes he thought that had been the origin of the problem, the fact that he wasn't a real Junior. It wasn't that cleaving to his father's legacy might have made a better man of him—from what he'd heard, his old man hadn't worked in years, and even then it was at a half-dead restaurant in the Quarter. But it was just another example of his not-quiteness, deficiencies he first noticed when he was asked to repeat kindergarten and that had culminated in his stay at the Orleans Parish Prison.

He was getting out today though, and maybe that meant something. It wasn't his first time in, but it was hard to count the weekend stint for stealing a bicycle from Bourbon Street. He didn't even mention that incident to his boys; it wasn't enough to earn him any street cred. Not that he sold drugs to impress anyone. No, he started smoking his second semester in college after his injury, and he found he could actually afford to buy in bulk by supplying his neighbors and friends. Plus, he wasn't going to lie, there was something soothing about the boys on his block ringing his bell all hours of the day. It hadn't been that way in grade school when it might have counted for something. He'd been a heavyset kid before basketball, and he wet the bed until he was twelve. He always passed on sleepovers—T.C. was not stupid—but he could never forgot that for so many years longer than was natural, he couldn't control such a basic function.

"You getting out today, huh, Lewis?" The CO was white and short, even for non-Lewis standards, so short he needed to crane his neck to ask T.C. a question.

"He'll be right back in though," the other CO shot in. Black like T.C. but full of undrained malice toward him. It happened like that sometimes.

The white one laughed.

T.C. joined in, best to stay on their good side. But what the CO had said wasn't true, not this time.

"Nah," T.C. said. "I got a little man on the way."

"So he'll be coming to visit you then?" This from the black one. "Him and his momma."

T.C. shook his head, but he didn't protest. *If you had to convince people who you were, it was too late*, isn't that what his grandmama always said? Anyway, he was in a good mood. The girl he'd been seeing before he got locked up had let him call her every night and wrote him letters from time to time. Her name was Natalia, but he called her Bon Bon. She was a hot little thing, and she was waiting for him at her mama's house Uptown. They hadn't done much before he left, low-level dibbling and dabbling that reminded him of his high school days, but she was all he'd been thinking about, and tonight that anticipation would bloom into something he could feel.

"Whatever you say, boss." He smiled at the CO who handed him his clothes. T.C. had forgotten he was wearing sweats and a T-shirt when he was brought in four months earlier. He was on his way to the grocery store when he got pulled over. The funny thing was, his mama had told him not to go, reminded him of that later during visitation.

"People think I'm crazy," she said, "but I'm never wrong. Your friend Daryl would be alive today if he had listened to me. Miss Patricia ain't been the same since, and she won't be; Miss Patricia might as well a died along with her boy." She paused then before going on. "It's a goddamn shame how the city blew up them levees. Just like Betsy. If they got a choice, they gon' always side with white."

T.C. ignored her when she went on like that, though it was true, his mama had predicted Katrina would take lives. Everybody knew it was coming, but half his friends banked on it being like the storms the year before that rerouted or lost force before they hit the city. T.C.'s mama had a dream the morning before the storm hit, though, called him from work, begging him to pack a suitcase. He obliged her only because she started crying. They were halfway to Alabama when the levees broke. Daryl, his brother from another mother, the friend he'd walked to school with every day for fifteen years, had decided to ride it out. They got word three weeks later that his body was found in his attic under a moldering sofa.

On the other hand, T.C.'s mama spilled out useless details, conspiracy theories, information from her childhood nobody wanted to hear, outright inventions, stream-of-consciousness commentary, and caustic affronts that sometimes held truth, sometimes didn't. Like the time she told Miss Patricia that she'd been ignoring her since she got her new house, but there was no new house. Then once when she was delivering a monologue to the TV screen, T.C. heard her say her mama had died when she was three years old. But her mama was still here, had let T.C. stay with her after he lost the scholarship in fact, and if it hadn't been for his MawMaw, he'd be doing much worse than selling weed by the eighth.

When he was done dressing, he walked with the COs to sign his release forms. Then they handed him the money left in his commissary, and he was free to go.

T.C. had called Tiger the day before, and sure enough here he was waiting in the parking lot leaning in front of his silver Honda Civic, fancy since T.C. last saw it, with new blacked-out twenty-two-inch rims. The two had met a few years back playing intramural basketball at Joe Brown Park. Tiger always ran with the wrong crowd, even went to juvie when they were in middle school, and T.C.'s mama banned him from kids like that his whole childhood. But things were different now: Tiger had been friends with Daryl too, and after the storm that was worth more than a good reputation.

"Whoa, nigga," Tiger called out. It was an expression that still stirred fear in T.C. Technically it just meant *come here* or *let me talk to you*, but it had been what the boys had called out before they jumped him in high school, and once before he even started hustling, three dudes cornered him with the same line before they pressed a gun against his temple.

"I'm just messing with you." Tiger walked up closer. "You know I'm just messing with you," he repeated, laughing so hard his shoulders shook. "You done gained weight, huh?" He leaned into T.C. and felt his biceps.

"You know it, ain't nothing else to do in there," T.C. said, feeling his heartbeat settle. He had an urge to knock the boy out for scaring him like that, but he took a couple of deep breaths like the counselor inside had taught him, told himself to calm down. "But looka you, you ridin' on them thangs, huh?" he asked after a while, nodding at the new rims.

"Yeah, yeah, you know how I do." They both walked closer to the car. "But looka you, your dreads all twisted up, and long. They

almost catchin up with mine." Tiger fingered T.C.'s thick, black
hair. His own hung past his bright green T-shirt, nearly touching
the top of his tapered jeans. He was shuffling his feet, socked up in
Adidas slippers.

"Still light bright and damn near white though," Tiger play-
scoffed. "That's why they let you out early? I thought you had another two weeks."

"Nah, overpopulation, nigga," T.C. said, laughing. "They need
to make room for the real menaces to society." T.C. was lucky—
he'd been headed to reup when he was caught and only had a few
ounces of weed on him; if it had been a day later, hell, a few hours
later, he'd be in jail two years minimum.

"Aw, nigga, they done made a mistake releasing you then," Tiger said. They laughed together finally, gave each other dap, then
came apart again.

"You look good though," Tiger added. "You must be getting
ready for the comeback, and we got competition now, boy. Right
after you caught your lil' bid, Spud got out."

"What?" T.C. leaned against the car, guessing they'd catch up
for a minute, then he'd ask Tiger to drive them the hell out of there.

"Yep, he been trying to reposition himself. I been spreading the
word that you coming back but nobody ain't hearing it. Half our
block been buying from him."

"Oh, yeah?" T.C. let out a nervous laugh. "Well, maybe that's
for the best."

"What you mean 'that's for the best,' nigga?"

Tiger looked at him as if he'd been joking, and maybe he was.
He didn't know.

"What you mean?" Tiger repeated. "We got to eat. What, you
plan on going back to Winn-Dixie?"

"Hell, no," T.C. said, then laughed suddenly, an awkward burst
of sound, but he had been thinking about it, had even calculated
how many hours he'd have to work to make enough to get an apartment over in Lakewind East on Bundy. It came out to a lot, but

people did it, some he went to school with, and he'd run into them bagging groceries on his late-night munchie runs.

"Bruh, I ain't trying to think about that right now," T.C. said. He opened the passenger door. The truth was it was all he had been thinking about. It was jailhouse policy to declare you weren't coming back. He didn't know anybody who hadn't screamed it across his cell at least once in a fit of rage or desperation, or repeated it to himself like a prayer during meal lineup, and that wasn't to say he didn't believe it. He did, but something happened when you walked away from those prison gates: Freedom and its expansive nature convinced you it could last forever. The promises you made to yourself flitted from the front of your consciousness. It was funny, but already, not even in the car that would take him away, he could remember the allure, the fast money, the easy power of his old life. The one thing was, he was really good at it, and there weren't too many other things he could say that about anymore.

"Anyway," T.C. went on. "I need you to ride me Uptown."

"What the hell? That's in the opposite direction of home."

"Is it that far?" He smiled his big goofy smile he'd gotten teased for in fifth grade. He didn't smile for a while after that year, but sometimes he couldn't help it.

Tiger started the car. Lil Wayne's "Right Above It" came on, still getting bumped on Q93 after four months inside. T.C. put his head back and sighed as they pulled out of the prison lot. They passed the St. Louis Cemetery, its white cement tombs like little houses above ground, then the old St. Bernard Projects. The city tore them down after Katrina, gutted the windows, razed the tall bricks. They were almost done building something new in its wake, but T.C. still didn't know where all the old residents had gone.

"It's hot as hell in here," he said. "You ain't got no air conditioning?"

"You see the windows down. It's broke, nigga."

"The windows being down ain't helping. That's just hot air comin in here then, nigga."

"Well, maybe I need to slow down and let yo' ass out. Maybe the air is cooler on the sidewalk."

T.C. laughed, felt the sweat start to roll down his balls.

"You not going out by Alicia, then, huh?" Tiger asked.

At the sound of her name, T.C.'s head shot back up. "Aww, hell no. She beaucoup pregnant, bruh. You can't fuck a woman when she big like that. I'd push a hole in my lil' baby's head."

Tiger laughed. "That ain't true, bruh. I went up in my old lady till the last minute with all my kids."

"Ain't one of your kids slow though?"

"Nah, bruh, all my kids is straight."

"Nah, bruh, you told me one of them niggas tried to fight a teacher and had to be put in the slow class."

"Nah, bruh, that teacher tried to sneak up on him one day, ya heard me. My man got them killer instincts like his daddy. He ain't gon' stand for that bullshit. Anyway you was in the slow class yourself, my nigga."

"Yeah, exactly, that's why I ain't trying to fuck no pregnant lady. My kid's gotta start out smarter than everybody else."

Tiger was turning onto Tulane. That was good, he was listening at least. T.C. just had to make sure he didn't try to stop at Popeyes. That fool couldn't get enough of their popcorn shrimp with a side of red beans and rice, and he was going to try to get T.C. to pay for them. Any other day that would have sounded like a plan, but four months was too long to be sneaking porn to hit it before the sun came up. He needed to release; the weight of the impulse was drilling a hole in his goddamn brain.

"Awright," T.C. said, "the traffic ain't bad at least."

"Aww, bruh, you still talking about that girl. If we gon' go Uptown, we might as well stop for a bite on Napoleon. Don't tell me you gon' make me drive out of my way, and you ain't even gon' break bread with me, dawg? That ain't right. You know that ain't right."

"Man, you ain't caught a bid in a while, you must not remember what it's like. I got somewhere I need to be. She waiting on me is the thing." His words came out frantic and out of order, reminding himself of his mother; it was what he meant about his needs taking over his body right now.

"Let's just stop at Popeyes, my man," Tiger said. "Get a couple orders of those Cajun fries. It's on the way. We'll be done in an hour, I'll carry you over there, you'll bust a nut by noon." He laughed, glancing at the dashboard for the time.

T.C. shook his head. "We could go out there tomorrow. And I got you, I promise. I really appreciate the ride and everything, but not today, bruh. I ain't gon' be good company anyway."

"Man, dawg," Tiger sighed.

T.C. couldn't tell if he had convinced him. Tiger had turned on South Broad, then left on Napoleon, but that was the way to Bon Bon's house too.

"That ain't even your old lady. She supposed to be your Betsy friend, and you treating her like the queen." Tiger turned for a second to gauge T.C.'s response, then looked back to traffic. That was T.C.'s weak spot, and Tiger knew it.

T.C.'s guilt came back on him and strong. Tiger was close with Alicia and thought T.C. should have married her by now. Back in the G when they used to kick it together real strong, T.C. thought he would too. But she went ham on him all the time, and she wasn't all the way right in the head. They'd be talking, laughing, he'd be feeling like the weight of existence was sliding off his shoulders, he'd shut his eyes, then she'd start screaming about something she found on his phone.

"Why you even going through my phone?" he'd yell back.

"I can't trust you, T.C.," she'd sigh. "I wish I could, but I can't."

The thing was, the most she ever found was flirtatious messaging with his lil' boos, and, yeah, they sent him pictures of their titties from time to time, but he hadn't ever stepped out on her; he hadn't ever wanted to.

"Awright, fine, nigga, I'll ride with you a lil' bit, get you the shrimp." It was too late anyway. T.C. felt the car slowing down in front of the restaurant's red awning. Another mile and they would have been at his lil' boo's, but it was all good. Either way he needed to change the subject. "You and this goddamn shrimp. You'd think they was mixing steak and lobster in the batter."

"Nah, bruh, I ain't got to beg. I got my own money. I just wanted to spend some time with you is all, go over our strategy and shit."

T.C. didn't say anything. He was still thinking about Alicia.

"How she doing anyway?" he asked.

"She all right, hanging in there. She stayin' by her mama and them again, getting the guest room ready for the baby. I think they got everything but the car seat."

"I'll get that."

Tiger didn't say anything.

"I was already planning to get it," T.C. insisted.

"Nobody said you wasn't." Tiger paused. "She still cry about you when your name get brought up."

"Aw, bruh, don't believe the hype. She the one kicked me out. I loved Alicia. I still do. But—" he stopped. There wasn't any use going into this again. He could feel his excitement over Bon Bon diminishing the longer he stayed on the topic, his uncertainty rushing in, his sadness, the fear. He was twenty-five, but he wasn't ready to be a daddy. He had told Alicia that, but she had gotten careless with her pills, and she wasn't scandalous by any means, but T.C. still wasn't sure she hadn't done that on purpose.

"Anyway, man, what else you gon' order?" he interrupted himself. "Them same red beans and rice? I could fuck up some chicken legs, I guess."

Tiger didn't answer him. "I'm not saying you did nothin' wrong. I know she crazy. All these bitches is. And she probably in the ninety-ninth percentile of crazy, you feel me?"

T.C. laughed. "You right about that."

"Especially now that she pregnant."

"I hear you," T.C. said. "I do hear you," he repeated. "But Alicia got to see there's consequences to her actions. She wouldn't stop. It got to be too much. Every day accusing me, and that kicked me out more than she did. Only so many times you could be told you a cheater before you become one. Even now, she got me thinking I'm doing something wrong and she the one told me to leave. She the one wouldn't take me back. I went back every day the first month, but she had her mama slam the door in my face. How many times I'm a go back for more of that? What kinda man would I be if I did?"

They pulled into a spot in the Popeyes lot, got out of the car, walked up. A cop car passed him, and T.C. felt his heart tense before he remembered he wasn't the same man he was a few months earlier. He didn't have anything on him for one; even if one of them po-po approached him, the most they would do was throw him up against the car, search his empty pants' pockets, and slap him up for their lost time. He walked into the restaurant with a new swagger to his step, even turned back and looked one of them dicks in the eye. Inside, there was a line of course. T.C. remembered he couldn't stand the smell of the place, a combination of stale frying oil and cleaning solution. Then the children running around knocking into his legs. One of them looked up at him as if he were on stilts at a circus. "Mama," she said "it's a giant." She was almost whimpering.

Tiger doubled over laughing. "It's good to be home, huh, my nigga?" he asked.

T.C. nodded, smiling that goofy-ass smile. "Yeah it is."

Tiger talked nonstop about the block.

Spud had swooped in when T.C. left; he was bringing in two thousand a week, even had middlemen riding out to Chalmette for him, and people were saying his weed was good, almost as good as T.C.'s.

"Almost as good," Tiger stressed again. "And that's cause half of them only touched the gas you bought, not the gas you made."

T.C. couldn't even front. He grew the best weed he'd ever smoked. There was something hypnotic about picking out the seeds, testing the levels, trimming the leaves, drying the buds. But he couldn't afford to grow enough to satisfy his base, so he supplemented, and some people got his creation, and some people got old regular bud.

"Once you back though," Tiger was still talking, "and they get the real deal, it's gon' be like taking candy from a baby. Thing is," he paused, "I don't think you got enough. See Spud, he don't even touch his own gas no mo. He fronts a lil' bit to his middleman, then takes the profits off the sales, and gives that lil' nigga a piece, and it's not as dangerous that way, cause he not the one out in the streets." He paused again. "If you did it that way, you'd have more time for your product, more time to be the creative genius you are."

T.C. nodded the whole while, dipping his chicken strips in a pool of ketchup and tossing them back, thinking about Bon Bon's titties.

"T.C.? Hello, T.C.?"

"Yeah?" He guessed Tiger had been trying to get his attention for some time.

"Did you hear what I was saying? When you get back tonight, maybe we could see about doubling up on them plants?"

T.C. nodded. "That's cool," he said, though the truth was Tiger's plan was stupid. Adding middlemen would take the power out of T.C.'s hands. One of the reasons he'd gotten caught dealing only once was because he sold to old basketball friends, students at Dillard. On the other hand, it wasn't sustainable. There was only so long you could sell before you got busted, and if he went in again for hustling, it was five years minimum. He didn't have it in him to serve that kind of time, not with a kid on the way. If he didn't have to worry about sales, he could grow more plants, put enough aside sooner to start his own business. He'd always thought he was going to be a basketball player, and it didn't work out, but maybe he could coach other kids like him, see to it they didn't make the same mistakes he did.

He wasn't going to get into it with Tiger though, not right now. He still needed that ride Uptown. And maybe he would be a different man after that encounter. It was possible whatever was waiting between Bon Bon's legs was going to be the magic he needed to go another way.

Tiger had always been a big eater, but today he put back two po'boys, not to mention the red beans and the French fries. He kept getting up to refill his Coke and after three trips he leaned his head back and let out a huge belch. Sure enough, when it had been time to pay, he hadn't lifted a single finger for his wallet.

"Aww, thanks," he had said, acting surprised when T.C. put the cash down. "I owe you. I'll get you back tonight then."

T.C. had nodded, though he didn't know what tonight would bring.

It was hard making it out of Tiger's car; even once they pulled up to the house, Tiger was still talking shit.

"Aww, man, this don't even seem like the kind of girl you want to be involved with. She stay all the way Uptown, don't have no car. At least Alicia had her own place. I mean she moved for the baby, but she always did for herself. She 'bout to get a nursing degree. This girl got a job, T.C.?"

He didn't answer, he just lifted his plastic bag of belongings and strapped it to his shoulder. He would need to call Tiger for a ride in the morning, but he didn't want to get into that now. The thing was, as far as Uptown was from New Orleans proper, T.C. enjoyed riding out here. The people in this neighborhood had been touched by Katrina too, but you wouldn't know it by looking, not like his own block. Sometimes he'd wake up screaming, remembering the flood marks nine feet up his wall, the refrigerator tossed to his bedroom, his baby pictures unrecognizable, and that smell, that God-awful smell of rotten food and mold, as if a skunk had died somewhere in the house underneath all the trash and they didn't know where to begin to look.

"I'll holla at you a little bit later, my nigga," T.C. called out over his shoulder, walking up to the front gate. He rang the bell, then looked down Freret Street while he waited. There were new kinds of restaurants opening up, pricey ones too, places where he had no business even reading the menus. And he wasn't saying it wasn't a good thing—he remembered the neighborhood before Katrina, the vacant storefronts, that his mama locked her car door when she drove through. It was just different, that was all, more to get accustomed to, but maybe one day he could take Bon Bon to one of these fancy spots, let her order whatever she liked without feeling his chest tense up.

He had expected Bon Bon to be at the door waiting for him, maybe dressed in something see-through, but no, her fat-ass mama opened the gate in a muumuu even though it was past eleven in the morning.

"Hey, how you doing? Good afternoon," he said in his best up-standing-citizen voice. He tried not to deliver that goofy-ass smile, but like he said, it just came out sometimes.

"I'm here for Bon Bon, I mean Natalia. She told me I could stop by and see her."

"Bay Bay," the mother screamed out to the back of the house. While they waited for the girl, the mama just looked him up and down as though she could smell the prison yard on his dreads, the disgusting lockdown food on his breath. Finally, Bon Bon came to the door. She wasn't wearing Victoria's Secret, but good enough. Little-ass jeans and a belly shirt. He thought about Alicia again. Last time he saw her, she had been big as a house, her belly button sticking out like a thumb already. The thing was, it had been beautiful to him, her carrying his seed. Of course he'd wanted to be married with a job, but just because it didn't go down like that didn't mean he couldn't find the joy.

The mama finally stepped out of the way, made room for her child. Bon Bon opened the door fully, and he pulled her into his arms. They stood like that, embracing for a while. She stepped back after a few minutes, but he didn't want to stop touching her. He could feel himself filling like a balloon getting ready to pop.

He followed her down a short hallway, holding her hand, her head barely at his chest, trying to stay far enough behind her that she didn't feel him pressing into her back.

Her room smelled like her, shampoo and Tide detergent. There wasn't much in terms of furniture: a bed, a desk, a dresser, but she had a stereo, speakers strapped to the wall beneath her window, a big-screen TV, two iPads. There were posters of whack-ass Drake all over the wall, the last person T.C. wanted to be looking at when he was inside somebody as fine as Bon Bon, but it'd have to do. He collapsed on her bed; it had been so long since he'd been on a real mattress that actually sank with his weight and then lifted again. He looked up; she was standing on the other side of the room.

"Come on over here," he said. "Let me see you."

She inched a little bit closer but stopped midway at the computer desk and leaned over to check her email.

He told himself to calm down. He had waited this long, he could go a few minutes longer.

"What?" he said, her back to him. "You nervous?"

She giggled, then turned around, twirling the ends of her long black hair. He looked at her, really looked at her, the smooth chestnut skin, the straight white teeth, the big lips. He'd like to get those lips around his—

"No, I'm not nervous," she said. She had such a sweet voice. Alicia's, on the other hand, was so low she got mistaken for a man on the telephone sometimes. Alicia carried herself like a grown woman was the thing, and her voice was just a part of that.

"Come over here," he repeated, stretching out his long thin fingers.

She came but with reluctance and sat on the bed beside him, not on his lap where he had wanted her.

"Let's just talk for a little bit," she said.

"We been talking though," T.C. said. If it had been any other day, he would have bit his tongue, but the truth was all they had done was talk. He called her more than he called his own Maw-Maw, and more times than not she would answer. Sometimes when they'd run the distance of their normal topics, her classes at UNO, how they would touch each other when the time came, she would just sit on the phone and breathe. That had been plenty for him then, but now—

"What you wanna talk about?" he asked, sighing.

"I don't know. How was your day?"

He laughed. He couldn't help it. "How was my day? You know I just got home from jail, right?"

She nodded.

"You know that then? So my day was nothing. I woke up, ate breakfast, stood up for roll call, I got processed out, now I'm here with you."

"You glad to see me then?" She smiled. She was teasing him now, seeming more comfortable.

"Hell, yeah, I'm glad to see you."

She started tracing her fingers along his chest. He wanted more than anything to move her hand down, but he restrained himself.

"Tell me again how glad you are to see me," she said.

He felt himself relax inside. This was the girl he knew, the girl who'd let him sneak his hand inside her jeans but wouldn't let him see what he was feeling. From what she'd been saying on the phone though, she was ready for the real thing.

She got on her knees and straddled him. It was on now. He pulled her down, closer to him, kissing her, his hands fumbling with her clothes in an awkward fever. It wasn't his style. Alicia used to tell him that he made love like a woman. He didn't like to hear it that way, but he knew what she meant, that he took his time, that he used his mouth, that he treated her body like it was holy ground, but this was a different story and one he would have to make up for later.

He flipped her on her back and climbed on top. He was startled by how slender her waist was, her titties round as buttermilk drops from McKenzie's before they closed down. He put them in his mouth one by one, alternating back and forth, feeling finally as if he was at home in his body, as if God had put her here with him now as an apology, and He was forgiven, for the half-crazy mother, the runaway father, the learning disability, the deferred basketball dreams. Sometimes in his early-morning thoughts he believed that God was condoning his drug activity. Where else would such pure inspiration have come from, the carefully laid-out plans? And he'd become angry with his Maker when he was caught, as if he'd been betrayed by the true author of the crime, but now all was forgiven. In this world, even if he hadn't come in as a completed man, he had been made one now.

"My turn," she said, and she eased her face down, down, down. His dick was throbbing now with the weight of the urge inside him. Ordinarily this was his favorite part, but there was something about this girl's titties that wouldn't let him go, that seemed to contain the whole of existence inside them, and if he could just stay connected—

She didn't have to pick his dick up to slide it in her mouth, it was already upright. She wrapped her big lips around it and bobbed her head up and down, up and down. She had done this before. He didn't have many more bobs left in him. After that, he would put his mouth between her legs. That wasn't his thang. He didn't love the smell of pussy and it seemed to always be there, lurking, no matter how clean the girl was, but she was earning it right now. She was giving him life and any minute a fraction of that very force was going to burst inside her.

He was so enshrined in the world of her bedroom he didn't hear the knocks, and it wasn't until Bon Bon yanked her mouth from him that he realized they had been sounding for some time. It must have been her goddamn mama, but Bon Bon would know what to shout to send her off, and in a minute they could get back to business.

Sure enough, Bon Bon yelled through the door, "Not now," but she darted around the room for her clothes too, sliding into her panties and some shorts. Before she could slip her top over her head, the door burst open and a man as big as T.C. was tall busted in. T.C. froze; he was still acclimating to the knocks let alone this new disruption, and he didn't know enough to search for his boxers, pull them over his dick, which was straight as an arrow despite everything.

"What the fuck is going on here?" the man shouted. He reached over to her desk and slammed her computer off it. T.C. heard it land with a crack. Then the man walked over to her drawers, pulled the top one out, turned it over, and emptied her socks, panties, and bras onto the floor. A receipt floated out too, drifted to the carpet. T.C. eyed it; whatever it had been for cost only $13.10, but for some reason Bon Bon had kept it.

Finally T.C. snapped back to attention, repeating the man almost verbatim. "What the fuck is going on?"

Bon Bon didn't say anything. She had managed to slide her shirt on. She tossed T.C. his pants, and he stepped into them, his eyes on the maniac in front of him, whose green eyes lit up as if they were electric.

"It's not what it looks like, baby," Bon Bon said, but T.C. wasn't sure which one of them she was talking to. He had decided once he got his clothes on, he was going to bolt for the door. Tiger would have just made it back to the Ninth Ward, but this was an emergency. This mothafucka was crazy, there was no doubt about that, and Bon Bon, just watching him ransack the place as if he came over every Saturday to throw her shit around, must have been nuts too.

He was pulling on his shirt when the man got in his face. Bon Bon stepped in then, trying to protect him, but she was 110 pounds soaking wet, and when the man pushed her out of his way, she fell onto the bed in a soft thud. There was nothing between them now, and T.C. couldn't do anything but back up when the man pushed closer. Before he knew it, he was cornered against a wall between the bed and the dresser; there was nowhere else to go.

"Look, man," T.C. said. "I didn't know nothin' about you. I thought she was free, we wasn't dating or nothin' like that, it wasn't nothin' serious. Let's just put it behind us." He had never been in this situation before, but because he was always the peacemaker among his friends, because he didn't love this girl, and because the comfort of his own bed beckoned to him, his words streamed out like gravy on a plate of rice.

The man didn't budge. It wasn't that T.C. was scared to fight, but he was tired. He'd had to become someone he wasn't the first few weeks of jail. You would think his height would have been a deterrent, but men made knives out of metal scraps from the ceiling, hid them in their boots in the Orleans Parish Prison, pulled them out if you so much as stepped in front of them in line. He would never lose the scar that stretched like a *Y* alongside his belly, and that was enough. The idea of bustin' this nigga's head open, which he was sure he could do, was like asking a man who had just finished a marathon to climb Mt. Everest. No, if he wasn't going to bust a nut, he needed to excuse himself and call Tiger. Maybe he should have gone home in the first place, to see if his mama made him a welcome-home meal.

T.C. repeated himself. "I told you, wasn't nothin' going on between me and her," but the man still didn't move.

"Nothing, Bakari, I swear, nothing," Bon Bon added, in her squeaky little-girl voice.

"Look, I promise you, you don't want none of this," T.C. said, his voice more solid this time. "I will crush you," he added when the man still hadn't backed up. "I will crush you," he repeated, his voice like stone.

The man pushed him now. T.C. didn't fall, but to his surprise, he staggered a bit. He began to wonder if the accumulation of his day—watching his hopes dashed, being on the other side of jail and still running into it—had taken something vital out of him. The man pushed him again, harder this time, and in the seconds it took him to regain his footing, the man pulled out a knife. Bon Bon had been trying to mediate from the sidelines still, but when she saw the knife, she stopped talking and started screaming.

T.C. looked at her instead of the knife itself. The adrenaline he'd experienced during altercations in jail, that force of survival, seemed to drain out of him now, and he didn't know if he was going to be able to get the knife out of the man's hands without slicing himself up, maybe somewhere you couldn't simply bandage up again.

He looked into the man's face. Where had he seen him before? Of course everybody in New Orleans was light bright and damn near white, but this man had red hair too, and those eyes—he recognized him from somewhere, even if it was just a picture. He was certain of that now.

Then the man waved the knife under T.C.'s chin, and he would have swiped him if T.C. had snapped his head out of the way a second later. T.C. looked up at the window behind him. He could try to climb up, but the man could cut his legs while he figured out the lock. He turned back to Bon Bon, begging her for help with his eyes the way he had been begging her a few minutes earlier for a different matter, but she was just as paralyzed as he was, her screams like sirens from that night four months back when he had been only a mile from home, and the door to his world had come crashing in. T.C. looked back at the knife and heard the click of a burner cocking across from him. They all turned to the doorway. Bon Bon's mama was there, pointing a Glock 19 in the air with both hands.

"I'll blow both y'all motherfuckers' heads off if you don't listen up," she said. "I tried to raise Bay Bay right," she went on. "I guess it wasn't enough, but I did what I could. Now I'm going to give you one minute to get your shit and get the fuck out of my house."

The man slipped the knife in his pocket and sprinted out of the bedroom door. T.C. wasn't cornered anymore, but he stayed where he was. What was he going to do? If he ran out now, he would just get sliced in the street, maybe more brutally because there was no mama to defend him. He looked at Bon Bon again. She was crying this time.

"Mama," she said in a soft, shaking voice. "It wasn't T. It was Bakari. You know how he is."

"All I know is I won't have that in my house," her mama said, looking as if she were mad enough to turn the burner on her own daughter. She was still aiming at T.C. though. Bon Bon got up and pushed her arm down. "It's okay," she said. "It's okay," she repeated.

But her mama was shaking her head. "It's not this kind of house. I won't have people thinking I'm running that kind of house." They were both crying now.

"Nobody thinks that, Mama. It was just a silly argument. Everybody has these silly arguments."

"No, they goddamn don't." The mama's hands were shaking and T.C. thought the burner might fall on the floor and go off.

"And not goddamn here." She turned to T.C. still shaking her head. "Now I know that nigga is out there waiting for you. You can stay for a few minutes, long enough for him to leave or for you to get your lil' skinny ass a ride. It's one o'clock. I'm gon' go in my room and watch my stories. If you still here when I'm done, I'm gon' call my husband. He got a permit for this gun, and he know how to use it, and I swear to God if you here when he get back, you gon' wish that man out there had sliced your dick clean off."

"Mama," the girl shouted.

"Don't you 'mama' me." The woman wobbled toward the door, the hem of her muumuu trailing behind her. "With your fast ass."

Bon Bon closed the door.

"What the fuck?" T.C. said, not as loud as he wanted to; he was still mindful of Mama Muumuu in the next room.

"I'm so sorry." Bon Bon was all over him once the door closed, petting him and kissing his face. "I didn't know he was coming."

"I guess you didn't," T.C. said. "And get offa me with all that." He shrugged her off of him, and she slid to the side of the bed.

She started crying again. "Don't do me like that," she whimpered. "I waited for you."

"You couldn't have waited that long, you got the green-eyed monster coming in here like he had some claim to you."

"No, baby, you don't get it. I haven't been with that nigga since back in the G, and even then that was just my lil' trade, but he's crazy. He won't leave me alone. He shows up every few months; I thought it was done 'cause I hadn't seen him in a while, but here he is. He's crazy, you gotta believe me, I waited for you." She edged closer to T.C. as she talked, rubbing his chest. "I waited for you," she repeated. By the time she was finished, she had wrapped her arms around his stomach.

"He always threatens me, but it ain't never got that ugly before." She leaned her head against his chest.

"What kind of threats he make?" T.C. asked.

"That if he sees me with another man, he's going to kill me, that kind of stuff." She was whispering in his ear. His dick was getting hard again.

"I wouldn't let that happen. I'm tired today, from everything, but if he came over here again like that, I would take care of him, you know I would," T.C. said.

"I know you would, T.C., that's what I love about you."

She was straddling him again now. He let her. What the hell. Mama Muumuu was in the next room with *The Bold and the Beautiful*. He could hear the theme song as he slid inside her daughter. It wasn't anything like what he'd imagined all those months, not with the terror of the past fifteen minutes hanging over him. No, it was more a physical release than an emotional satisfaction, but he would take it.

He didn't last long, and he rolled over as soon as he was done. The mother's show was coming off, he could hear the song again. Bon Bon was laid out beside him, snoring; maybe he was better than he gave himself credit for. He dialed up his boy Tiger.

"Already, my nigga?"

"Yeah, and hurry up too. I gotta story for you."

When the horn sounded twenty minutes later, T.C. opened the front door, glanced in both directions, and ran out like suicides at basketball practice. He jumped in the car, and Tiger sped off.

T.C.'s mama hadn't made a welcome-home dinner nor was she in such a welcome-home mood. The block looked good though. It had been only four months, but Miss Patricia had finally finished her house, gotten rid of that FEMA trailer that hugged the brown grass beneath it. New Orleans East wasn't Uptown, but it was coming back together. Most of the brick houses of his childhood had been gutted and restored. Yeah, some off in the distance still had windows boarded up, roofs torn down. T.C. had to squint to see them though.

His mama gave him a hug—one long tight squeeze—reached up to the side of his head, and cupped his ear in her hand the way she used to.

She was on beer number two, and she sat back down to tend to it. Unfolded laundry covered the rest of the couch and potato chip crumbs ground into the carpet at her feet. T.C. sat on the edge of a table crowded with stacks of coupons and unopened bills. He hadn't been into the kitchen behind him yet, but he could smell the dirty dishes no doubt lining the sink. Alicia used to tell him that he had OCD, he was so anal about organizing drawers and making up beds, but for most of his life, his room at the end of the hallway had been the only one he could keep clean.

"I thought you had another two weeks," his mama said.

"Overpopulation," he said. "They wanted to make room for the real criminals, Ma." He laughed, a short grunt. She didn't join him.

"Hmph. I woulda picked you up." Her taped stories were on pause, but she was still staring at the screen stuffing cheese puffs in her mouth, the orange powder shining on the tips of her fingers.

"It's all right, Ma, Tiger got me," he said.

She opened her mouth to respond to that but shut it before any words came out. T.C. knew she still blamed Tiger for his selling drugs in the first place.

"You know I would have," she repeated, turning to look in his eyes for the first time. "It's not like I'm still teaching." She had taught art education at Schaumburg Elementary for fifteen years, but after the storm the state took over the school districts, fired 4,500 teachers; his mama just happened to be one of them.

He decided to change the subject. "I saw Miss Patricia finally got out the FEMA trailer," he said. "It looks good."

"Umhmm. And she finally got that extra room in the back she wanted. Pool table and everything."

"I didn't know she played pool."

"She don't."

T.C. and his mama had spent three years in a trailer themselves. Most of the block had. Most people didn't have the money to rebuild outright. The Road Home program was supposed to pay the costs, but the government used the prestorm value of the house to calculate aid. For T.C. and his neighbors, out there in the East where there was no central plaza, no fancy restaurants and no whites, that money came out to much less than it would cost to repair.

"And Tiger told me they plan on building a hospital out here," he went on.

"Why? You plan on getting sick? Anyway, your aunt Sybil called," she said before he could answer.

T.C. rolled his eyes. His aunt had been his favorite at one time, but she turned her back on him after the conviction.

"What for, to dog me out about going in in the first place?"

"She means well, and she's your aunt," his mama said, but it came out flat. His mama didn't like her older sister either.

"Well, I'm out now," T.C. said.

"Just call her back. I won't have her thinking I didn't pass the message along." She paused. "You might as well know your Maw-Maw is still on dialysis," she went on.

T.C. nodded. "I figured."

"Doctors said two more years of it, then—" she cut her hand across her neck. "You betta go visit her now while you can."

"I was gonna go."

She sucked her teeth as if to say, *Don't get smart with me, boy. You ain't too big for me to backhand slap you.* But she didn't say that, only "You never know. You went to Tiger before you came home, so I had to say." Then she downed the rest of her beer. "Aunt Ruby buried her third husband while you was locked up," she went on after she let out a long, burly belch.

"I know, Mama, you told me."

She ignored that part. "Been a mess about it too. I think she loved this one the most. Woulda been nice if you could have been at the funeral. Everybody was there, Mookie, Alonzo, Cynt—"

She was still naming names as he walked to the back of the house.

"Sloppy Joes in the fridge," she shouted, her voice like gravel though she'd never smoked. His stomach heaved.

"I ate," he yelled back.

He had stopped eating her cooking after he came home from college. He still remembered the day. He'd told her the macaroni she made from powdered milk tasted like poor people food, and she slapped his face, then ran from the kitchen crying. After that he mostly ate at his MawMaw's. His mama still cooked for him, and sometimes he'd indulge her on simple stuff: pancakes and biscuits, or her annual gumbo. It wasn't that her food wasn't good, it was that he knew too much about how long her dishes sat in the sink, that she didn't wash her dish towels, that sometimes she'd leave the bathroom and he'd hear the toilet flush but not the run of faucet water. She wasn't always like that. She was the one who got him playing ball in the first place. She didn't know much about it herself, but she enlisted the best coaches; she worked summers delivering pizzas to pay for the most competitive camps; she went to every basketball game dressed to the nines, and every one of his friends wanted to holla. But it was like that high-end version of herself was too lofty to maintain for long. Every few years she'd relapse into what he saw today. Sometimes as a kid, he'd stare at pictures of her in her good days—slender as one of those models in the white magazines, in her beige suits with hair down her back—and wonder what happened. It wasn't just her looks that had suffered. When she was out of commission, she'd either spend hours going ham on him for made-up slights or look straight past him with a glaze over her face. Times like those, he didn't think she even saw him really.

He needed to lie down for a minute and just think. Tiger had been talking about expanding, and T.C. had thought Bon Bon was going to clear his head, but his thoughts seemed more convoluted than ever.

When he woke up, it was past dark. "Shit," he called out to no one in particular. He checked his phone: 9:00. His mama would be off at her night job, tending to that old lady with dementia. Maw-Maw stayed up until midnight, but he didn't want to bother her so late. He would just have to make it quick though; there was no way he wasn't going to see her, and his mama knew that too. Wasn't that what she was so mad about?

He rummaged around for some resin, hideaway bud beneath the mattress or under his lone shelf of books, but no, his mama must have come in and cleaned the place. It used to be that his MawMaw was the one person he didn't need to be high around, but he didn't like to see her the way she was now, crumpled in on herself like a paper napkin getting ready to be discarded, and he could handle it if she was going out today or tomorrow, but his mama was talking about two years.

He got dressed for the two-mile-long walk.

Moving to their neighborhood when he was ten had been a miracle. His house hadn't been much even then, just three bedrooms, 1,200 square feet, but they'd been staying in apartments since he was born, and once when his mama got laid off, they'd spent a month in the Magnolia Projects. It had been a dream to come out east, if only for the peace and quiet. His mama enrolled him at the Catholic school down the block, and he'd walk there and back without worrying about getting jumped. Now since Katrina, nobody stayed out past dark. The storm was more than five years before, but most of the lower Ninth Ward was still uprooted, and the people who had lived there, who had evacuated to places like Houston and Baton Rouge, just stayed. The ones who did come back were poor and newly homeless, and since the East had been on a gradual decline anyway, the city tipped the balance and infused T.C.'s neighborhood with Section 8 housing. It took only a year for T.C.'s neighbors to go from teachers and secretaries to thugs and prostitutes. He had been square before Katrina. Even after he lost his scholarship at LSU, he took classes at Dillard University and bagged groceries at the neighborhood supermarket, but the New Orleans he knew didn't survive the storm, and in its wake he'd become somebody different too.

Still, selling weed out of his house didn't mean he didn't feel scared anymore. Instead he had more to fear. Everybody he passed knew he grew plants in his mama's guest room, that he always carried the product on him, the product and his proceeds. He was tapped right now, but they didn't know that. Also, there was that new element that was creeping in, cars that didn't belong on this run-off block, like the black Grand Prix he had never seen before, creeping by at five miles per hour then turning back down the street for Hammond. Before he went to jail, there had been a splurge of home invasions and armed robberies, and from what he'd heard, they hadn't let up. Now he couldn't help but look over his shoulder and wonder where po-po was. When he was up to no good, they were surrounding him.

T.C. began to calm down when he got closer to MawMaw's. The houses on Lake Forest had always been nicer, and after the storm, people didn't take as long to return them to their original state. MawMaw for instance had never lived in a trailer. She just rented a condo in Baton Rouge until the contractors were finished rebuilding. When she came back, everything was close to normal, and sometimes he wondered if she could convince herself that nothing had ever happened. He walked up her porch steps, sidestepped the lawn chairs and potted plants—one with an open pink flower he could have sworn she had told him was a petunia—and knocked on the door through the barred gate.

She made him say his name before she opened the door. It had been only four months, but he had braced himself for this, that she would look different than the woman who'd raised him, the woman who manicured her nails every week and treated herself to MAC foundation. She hadn't had to waste money at a beauty salon, she always bragged, but now she wore a wig that pressed on her scalp like a helmet. Her collarbones peeked out of the neckline of her shirt, and she'd already taken her dentures out for the night. Still, he told himself to notice her face. Wasn't her skin as smooth and fine as it had been when he'd stare up at her as a boy, as she peeled crawfish over newspapers, sucking the heads out with her pink lips?

Once she saw it was him, she dropped her cane in a clang and opened her arms.

"Your mama didn't tell me you were out. Boy, get over here and give me a kiss."

"I'm early, I wanted to surprise you," he said. He almost repeated the line he'd told Tiger and his mother, that they needed to make room for the real criminals, but he wanted to get through this visit without mentioning that place if he could.

"Now you know you don't go surprising people with heart conditions," she said, and her smile lit up her face, the light brown eyes and pale skin. "Well," she looked him over. "You're certainly looking good." She let out a loud laugh, sweet though, so sweet he wasn't put off by her empty gums.

They walked to the sofa. The TV was on in the front center of the room, commanding as much attention as another person's voice. She always kept it on now that PawPaw was dead.

"Your aunt Ruby just left," she said. "I'm so glad," she went on, though T.C. knew that wasn't true. "I couldn't handle another minute of her complaining. Another one of her grandkids moved in with her. I said, Ruby, if you didn't want a big family, you shouldn't have had seven kids."

T.C. chuckled. There was a picture of MawMaw's brother out on one of the TV trays and he picked it up.

"Ruby and I were just talking about Brother," MawMaw said. "It was his birthday today. He would have been eighty."

T.C. tried not to look at the photo too long; people always said he resembled his great-uncle; looking at him now, he could see the similarities around the eyes. The man had died at forty-two of a heroin overdose.

MawMaw snatched the picture from him, slipped it into one of her albums, and filed it away.

"What about you?" she asked. "Now that you're out, you better stay out, you hear?" Then she looked away. "You might as well know, your MawMaw isn't doing too well."

He nodded. "You looking good though."

"I look like hell, and you know it," she said, rumpling up her shirt as if it were to blame.

"But that's all right. That's why you have kids. That's the secret, you know. To everlasting life. Well, first there's Jesus, but the other part they don't tell you about is reproduction. I did my part, and through all of you all I intend to live forever." She beamed saying this, and the light of her smile seemed to strengthen her whole body. Small and weak as she was, she sat straight up in her chair, and it seemed like if she wanted to, she could carry him into the kitchen for his supper. She leaned over and tapped him on the knee.

"The girlfriend? Your mama tells me she's pregnant?"

He nodded, feeling blood heat his face. MawMaw was a high-end Creole woman. It would have been blasphemy for her to get pregnant before she was married. She had taught them the right way, but he had gone ahead and shamed her anyway.

MawMaw smiled at him though. "That's your ticket out, you had a little fun, you lived a high life, but now it's time to settle down, start a family. You love the girl right?"

He shrugged. "I don't know, it's complicated MawMaw."

"Is it? What complicates it? The money?" She stuck her hand down her shirt.

He raised his hand. "No, MawMaw. I'm straight."

"Now don't be too proud. I know they don't make it easy for you young men, plopping you in jail by the dozens, and I notice it's always right around election time. You noticed that? I got up and voted the morning after you went in. I went to church first, prayed the Rosary over your soul, but then I went to vote."

"Aww, I wasn't going to vote in those little elections anyway, MawMaw," he said, trying to shut down her concern.

She sat up even higher in her chair. "I'd vote for the school bus driver if they let me."

"Well, I do it when it's important. Like for Obama." He smiled. "Yeah. I was able to vote for Obama."

"That's it now though, huh?" She didn't come right out and say what she meant, just kept going. "And now it's going to be impossible to get a job too. Oprah was just saying something along those lines. How do they expect you to make ends meet? No wonder you don't want to take on a wife—"

"It's not about the money," he said without thinking.

"Oh?" She leaned back in her chair.

He wished he hadn't said anything.

"What's it about then?" she asked, tapping the spot in her bra where her money had been.

He didn't answer her. He didn't know what to say. Why was it so unfathomable that he and Alicia would settle down, buy a house, raise their kid, in a few years add another to the brood? Part of it was that all that shit was expensive, but there was another piece too that he couldn't quite wrap his fingers around.

"I wish you would have met your father," she said with a sigh.

He waved the comment away. There had been a time when that was all he wanted. He begged anyone who'd seen the bastard cross a street for details about his stride. He went to bed praying that he would reappear, conjured him up in his dreams at night. But all that was over now.

"I didn't need him." He started the speech he gave whenever the man's name came up.

MawMaw cut him off. "I know that, I'm the one who told you to say that. And it's certainly true, but you don't believe it. That's the problem. If you had met him, maybe if you had met him as a grown man, you wouldn't need to take my word for it."

She stood up to fix his dinner. He didn't want to burden her. He knew she had dialysis in the morning, and though she went to sleep late, she retired to bed around ten to watch the evening news. But, as always, she insisted, dished him a plate of hot white beans over rice, and a tomato salad. She'd picked him up from school every day when he was a kid, and he'd be starving, but when she got him, she'd fix him a double-stuffed sandwich, then set about stewing or boiling her own evening meal. When she was done, she'd feed him as many servings as he could stomach, trying to fill a hunger that was never satisfied.

Tonight, after he filed his plate away in the dishwasher, she walked him to the door and slipped a check into his back pocket. Her wig had tilted and the curls on the edges of her scalp were grey and sparse. In the bathroom he'd seen a pack of those undergarments they advertised on TV. The tender weight of all this tugged at his heart now. He hadn't had anything to roll up before he left, but he'd need to find something fast. Maybe it was time to reup in general.

•

When he got home, the door was open, though he was sure he'd locked it. He rattled the knob to warn whomever he was coming. He stepped in and heard something shuffling inside.

He turned the hall light on, called out, "Who's there?"

He had found his old pocketknife in his closet and he pulled it out now.

"I said, who's there, nigga?" he called out again.

More shuffling. The noise was coming from the living room.

As he rounded the corner, he heard somebody scream out, "Whoa nigga." Then laughing. T.C. turned on the living room light.

Tiger's ass was bent down belly laughing in his mama's chair.

"I got you," Tiger said through laughs. "You was all like, 'I said who's here?'"

He looked at T.C.'s hand and started laughing even louder. "Boy, what you was gon' do with that knife? Nothing! You know everybody out here is strapped now, right? With at least one."

"How the fuck you get in here?" T.C. shouted.

"The same way I used to get in to see to yo' plants, nigga. You don't remember that summer I spent robbing houses? Too dangerous now though. Everybody got them alarms with the cameras. Anyway, you said we was gon' meet up tonight."

T.C. sat down.

"Mothafucka, you lookin' like you seen a ghost. Where you coming from all paranoid?"

"That place, nigga, jail, that's where I'm coming from all paranoid." T.C. was surprised to hear himself shout. He was still worn-out from MawMaw's, plus this wasn't funny.

"Aw, I'm sorry, nigga, calm down. Calm down. You said we was going to meet up, you don't remember?" Tiger repeated.

T.C. shook his head.

"Anyway lemme holla at you, dawg. They been feedin' you for free in that place, but I'm hungry, nigga. I told you about Spud, not even moving the gas himself, letting other people do that shit for him so he out of the limelight. That would save you twenty hours a week, at least. You growing a quarter pound a month now; you could quadruple that. Sell the same amount, but the proceeds are all yours, and a little bit would go to me of course," he chuckled.

T.C. didn't even look at him, just down at his own feet, his white socks and Adidas slippers. He had never wanted much. Even when he was young and MawMaw would try to buy him the newest Jordans, the Girbaud jeans, he would take them because it made her happy, but he never really needed all this.

"Before you say anything," Tiger went on, "just listen. That's the problem; earlier today, I could tell you wasn't listening, and this is complicated shit. It's not like before. We can't just sell to yo random-ass friends. You too good at what you do to be depriving the public, nigga; this is a goldmine and we gotta capitalize on it while it's hot."

And then MawMaw going and mentioning his daddy. He hadn't thought about him in years, not the way he was thinking about him now, with longing, that old hurt he buried rising back.

"So my cousin is moving out, I'm thinking we take over his old room, switch to hydro, grow twelve plants, turn out four ounces each. So that's three pounds, and nigga, it's all ours to keep."

Now there was his little boy. He spent his whole childhood fantasizing about how different he was going to be with his own, but he wasn't sure he was going to swing it. He wasn't stupid. You reached a certain depth in the drug world, and it was inevitable you'd be caught, but that took years; he was still riding on beginner's luck, and all he needed was a few more months to spark a turnaround. Something big to help him scale the next bend in his life.

"And this ain't the kind of thing you gotta do forever. I'm talking six months at the most, we get a big yield, turn a profit off it, and we set; you want to open a restaurant, do it. You want to open a clothing store, do it. The sky's the limit, my nigga. But you gotta be ready to turn the whole thing up a notch." He paused. "My only question is, how much it cost to buy more plants?"

The plants weren't the half of it. It was the lamps, the power to fuel them. But maybe MawMaw knew there was something on the horizon of his life; maybe she could divine he was on the verge of something greater, and maybe she couldn't determine the shape of it, but she could see its outline, she could estimate its weight.

"It's cool," T.C. nearly whispered.

"What? That's it?"

T.C. nodded.

Tiger paused.

"All right then," Tiger said after a minute. "All right then, dawg. That lil' boo musta gave you what you needed 'cause you was trippin' this morning. I thought that place had turned you out, dawg."

"When were you thinking we could start?" T.C. asked.

"Today, my nigga. I got my contact who sell the seeds. They got the ride and everything. They'll come right over."

"Call him then," T.C. got up for the bathroom. He remembered MawMaw, the pad bulging in her pants, the loose shirt sneaking down past her shoulder blade. He shook the image out of his head. At least when they reup'ed he could roll a blunt. He and Tiger could sit on his patio like old times stuffing their faces with Domino's slices, or maybe they'd stay in, play *Mario Kart*. He had won a bronze trophy before he left, and he might as well start making plays for silver.

Evelyn

Summer 1944

A few weeks after the dinner, Evelyn sat in her bedroom finishing her homework, when Ruby stormed in.

Evelyn asked what was wrong, but she didn't look up. She didn't imagine anything substantive could be the matter. Ruby had Andrew, she had Daddy's approval, what more did she need?

Ruby mumbled something, but Evelyn didn't understand it and instead of digging further, she started preparing for bed.

"He's leaving me," Ruby repeated, this time belting it out across the room.

"Oh," Evelyn said, with more emotion than she'd given her previous comment but far less than the situation might have appeared to require. She was surprised, and then she wasn't. The more she'd gotten to know Andrew, the more it seemed he was a sensible type of guy. She didn't understand what had taken him so long to see her sister wasn't his equivalent. On the other hand, everything had been going so well.

"You're not going to say anything else?" Ruby asked. "You're just going to stand there and finish undressing."

Evelyn sighed. "Was it another girl, Ruby?"

"What?" Ruby hustled up behind her. "If it was another girl, you think I'd be here crying? I'd be out somewhere screaming, I might even be swinging, but I wouldn't be crying."

Is that so? Evelyn wanted to say. She remembered Ruby in the exact same position when old Langston had strayed, but Evelyn only nodded and said, "Okay then."

Ruby got tired of waiting for a proper response and threw her handkerchief down on the floor.

"He's going to the war," she said, her words sputtering out, except for the last word, *war,* which sealed the rest of them together.

Evelyn looked up then. "What do you mean?"

"Oh, so now you're cooking with gas. What do you think I mean? He's going to war. He's leaving in a couple weeks. He may never come back. What else do you need to know, Evelyn? Looks like those are the only few details that matter."

Mother opened the door then, gleaned the problem from Ruby's display, and wrapped her arms around her child.

"That's okay now, my pretty baby; *ah, la pauv' piti.*"

Evelyn felt sick witnessing her sister being comforted, and when Mother whispered for Evelyn to get a towel, she was happy to oblige.

Mother smiled when Evelyn handed it over, and Evelyn smiled back. She'd held a tender spot in her heart for the woman since the dinner, and a repulsion toward her father that couldn't be tamed. It was as if all her affection toward him had shifted over to Renard. Her beau's naïve belief that her father approved of him, his security in it, only made her love him more.

She left her mother and Ruby to mope and went out on the porch. She could hear Brother and his friends playing cops and robbers a block away. It was summer, and the orange nasturtiums and red zinnias bloomed across the street on the porch beside Miss Georgia's rocking chair. Evelyn had already met Renard that day on North Claiborne, but some nights when he needed to see her sooner than the following afternoon, he came for her here. He'd walk by the house, kneel behind the petunia tree, and whistle. They'd walk the few blocks to a bench and though they scarcely did more than kiss, she'd been tending an irrepressible urge to allow him to make a woman out of her. Even tonight as she waited, she wondered if this night would be the one.

She dallied on the swing almost an hour—the full heat of daytime had become unbearable, but the cool night breeze felt nice on her skin. When he didn't come, she told herself he was probably with Andrew, and she went back inside. Ruby was asleep; her mother had retired upstairs. Evelyn stood over her sister, stared at her, trying to glimpse a change. What happened to the face of a broken woman? Did it turn to convey the loss or did it conspire with her heart to hide it? Looking at her, she thought it was the former. She remembered seeing Ruby so crumpled only when she was a toddler and their mother would leave her. Now as an adult, Evelyn felt genuine sympathy for her for the first time in her life. She sat on the edge of Ruby's bed and stroked her hair, but when Ruby stirred, Evelyn retreated back to her own corner of the room, back to her own life.

The next morning she went out in search of Renard. It was a Saturday, and she thought he'd told her he'd be working at the French Quarter restaurant that weekend. She chose one of her Sunday dresses, pinned her hair up, and dabbed a touch of lipstick on her cheek for color the way she'd seen Ruby do. Aside from Andrew, she had never been introduced to anyone in his life before, and she wanted to make a good impression.

She walked to North Claiborne, then St. Bernard, stood amid

the mothers buying snap peas and chickens for their evening meal, the bakers unloading mounds of white bread. She stepped onto the bus. It was so crowded the whites were seated in the Negro section. Evelyn didn't mind standing though, not today. The closer she got to her stop, the more excited she became. She could see Renard through the restaurant window before the bus came to a complete stop. She watched him while she waited for the whites to disembark. He didn't even know she was there. He moved in a steady rhythm, bending down to pack boxes, taping them, lifting them and stacking them in a large pile. An air of peace shone through him while he worked, almost as if he had merged with the movement itself and they were bound together on some mission that surpassed what lay ostensibly before him. She didn't want to interrupt him; she didn't want to interrupt something so sacred; she would say hello quickly, then head back home. She stepped off the bus and walked toward him. She was only a few feet away when a policeman approached the restaurant window. He tapped on it loudly until Renard came out, then he shouted, "There's some trash from your store in the street, boy. Old fruit and the such. It's starting to stink."

"I'm mighty sorry, sir. Mighty sorry." Renard bent his head for the officer in front of him. "I'll have someone clean it right away."

The officer smiled, a slow stretch across his face that felt more malicious than joyful. "Is that right, boy? You'll have someone see to it?" His smile stretched even wider, and he leaned into the backs of his polished black shoes. "Just who do you think you are, boy?"

"No, sir, I mean, yes, sir, I'll see to it myself right away, sir."

"That's more like it, boy. That's more like it." The officer stepped back and watched Renard fumble through the street, lifting particles of trash near the store and even stray bottles from the billiard room next door. When he was done, he wiped his hands on his white apron and walked back over to the police officer, reached in his pocket, and slipped him a bill of cash. The officer yanked it from his hand, and it was Renard who said thank you. He watched the officer walk off until he was out of sight, then he ducked back into the shop.

Evelyn would have gone in then. Renard went back to hunching over the boxes, oblivious to the fact that she'd seen him, and she longed to touch him, join him in his oblivion. Each time a box hit the dolly, she started toward him. She told herself she should go at that very moment, but something glued her to the road, and when finally he went out to check the street once more for litter, she ran away so she wouldn't be seen.

Evelyn didn't see Renard again until a couple of days later, and she had to run into him in front of the Sweet Tooth, the way the insurance man would meet her neighbors out in their driveways sometimes. After she left the restaurant the other day, she waited for him on her swing but he never came. She wondered if it had something to do with that officer, the way he'd spoken to Renard, but Evelyn didn't have reason to believe the officer didn't speak to him that way every day. Why would one encounter effect change? Still, she was glad she hadn't revealed her presence. She hadn't been embarrassed for him, only sad. If he knew she was there, though, he'd be embarrassed for himself, and he might not be able to recover.

Now, the way he was standing, with his hands in his pocket and his head down as if he didn't have every pure thing in the world ahead of him, she wondered if it was her Renard, or if she was seeing visions. Of course it was him. She approached him slowly. When he caught sight of her, there was only faint recognition.

He nodded at her instead of speaking.

She tugged at his arm. "Renard, where have you been? I've been so worried about you."

"Nothing to worry about, girl." He smiled a distant smile.

"What do you mean, 'nothing to worry about'? You were supposed to come by yesterday, and the day before that. Where were you?"

He looked off to the side. His eyes appeared misty, not as if he had been crying, but as though he had obscured them to avoid seeing. "Look, Andrew and I been busy with some things. I just didn't get to it."

"You didn't get to it?" Everyone around them turned to stare, but she barely noticed her voice rising. She lifted her hands to pummel them into his chest, and only then did he really seem to see her. His face sort of softened then, but she wasn't sure, there was so far he had to go. "What is it, baby?" she asked.

He pulled her by the wrist behind him. They walked for seven blocks before they slowed, then turned down several roads in a confusing wind. When he finally stopped in a secluded street she hadn't known existed, he let go of her hand. He lifted both of his own, then dropped them at his side, like a balloon expanding and deflating.

"I'm going to the war," he said.

Evelyn sighed. After his behavior she had been expecting worse, though when she thought about it now, there wasn't a worse scenario she could pick out and name. No, this was as bad as she could fathom. She shook her head, wanting to bar the news from penetrating. "But that means you can't come by? That means you forget about me?"

He sighed, a deep heavy release. "I didn't forget about you, Evelyn. I could never forget about you. But I wanted you to forget about me. They're starting to let more Negroes fight now. I may not come back, and if I do, who knows what shape I'll be in? Andrew's brother lost his legs. He ain't no use for nobody." He talked in a matter-of-fact manner as if he were explaining to someone how he cracked the chickens' necks each Saturday.

"Well, can't you tell them things changed? You're a student now, and of medicine. I thought if you showed proof of your studies, you could—"

"Even if it did work—" he paused. "I didn't want to worry you, but the money Andrew's mama was giving me didn't come through this semester, so I'm not a student. So there's no excuse."

Evelyn didn't say anything for a while. What was there to say?

"I could talk to my daddy," she started. "He'll know his way out of this. He always has a plan. What he says is, 'Every problem has a solution.' He says it's a law. By virtue of there being a problem, there has to be a way out of it. You just have to identify it."

Renard shook his head violently. "Is you that naïve?"

Are, she wanted to say.

He grabbed her elbow and shook her whole body. "Well, is you? You think your daddy know a way out of doing what the government tell you to do? You think your daddy know a way out of war itself? I know he over there living his life like a white man, but that don't mean he turned into Jesus Christ overnight." With that final display of rage, Renard seemed to come to, and his body quieted along with his voice. "I didn't mean to say that," he started to stammer. "I always respected your daddy."

Evelyn might have cried over any aspect of the last few days—just the drafting and not the outburst, just the distance and not the war—but she snuffed out any urge she had to do so now, forbidding herself from breaking down in front of a man who had enough anger in him to overpower his love; if their roles had been reversed, she didn't know if any other emotion inside her could have outshined what she had come to feel for him. She lifted her head.

"You didn't have to say that about my daddy," she said. "My daddy always was kind to you. He's an honest man and works an honest living. Is that a crime all of a sudden?" She held on to the self-righteousness that was duly hers in that moment. She didn't care so much about what Renard had said—she still hadn't forgiven her daddy for the conversation she'd overheard—but it was his ability to distance himself that had broken her.

"No, no, it most certainly isn't," Renard said.

"Well, then, I didn't think so." She reached down for her bag, which had dropped in the uproar. "I guess I ought to be going then," she said, willing herself now to hold back her tears. "I'm awful sorry to hear about you being drafted, and I'll pray for you then."

She turned and walked toward the bench where she'd left her books. She hadn't walked far before she heard footsteps behind her.

She turned. He had followed her. Her relief rose, but when she remembered his rage, it fell again.

"There's nothing really to talk about," she said.

"I leave in a month for basic training."

"You and Andrew going to the same place?"

He nodded. "For training at least."

"Well, that's good then. You can keep each other company, watch out for each other." Her voice cracked then under the weight of all the heavy suppression.

He pulled her to him. "I'm so sorry. I didn't know how to handle it. And then yo daddy, who was I to say a word against yo kind daddy, I ain't been myself is all. I'm so scared, and you the first one I been able to say that aloud to, I'm so scared." His words came out from all directions in sharp spurts, running into each other, stepping back, and turning in the opposite direction just to collide again.

Evelyn felt herself collapse inside. "Oh, I wish you would have said all that straight out. We could have avoided all that other—"

"I didn't know how to say it until now. If I had known, I woulda, but I didn't know how to say it."

They held each other tighter.

"A month is a long time. I've heard of men getting less," she said. "There's a lot we could do in a month."

"I could stand here just like I'm standing right now and be content."

Evelyn looked around. The evening was just starting to come, and the street was filling up with people hustling home for dinner. "It's so early in the night," she said. "I got at least a few hours before my daddy starts looking."

Over the next week, Ruby stayed in bed, and their mother catered to her, extra honey buns and jars of pig lips. While Ruby napped, Mother would sit at the table plodding through beads of the Rosary, her mouth moving in silence. While she prayed, Evelyn stood in the bathroom mirror, spraying her wrists with her sister's perfume, reddening her cheeks with her lipstick. She even borrowed Ruby's new clothes; her favorite was a short black slipper satin dress that reached her knees. It left her shoulders bare, so she begged Miss Georgia to spare ribbons of material she could drape over them. Then she'd stand in the mirror and just stare at her reflection. She began to understand why it took Ruby over an hour to get ready to see Andrew. For most of that time, she was already complete, but she was surveying her work, admiring it, spinning around and catching it from distinct angles. Now that Renard was leaving, Evelyn intended to spend every minute with him. She invented outright lies about where she was headed, more out of habit than out of concern for what her parents would think. Her mother barely lifted her head as Evelyn's heels tapped against the hardwood floor, but her father burrowed into her lies, seeming more fascinated by the evidence of her new disregard than by the content itself.

That night, as she sat on the front porch waiting for Renard, her daddy walked outside to smoke a cigar.

"I'm just going off to study with some of the girls from school," she hurried to say, to ward off any serious conversation.

Silence.

"We have a big final coming up, and I joined a study group."

Her father sat beside her, and the swing creaked under his weight. "Don't lie to me, Evelyn."

"The girls came to me, I didn't need it, but I wanted to help people who weren't as well off as I am," she continued.

"You know we don't lie to each other in this house."

"Like I said, I didn't need it, but I thought about what you always say. 'To give is to get. The Lord sees people as interchangeable and so should we.' So I didn't need it, but I remembered how you felt on the matter, and I obliged them."

He sighed. She hoped he could feel the punch she intended.

"Look, little girl, I know what you're doing, and I can't lock you up." He lifted his palms then dropped them at his side.

"Your mother must have told you how I feel. I know you don't agree now, but I promise one day you'll have some perspective. If you even waited a few weeks, you might see your old man knows what he's talking about. I'm not the smartest man, but I'm not new to this world, Evelyn. I've sheltered you and your sister, so you think life starts and ends on Miro Street. You don't know it's only easy for you because I made it easy. A different kind of man might not."

"He's going to be a doctor just like you, Daddy," Evelyn said, but her voice was shaking.

"He's going to try to be a doctor," her father corrected, "and Lord knows I want to see him succeed, but the odds are some obstacle is going to come along and trip him up. And it doesn't mean he's not a good man, it's the world we're living in, baby; it's the world I want to protect you from."

He reached for her hand, and she yanked it from him, dropped it on her own lap.

"I hear he's going off to war, huh? Real heroic. Going off to fight somebody else's battle when the real work could have been done here. Imagine how many lives he could have saved in New Orleans. I don't just mean that literally. It does something to a young Negro boy to see me walk in his house to deliver his mama's babies. I see it every time in their eyes, and it's an awesome wonder to watch their pride develop inside."

"He didn't have a choice. He was drafted."

She could hear her daddy's soft chuckle, then out of the corner of her eye she saw the smirk.

"Oh, okay," he said in a soft tone. "You're right."

But in his resignation, Evelyn understood that she was wrong. She remembered the conversation earlier that day in the alley; he hadn't actually said he was drafted. She had just assumed that he was. But why would he volunteer? Of course she had heard of men who did, men who thought aligning themselves with this country would benefit them in some regard when they returned. Renard and Andrew had debated that very issue their first night over for dinner, but it had been Andrew who was promoting that angle. Renard, she thought, hadn't agreed. At the heart of her shock of course was the fact that if he had volunteered—and her father's tone had convinced her he had—he hadn't discussed it with her first, and what did that say about his feelings for her? What did that say about the likelihood they would make it through this?

She put the matter out of her mind; she had so little time left with Renard and she didn't want to squander it, but she hated her father just then for the very trait that typically endeared her to him, that he was always right, and her anger stripped her of anything else she might have said. She fumed inside, but she quivered too. If she were to speak, she didn't know if she would strike him or cry out.

"You could have any boy in this neighborhood, in this country, I might dare to say. You have your whole life ahead of you. Who knows whom you'll meet out there? You're so young. You don't know what it means to have choices. Don't throw your life away over a low imagination."

Low imagination, it might as well have been her nickname, she'd heard those words so often growing up, but never out of her father's mouth. No, that was her mother's expression for her, applied about once a week, usually after Evelyn said there were no groceries in the kitchen when there was rice, green beans, and salt pork. Or when she bought the beef the butcher offered her instead of demanding the choice cut. But this time her daddy had adopted his wife's tool, kneaded it into Evelyn's chest with his fingers.

Miss Georgia snuck out on her porch just then, and Daddy waved. Then he reached for Evelyn's arm one more time. She made a show of refusing him so Miss Georgia could see it, and he sighed, tapped his cigar out, and walked back into the house.

Evelyn began pumping her legs harder. The cool wind slapped her face as she swung, and with each lift, she quieted inside. There was no more pretense. She would go to see Renard and stay out as long as she pleased, and everyone would know where she was, including Miss Georgia, who peeked out from behind her zinnias.

"It's a beautiful day, little girl, isn't it?" Miss Georgia called out, but Evelyn didn't respond.

She just stared back without flinching; there were tears leaving her eyes, but she could hardly feel them.

It was harder to maintain her guard with Renard. He'd found a patch of grass across the street from the Sweet Tooth where they could sit, and he'd bought a bag of crawfish from Dufon's, picked meat out for her the way her father always had, the juice of the heads trickling from his mouth. But she barely touched them.

"What's wrong?" he repeated.

She shook her head each time. If she told him about her talk with her father, she'd have to share her father's real opinion with him, and she didn't want to offend him. He was already going through so much. He hadn't mentioned his fear since the day he'd told her he was going to war, but she could hear it in his voice, too high-pitched, as he listed each sibling he had to visit, that he'd already seen half, that they all served gumbo, and he was so sick of okra he thought if he smelled it again, he might vomit.

He looked up from one of his stories, expecting her to laugh, and she tried to twist her mouth and her voice into something that might resemble that sound, but a cry escaped. It was in that moment that she let it all come out, every detail since the dinner that he thought had gone so well. She kept looking up at him as she spoke, oddly seeking the betrayal in his eyes so she could share the feeling with someone, but he only stared ahead nodding, his face as cold as stone.

When she was done, he didn't say a word.

"I knew it was too good to be true," he said finally.

"What's that?"

"Your daddy's approval. I believed it because I wanted to, but now that I think about it with a solid mind, I can see that it was all too good to be true." He paused. "And I understand it. I mean if I had a daughter, I would want better for her too, better than a janitor's son. My mother was a schoolteacher."

He seemed to look up then for a glimpse of her approval, but there was none. Evelyn was as impressed as she would be by him already; he himself had been enough.

He lowered his eyes again. "But that was so long ago and I never met her. I was raised by a janitor and—"

He laughed, jarring only because it came out so authentic, the same sound he'd delivered when she'd told him stories about how long it took Ruby to get ready, or how Brother still begged for hog head cheese sandwiches.

"I had a teacher in the fifth grade," he went on, "and he used to say to us, 'Nobody's going to get any free rides in this classroom. The last thing I'd want to do is deprive the world of a good garbageman.'" Renard laughed again, his eyes watering, his voice shaking out into a low-pitched dance. "I never thought he was talking to me."

"He wasn't talking to you," Evelyn said.

Renard took his time answering. "Maybe. Maybe not. Either way. I just want to enjoy these moments with you." He pulled her to him, and she relented, but she held her head away from his chest.

She tried to relax, but she couldn't go with it. "I don't like to hear you talk about yourself that way, what you were saying about the janitor and the garbageman," she said.

"Aw, I'm just talking, Evelyn, you don't have to worry about it. I know who I am. I'm just sad, that's all. It's been a rough week."

"You sure?"

"I'm sure."

She leaned closer into him now. "Well, Renard, I haven't known you long, but I know you well, and the man I fell in love with is a fighter. He wouldn't let somebody else define him one way or the other. He wouldn't give up hope, not now, not when he needed it more than ever."

"Look, if I can get myself back here in one piece, you won't have to worry about me one way or another, I promise you that."

"That's what I mean. Not *if*."

"What?"

"Not *if, when*. Just decide right here and right now that you're coming back."

He looked at her as if she had become something foreign to him. "That's not something I can decide."

"It is," she said. She almost quoted her daddy again but remembered it was the Bible she was remembering. "As a man thinketh, so is he," she said.

He nodded. "That was one of my mama's favorite scriptures. They tell me, she knitted it into a pillow, she loved it so. I still have that pillow. When I get back, I'll give it to you."

Evelyn sat up, her body stiffening with excitement. "That's what I mean, baby. You said *when*. Not *if*, but *when*." She beamed.

"Well, if anything would get me back here, it's you."

"What about me?" She smiled.

He traced his fingers alongside the edge of her bra strap. She leaned into him to kiss his neck. Every day since the news of the draft, they'd gone further than the day before. The night before she had allowed him to rub the outside of her panties, and she'd had to rinse them out when she got home and hang them over the tub. As far as what was coming, she couldn't say. She always thought she'd wait until marriage, but now that he was leaving, the order of things that had been pumped into her since birth seemed to fold into itself, and she thought this new version of her might be a product of the times, refined under the severity of them, whetted and changed.

"Those eyes, those lips," he answered. "Kissing them is making me want to put my mouth all over you, baby."

She moaned, moving onto his lap.

"Andrew said I could borrow his car," he said. "I could come by and get you. Would that be something you would like?" His voice had softened into a fraction of itself she hadn't been privy to before. She could feel him pounding against her, the intensity matching the ardor of her heart. She nodded. She lingered for a while on top, shifting herself against his pants until he said he couldn't take anymore. When they stood to leave, she looked up at him.

"Why'd you do it?" she asked.

"Do what?"

"Why'd you volunteer?"

He shook his head, sighed, shrugged. "They said they would pay for my schooling. Andrew's mama can't pay anymore, and I promised myself I would finish, no matter what. What other option did I have, work at Todd's for the rest of my life, saying 'Yessir' to the manager with my eyes on my shoes, pay officers half my pay just so they'll leave me be?" He paused, looked at her, his brown eyes shining. "It's no way to live, but I could have survived it if I hadn't met you. I want better for you; I want better for us."

Evelyn remembered the episode she witnessed between him and the officer and felt guilty she'd even questioned him. She pulled him to her. "But you don't agree with Andrew, all those lies he spouted, about it being our duty, about it demanding equality. You told Daddy you didn't agree."

"I didn't know what I thought. I didn't say one way or another. I only spoke about the matters that felt true to me, but listening to Andrew more, I don't know. I wonder if this is our ticket to full manhood in this country. Maybe if not for me, for my children."

When Evelyn got home, Ruby was lying facedown in bed, flipping through one of Mother's old issues of *Life* magazine.

Evelyn sat down beside her. "Shouldn't you be with Andrew?" she asked.

"Hmph, I'm not married just yet, you know. I do have my own life. Anyway," she went on, "he's with his family. Normally he asks me to go with them, but these are difficult circumstances, now aren't they?"

Evelyn smiled. She had been glad for some distance between her and her sister, but she had missed her too. She rested her head on her back.

"What's gotten into you?" Ruby asked, trying to scoot over but failing.

"Can't I spend time with my sister without causing alarm?"

"Hmph. You haven't said two words to me in a month, now you're laying all on me like it's not one hundred degrees in this house. Girl, it's too hot for all that."

Evelyn sat up, still smiling though. Her sister had turned back to the magazine, but Evelyn could tell she was smiling too.

Evelyn bent over and reached for Ruby's waist. Their whole childhood, she'd known just where to tickle her. When Ruby was in a bad mood, Evelyn would grab her around the middle, the palms of her feet or under her arms. Her sister would laugh and laugh until spit trickled down her chin, then she'd beg for Evelyn to stop in grunts more than words. This time was the same. They both laughed until tears formed, and Ruby called out, "Girl, you're crazy. I do believe Renard is running you clear out of your mind."

Evelyn conjured her sister that night. She wondered if without knowing it that had been why she'd needed to be so close to Ruby, to sit on her bed, to smell the perfume she sprayed on her wrists and between her legs. Ruby had never confessed to the things she'd done with men, but Evelyn could infer it from her guarded diary entries, the smug looks her sister shot her some mornings, and maybe connecting with her that day had been preparation for now, when she said words so dirty she didn't know they were inside her, when she climbed on top of Renard and growled like a dog, when she touched herself and moaned like she was possessed.

It was her imagination of how aroused he must have been that aroused her in return. By the time he was inside her, she was so slick, it didn't hurt as much as she'd feared it might, and though she had to bite her lip to keep from crying out, she clung to him and begged him not to leave her.

Renard had been gone two months when Evelyn learned she was pregnant. She sat on the information as long as she could. She had been forced to share so much with her family for so long, considering such a supremely important matter in private replenished her. Otherwise, her house felt as if it might break under the weight of its own gloom: Her parents hadn't spoken to each other much since Daddy and Mother's disagreement about Renard; Ruby stopped eating once Andrew left; Brother stayed out; Mother prayed the Rosary; and Evelyn's loneliness was fiercer than she'd ever known.

She filled her days with the same few questions, reshuffled so it seemed to her mind she was putting it to use. What was Renard doing over there in another continent? Was he safe? Would he return? When? Would he want her once he was back? And that last question slipped in not because of her new condition, which wasn't altogether real to her, but because his absence had dulled time's sharp edges. She felt as if the last few months had been years. Her feelings were the same, but she had scarcely left the house she'd lived in when they'd fallen in love. He wasn't off on a European vacation, but surely there were peaks beneath the cloak of war too; there were new faces to learn and places to discover. In her most desperate and selfish times she wondered if he even thought about her.

Meanwhile, she barely had the stamina to check the mail, and all the energy she'd spent pouring into memorizations and recitations drained out of her. She found herself sleeping through classes, coming home to eat, then retiring to her room for more sleeping. She'd attempt to do her homework in the beginning, but after a few days of lapses there seemed to be so much of it, and the parts of her mind she might have used to tackle it before seemed bent or dull, no longer available for use.

Still, despite the vague knowledge that her life as she knew it was slipping away, she was surprised when the president called her into his office and asked her to take a leave of absence. Disrupted from a routine, but oddly not devastated, Evelyn still pretended to attend. She'd wake up in the morning at the same time as she always did and walk with Ruby until she arrived at her sister's vocational school, then she'd turn at the next block—where she would have gone straight before to her own campus—and head over to the Sweet Tooth for apple pie. She physically craved ice cream, but something in her mind wouldn't allow it, and she was grateful for that, afraid of what the memory of the smell might do to her insides. She had managed to avoid crying, and she wanted to keep it that way.

One day when she returned home at the time she would have if she were still a student, her brother passed her an envelope postmarked from France. She locked herself in the bathroom and tore it open before she could sit. She read the last paragraph first, knowing everything important about a beginning could be gleaned from its ending. Renard had signed it with the words, "Everything my heart could give." Her legs gave way and she sank onto the bathroom floor. Once she had read it all the way through, she turned back to start over from the beginning.

He was fine, he said. And he'd heard that Andrew was too. He drove the same route every day, carrying gas, oil, and food between the beachhead and the city of Chartres, just outside Paris. They had met nice men, some of the nicest men he'd ever known, and he spent a lot of time with them, talking, playing cards, and bragging about their women. Everyone pretended they had each other beat, but several of the guys had taken him aside and told him he sure was a lucky nigger. He kept a picture she'd given him above his bed at night to make sure she was his first and last thought on both ends of the day. He didn't know when he was coming home, but he'd know soon, and he'd write her when he did. "Don't worry about anything, I'm safe, and I'm yours" was the last line, and Evelyn turned it over and over in her mind until she had drained it of all its magic.

The note not only fueled her love for Renard, it bred her confidence that when he returned they'd start their life together.

So she rubbed her stomach with cocoa butter not because it would prevent stretch marks, but because she wanted her child to know she'd been cooed over. She ate two portions of the breakfast sausage Ruby had forsaken. And she considered names like Sybil or Jacqueline, the latter the name of one of the girls at Dillard who without Evelyn present would surely finish first in their class.

In the months after Evelyn's tiredness eased, her weight came upon her, and she snuck through Ruby's clothes while she was at school. It didn't take long for Ruby to notice. She'd smirk at dinner as Evelyn reached for another helping, or she'd pinch the flab of flesh hanging over the top of Evelyn's panties. Evelyn expected her to press for the source of the change, but if she knew why Evelyn was growing, she didn't say. And one day that same week, Evelyn walked up to her bed and found pants and skirts from Ruby's closet folded in a neat pile.

There was still her mother to avoid though. Evelyn tried not to be in the house alone with her. If there were other people in the room, her mother would overlook her, but when it was just the two of them, the older woman had no choice but to notice how much mayonnaise Evelyn added to her sugar sandwiches, or how she answered questions about school too fast or too slow, Evelyn couldn't be sure which.

Thursday afternoon, though, when Ruby was still at school and Brother was with the twins and Daddy was at work, Evelyn was so hungry she couldn't bear to wait for her mother to finish her coffee before she did something about it.

She backed more than walked into the kitchen, never facing the table where her mother sat flipping through the news. When she made it to the giant jar of pig lips in the corner, she tried to make so little of a disturbance her mother wouldn't lift her head, but when she finally managed the lid, and leaned the container over to fish for the biggest piece, the juice spilled onto her dress in a dark circle she couldn't be bothered to wipe.

That was when her mother set the paper down and cleared her throat.

"Since when do you eat pickled pig lips?"

"I've always eaten them," Evelyn said, turning toward her mother.

"No, that's a dish I get for Ruby, not you."

Then the moment Evelyn had dreaded came to pass. Her mother looked at the dress Evelyn wore. It was one of Ruby's loosest, the one she wore a week after she found out about Langston, but it still clung to Evelyn's middle. Evelyn held the pig lip mid-bite, waiting for her mother's commentary.

But her mother just turned back to her paper, flipped through it. Evelyn continued with her snack, lost herself in the salt, the sourness, the chewy fat.

"You satisfied with yourself gaining so much weight?" her mother asked, not even looking up, once Evelyn had finished one and was fishing through the jar for her second. "You think that's a way to attract another boy, thickening yourself past recognition?" her mother went on.

Evelyn was so startled by the question—she had been so convinced she had cleared a reaction from her mother—she had to wait a while before an answer came to her.

"Ruby never had a problem getting men," she said after many seconds. "I'm still not as big as she is."

"Not everybody carries weight the same."

No, they didn't. Still Evelyn wondered about the pig lips. She was almost finished with this one, and she had anticipated putting a third on some white bread and spreading a spoonful of mayonnaise over it.

Evelyn's mother sighed, and she looked down at her daughter's feet. Gazing at her from that angle, she said, "I can imagine how you must be feeling, and for that reason I've given it three months. I know you loved that boy, and he loved you, but I just—" she paused here, "*Bon-temps fait crapaud manque bounda.* I just don't want you to throw your life away."

"I'm not, Mother," Evelyn said, tempering the part of herself that wanted to exclaim that her life was just beginning really, that maybe it wouldn't proceed in the appropriate order, but no one would remember that part once Renard was home again.

"I hardly ever see you studying anymore."

"We're on a break, Mother."

"You don't even read your old books. You just mope around the house, eating, and sleeping, like you're somebody's widow. I didn't raise you to fall apart because some man left you. Look at Ruby; she mourned for a while, but at least she's going out now. She's resuming her old life—"

"He's not just 'some man,' Mother," Evelyn cut her off.

Her mother sighed again. "That's not my point, Evelyn. Whether you knew him well or not—"

"There's no question about it really, whether I knew him. I did."

"I just don't want to see you lose yourself, sweetie."

At that, her father walked in, and her mother stood to fix him a plate he wouldn't eat. Evelyn noticed for the first time that if she had changed in those last months, he had too, that his hair had thinned around the middle and that his pants were bulky between his legs. He didn't look up at her. He didn't look at any of them anymore. He passed through more than occupied the place, his head down, his shoulders hunched.

Evelyn looked away too; she hardened any pity she felt toward him, the way she calcified her sadness after Renard left, and she realized how flat her life before him had been.

Renard was coming home though; in his last note he had said it, then he'd signed it "Don't worry about anything, I'm safe, and I'm yours," but she had considered the sentiment so much at that point the words themselves had no effect.

She reached back into the jar.

She thought about Renard in some unimaginable place across the sea, her picture the one she'd taken at her last debutante ball, upright beside his bed frame, and she smiled to herself. She walked to the icebox and swiveled a dollop of mayonnaise out of the jar with her finger, stuffed it in her mouth, then bit halfway into a pig lip.

It was November in New Orleans but still unseasonably hot, and Evelyn had taken to dimming the lights, drawing the drapes, and running ice cubes over her skin. She still kept up the charade of going to school, and sometimes she'd carry a book to bed before she fell asleep inside it. Otherwise, the house motored on without her. As Mother had said, Ruby was perking up, going out most Saturday nights. Evelyn didn't think there was another man in the picture yet, but knowing Ruby, he was just around the corner. Daddy came home for dinner as if in allegiance to the family they had been, but instead of complimenting their mother on the meal, he spread it around on his plate, then excused himself. And Mother could be found upstairs any hour of the day, limp amid the out-of-season drapes and rugs.

A scene like that might have depressed Evelyn if she were living inside it, but it was impossible to notice it beside her world of promise. She knew just the place her own family would live, a little shotgun in Tremé, so close that she could see her parents but set apart from her childhood house enough that she and Renard could start their own life. She hadn't decided how she'd get the money, but she knew with nearly two years of college, she could pick up a secretarial position. She was too big now, but once the baby was here, she could leave it with Miss Georgia and set to looking. In her airier dreams, her husband Dr. Renard August Williams, was head of hematology at the Negro hospital at Flint-Goodrich, and since she had graduated top of her class at Dillard, he often called on her to assist him.

She'd tried to get more detailed in her imaginings, but what did she know about hematology? She'd quit nursing school halfway through, and that was three months ago, one third of the way through a pregnancy that was gobbling up her mind. So she'd think about the house, how it would be so fine her mother would be embarrassed to remember how she'd treated her. Evelyn would learn the proper way to prepare tea for a lady, what order to serve the snacks in, which fingers to lace around the arm of the teacup, who should pour the first cup. Her daddy would visit every Sunday and hold her hand on the way out to the Cadillac she and Renard had bought him. He might not say anything, or maybe he would, but either way she would know he felt silly for how wrong he'd been. That baby of hers, he'd say or want to say, had salvaged not only Evelyn but all of them.

"You just going to lie around all day dreaming?" Ruby walked hard into the bedroom where Evelyn was draped over her bed.

"What else is there to do?" Evelyn barely looked up from her pillow.

Ruby stomped her foot in front of her. "School for one, girl. But I guess you forgot about that. I ran into Rose Haydel today, and she told me that you haven't gone in months. I argued with her. I called her a two-faced low-life lying sack of potatoes right there in front of everyone, said she was just trying to spite me and my family by making up garbage, but then her worst enemy got in my face and repeated her, said everybody knew it." Ruby paused then, seemingly for effect. "I looked around the circle that had formed, and it was true, everyone was nodding their heads. God, Evelyn." Her voice rose and it didn't seem as if she were putting on a show anymore. "I've never been so humiliated in my entire life. I walked all the way home thinking about what they'd said, going over it in my mind. I thought the worst part was how foolish I looked out there, but the more I thought about it, the worst part was that you've been walking with me every day for two months just pretending, and for what, all in the service of a lie?"

Ruby walked closer to the bed now, so close she could touch Evelyn if she stuck her hand out.

"What kind of sickness has crept in your brain that you would do something like that? And to me?" Her voice was breaking now. "Answer me. I thought we were close. Sisters, yes, but more than that, I thought we were friends."

"I didn't say we weren't." Evelyn still faced the pillow.

Ruby yanked it from under her face and threw it at her. *"You didn't say we weren't. You didn't say we weren't.* Girl, wake up. Either you're heartsick or you're brain-dead or you're—"

She stopped talking, surveying her sister's body. She shook her head. "Can't be." She pulled up Evelyn's nightgown without a fight, gasped at what she found.

"Oh, my God," Ruby whispered.

Evelyn could see tears spring up in her eyes.

"Oh, my dear Lord," she repeated, still shaking her head.

The relief that half the weight of all she'd been carrying was finally in someone else's hands sent Evelyn's words sputtering out. "I haven't heard from Renard in weeks. I don't know if he's dead or alive. And even if he is alive, what if he changed his mind about me? Or what if it's not me, if he just doesn't want a baby?" She pulled her sister to her, buried her head in her shirt, still talking but incoherent to her own ears.

"Shh, shh." Ruby rubbed her back. "You don't want Daddy to hear you."

"He's going to have to know eventually, Ruby," Evelyn almost screamed.

"Yeah, but not like this. Mama can help us figure out how to piece it together for him."

Evelyn thought she'd rather have Daddy find out because

one of his doctor friends delivered the baby than have him learn about it from their mother. All her life, she'd tried to combat that woman's low opinion of her, convince her she was okay, not better than Ruby but equal. Now the thought that Mother might have been right meant something worse than inferiority. It meant that in all Evelyn's searching for esteem, she had missed the lesson; she had tried to do things differently in choosing nursing, even in pursuing Renard, but she had ended up in the very same place her mother had predicted. Ruby, on the other hand, might go out there and do something big with her life. Whether she did or not was beside the point; she still had the chance to, and even the freedom of that desire was such a privilege.

Still, Evelyn didn't try to convince her sister to keep silent. What would have been the point? She was six months along, and a doctor had never looked at her. If, heaven forbid, Renard didn't come back, her mother would be the one to teach her how to bathe and feed a baby; her mother who had failed her would be most privy to Evelyn's own failure, and that, more than the uncertainty of her situation, caused her to sob. Ruby stood and hurried for the door. A few minutes later, Evelyn's mother walked in alone. When she saw Evelyn, she ran to her, pulled her up into her arms.

"*La pauv' piti*, it's okay, Mama's going to make it okay."

Evelyn shook her head. "I'm so sorry, Mama. You were right, I'm so sorry."

"Hush your mouth, girl. That's a life in there, a precious, precious life. And God deemed you worthy enough to carry it."

Jackie

Fall 1986

The next morning Terry got up to make blueberry pancakes, bacon, and eggs. He dressed the baby so Jackie had more time to focus on herself, iron her clothes, set her hair with hot rollers, apply a little lipstick on her cheeks for blush. People at the nursery noticed the change.

Her mother was the first one to comment. "Jackie Marie, are you humming in this classroom?" This during her break as Jackie stapled leaves and pumpkins to the bulletin board.

"No, ma'am," she said on instinct, though she supposed she had been. "It was just a song that I heard on the radio this morning," she added when she realized her lie wouldn't hold.

"Oh, I know, I recognized Anita Baker. But"—Mama paused, smiling—"is there something you need to tell me about? A new friend maybe?" She let her smile extend.

Mama had been pushing Jackie to start seeing new people, at least go out with her old friends, but she hadn't been ready to socialize, not then. This morning, though, she felt like calling all her girlfriends, inviting them over for one of her fish fries.

"No, Mama," she said, "just getting back into the swing of things, I guess."

Her mother paused, looked up at her on the ladder with her eyebrows arched. "Well, good, then," she said. "That's real good. I can't tell you how happy that makes me," and she clutched her heart.

She stood there for a minute longer, waiting to hear more, but there was no way Jackie was about to tell her what the real source of the change was. She remembered the last time Terry came back, that he stayed months, that he'd said all the right things, meant them even, that the baby had started to go to him just like he went to Jackie. But that didn't stop Terry from leaving, that didn't stop her from having to tell her family that he was gone, that didn't stop Sybil from saying *I told you so*, and Jackie would be damned if she put herself in that position again.

On the other hand, what was it he had said about staying in the moment? No promises? What was wrong with her enjoying this reprieve no matter how long it played out?

Thinking about it that way, she relaxed into their new routine. She'd come home to elaborate dinners, crawfish étouffée, his mother's recipe, or smothered chicken and rice. They'd watch movies, *Raiders of the Lost Ark* or *Friday the 13th*, play rummy or just marvel over their baby's sleeping body, how his hairline was just like Terry's, a sweet little *M*, or how he turned his nose up at strangers the way Jackie could sometimes. Jackie relished those moments she hadn't even known she'd missed. It was rare to find someone who was as invested in talking about T.C. as she was. Even with her mama, she parceled her bragging out. She didn't tell her the baby was trying to crawl already, that he had said the word *Mama*; she didn't admit she wanted him to be the first black president, but with Terry, she could gush, point out that it wasn't just *Mama*, T.C. was forming other words too. And they would have to childproof soon because he reached for everything in sight—did Terry see that the other day he'd grasped the remote? Not only that, but he already fit in eighteen-month-size clothes, he slept through the night, he cried only when he was hungry, and all those factors together had to say something, anything, about the prospect of them as a family.

Jackie even called her old friends again; she didn't tell them Terry was back, but she let them catch her up on the old neighborhood, who had gotten married, lost jobs, found a hookup since. She'd hang up the phone refreshed, as if life was on her side all of a sudden, as if she had accessed the formula for riding it instead of letting it ride her. Then she'd climb into bed and rest her head on Terry's chest, listen to his heartbeat like a second hand ticking, and in the morning he'd still be there.

One day about a month after Terry had returned, she woke up to the baby's coughs. The doctor said she didn't have to take him in, but he had never even had a runny nose and she decided to keep him home. She called her mama to let her know they'd be missing school, then nursed him twice as much as normal. She'd been on a cleaning streak already, but she took it to another level that morning, crawling on her hands and knees to clean the baseboards with scotch tape, pouring baking soda and vinegar into the cracks in the kitchen floors, vacuuming the carpet, changing the sheets, bleaching every surface of the house someone might think to touch. When she was done, she sat down for a breather. The baby was still sleeping. She thought about making Terry a welcome-home meal. He was out looking for work; he left every morning when she did and didn't return until shortly before, but she knew there was only so long he could slog through this city asking for something that didn't seem to be there without becoming discouraged. She'd caught glimpses of his frustration already. Once or twice, he came home barely talking, looking off to the side of the room instead of right at her, reminding Jackie of a man she'd seen before, weeks before a relapse. She didn't know if his favorite meal could preempt that route, but he loved her jambalaya and she'd baked some chicken thighs that might go well with it.

The doorbell rang. She couldn't imagine who it might be, possibly one of the neighbors; Terry had his own key back now. Of course, Jackie would tell whomever that it wasn't a good time. The baby would be up in thirty minutes and she had to boil that rice. She walked toward the door, opened it without looking through the peephole, prepared to hand out some tired excuse. She would have gasped when she saw Sybil, but she wouldn't give her sister the power of knowing she had rattled her. She couldn't form a single word, and it was Sybil who spoke first.

"Aren't you going to let me in?"

By habit Jackie did as she was told, though the truth was she should have made up an excuse, any excuse, as to why she couldn't be hospitable. Terry would be home any minute.

"You want some Kool-Aid or something like that?" Jackie asked.

"I'll take a Coke, diet if you have it," Sybil called out, and Jackie moved to the kitchen as though she were on autopilot.

"It's looking good in here, Jackie Marie. I expected a cyclone like the last few times. Mama said you were getting it together, but I had to see for myself." Jackie was back now with the drink. Sybil took a sip before adding. "It's good to see that you're everything she said you were."

Jackie sat opposite her sister. In a minute she would get herself together enough to ask her to leave. She would be polite about it, but assertive, and she wouldn't let up until Sybil was out the door. Any minute now she would figure out how to do that very thing.

"I was just in the neighborhood," Sybil went on. "I have a client out here. I don't usually make house calls of course, they come to me, but this one"—she shook her head—"I can't trust him to lead himself to the bathroom on time, much less make it downtown to my office."

"What'd he do?" Jackie asked to extend the time between the present and the moment she'd act.

Sybil shook her head again. "Selling. It's a favor for one of Mama's friends' sons. You know I don't represent those lowlifes anymore. But any day now, I'm going to get that contract, and all of this is going to be behind me, favor or not. See, these corporations don't want to go to trial, they can't risk a bad reputation, they'd rather just write a big check and forget somebody ever slipped in their bathroom, or that a whole class of kids got food poisoning from their meat. It's easy money with them, not like this nigger mess." She took another sip from her can, a sip so dainty Jackie couldn't even see her swallow. "Like for instance, this man today said he was done, right, but in the few minutes I was at his house, five crackheads knocked at the door, skinny as light poles, eyes darting everywhere, no teeth. I don't know how these people start this junk, don't they see what it does to everybody around them?" She shook her head again. "And I damn sure don't know how you do it, Jackie, living next door to these clowns. My client might as well be your neighbor, he's just a few blocks away, been dealing for a full year, just got caught for the first time, and wants to tell me it's not fair. He didn't have a choice. He's listing off the people who depend on him. Of course he's got two kids. He's barely twenty. His mama's in a wheelchair, his daddy's in jail, blah blah blah. I should carry a harp around in my briefcase."

Sybil kept going, oblivious to the fact Jackie had tuned her out. Jackie heard the baby stir, and she jumped up.

"Sybil, I've got to take T.C. to the doctor," she said. "That's why I'm home today, he woke up sick, so I made an appointment"—she checked her watch—"for four thirty, so I need to get him dressed."

"Oh, I know, Mama told me; my poor baby, let me see him," Sybil stood with her and headed to the back of the house where he slept.

Jackie passed the window on the way to her bedroom, peered out to see if her car was pulling into the lot, but no, not yet. By the time she reached the baby, Sybil had scooped him up, was petting his back, and he'd resettled on her shoulder.

"It was good to see you but—" Jackie started.

"Let me help you get ready, Jackie," Sybil said.

Usually when Sybil talked she carried an air of authority, and what could Jackie say to refute it, because it had been earned? But now she sounded more desperate than assertive, as though holding this child was the best thing that would happen to her all day, all week even, and she wasn't going to push her way in, but that didn't mean she didn't need it.

"Okay," Jackie said. "Okay," she repeated.

Jackie changed the baby's diaper, and Sybil peered over her shoulder. Jackie found with her sister watching, her hands shook; she had changed thousands of diapers in the past seven months, but she tore the tape off the first one and had to start again. In the meantime the baby peed in the air, sprinkling them both. Jackie was mortified—ordinarily, she never left his penis uncovered—but with her sister there, she'd forgotten. Sybil just laughed though, a deep guttural sound that seemed genuine.

When they were done, they walked back to the living room. Sybil held the baby while Jackie packed her diaper bag. Jackie began to relax; it seemed as if she just might have enough time to push her sister out before Terry came home. Of course there was no doctor's appointment, but Jackie could drive in that direction then veer off to the grocery store or the park. She hitched her bag on her shoulder, reached out for the baby.

"I can carry him to the car," Sybil said. "Give you a break."

Jackie nodded. What was the use in fighting now? She had made it. She was a few feet from the door when she heard keys jingling in the lock, saw the knob turning. Jackie stopped where she was. She wasn't surprised, nor angry, nor disappointed even, just resigned. She had been expecting it all along she saw now, and maybe it was ordained. Sybil turned to her but Jackie just looked straight ahead, waiting.

The door swung open and Terry started to walk in, then stopped.

They all stood in silence, even the baby, who seemed to sense the tension of the moment.

Finally, Terry walked over and hugged Sybil.

"You're looking good, girl," he said. "Looking real good. Jackie tells me you're big-time now."

Sybil nodded, speechless, but unwilling to ignore a compliment.

"I don't know how much you know," he went on, "but"—he walked over to Jackie and grabbed her hand—"I've been clean and sober for going on three months now; I'm getting myself together. It's a process, but I'm taking it day by day."

Moment by moment, Jackie thought to add but stayed silent. He was explaining enough for both of them, and she couldn't help but notice that all the extra talk weakened his case. Still, she grabbed his hand.

"And then, Jackie," he turned to her, smiling, then glanced back at Sybil, "Jackie doesn't know this yet, but I got a job today."

"Where?" Sybil asked. It was the first thing she'd said, and it came out cold.

"At a mail-order specialty pharmacy," he paused, "in the Lower Ninth Ward. Not at the Walgreens or anything like that." He looked down. "It's going to take time to get back to that level."

Sybil nodded, smug, seeming to smirk. She had been holding the baby but she passed him over to his father.

"Well, you have a lot of motivation in this one." She smacked a kiss on the baby's face, didn't bother to wipe the lipstick lingering on his chin.

T.C. cried when his father took him, and Jackie had to console him.

"He never does that," Jackie said to no one in particular but loud enough for her sister to hear. "He's so crazy about his daddy, he never does that," she repeated.

Sybil smiled that smug smile again, then headed for the door. A few minutes later Jackie heard her sister's BMW engine start, but it was as if Sybil were still there. Her doubt had rubbed off on Jackie, and she stood in the hallway for a while after the door closed, feeling dashed. It was only after a few minutes that she remembered she should congratulate her husband.

She smiled the way she would before he'd come back and she needed to convince the world she was handling his absence okay. She spoke in staccato, her volume rising and falling in big loops.

"I'm so proud of you," she said, and she supposed she was, or she would have been if her sister hadn't come over and transplanted her mind into Jackie's, if Jackie had time to just sit with the news and process it according to her own values and dreams.

"You don't seem excited," Terry said over dinner. "What is it?"

Jackie didn't know how to respond, so she focused on her plate, fumbled with the napkin in her lap. She had added too much salt to the greens, but the chicken was tender and the rice wasn't overcooked.

"What is it?" he repeated. "I know it's not what we're used to, but the pay is all right, it's something, and it'll get me started. My sponsor says it's important for me to have a routine. It'll help set me back where I was before all this." He waved his hand in a broad swoop, seeming to indicate the apartment, the neighborhood beyond it.

Hearing him express so much pride over a job he wouldn't have considered a year earlier filled Jackie with a guilt that she didn't think she'd be able to discard, it wrapped so thoroughly around her insides. Still she tried.

"No, baby," she said, grabbing his hand, "it's not you, it's me; well, it's my goddamn sister." She heard her voice stretch, rise. "I didn't invite her over here, you know; she just came. She just let herself in, she just took over like always, and now—well, we'd decided we'd wait to tell my family, that it would just add another layer of pressure, a group of people waiting on you to fail."

"I don't think they're waiting on me to fail," Terry said softly.

Jackie didn't respond.

"I don't think that," he repeated. "I think they want me to do well, I think they want us to do well, but they feel like they can't trust me, understandably so." He paused. "Sometimes I think I can't trust myself." He dropped her hand.

"She didn't seem upset though," Jackie went on, not noticing Terry had turned away from her. "Maybe she won't even mention it to my parents." Jackie had barely got the thought out before she realized how ludicrous it sounded. Sybil had told on her for smoking a cigarette outside the mall when she was fourteen. She had told on her for scamming the liquor store into delivering beer by ordering it alongside her pizza. She had told on her when she found a condom wrapper in her wastebasket when she was seventeen. So there was no way Sybil was keeping this to herself. "Maybe my parents won't care."

"Goddamn it, Jackie," Terry shouted. He threw his napkin against the table with such force Jackie expected it to make a sound, but it just fell flat. "You're not fourteen years old anymore, girl. It doesn't matter what they think; this is about us."

She was startled by his outburst, but it leveled her, brought her back to where she was sitting, the man she was sitting beside.

She shook her head. She knew he was right, but it wouldn't have occurred to her if he hadn't mentioned it. She had always been young-minded, leaned too hard on her family's opinion of her, but there was more to it now. She had a reason to rely on them, to care what they thought. For the last few months, they'd been all that she had.

"What do you want me to say?" she belted out. "I have to think about what they want, what they care about, because if this doesn't go well, they're all I have to depend on." She paused. She wondered if she should have let him into her worry, if it would infect him, send him back on those streets. She kept going. "I'm afraid, Terry. I'm terrified. I'm trying to stay in the moment, but I told myself I'd never let you in again, and here I am, looking forward to you coming home, letting the baby warm up to you." She started crying when she thought about her son. "I didn't think it would be this easy to fall back into where we were."

"I didn't think so either," he said. He reached for her hand again. "I'm scared too," he added. "I'm scared too."

The next morning Jackie woke up with a new resolve. Nothing had happened in the night. She and Terry hadn't said much after their conversation at dinner, just drifted off into sleep at different times in front of *MacGyver*. But she woke up as if they'd had a healing discussion, as if she'd been shown a reel from their future, a future she'd designed with her decision to accept him, and in it they were impenetrable to threat.

"I'm so sorry about yesterday," she said as she dressed.

"Don't be sorry." He was still waking up and he grunted more than spoke. "I get it. I'm the one who should be sorry."

"No, really, listen." She hobbled over to him, her legs only halfway inside her pantyhose, hot rollers clipped in her hair. "I want to celebrate you. You deserve to be celebrated. Two months without—" she couldn't even say the word *crack,* she didn't think she would need to say it again. "That's something. I don't know how hard it is, but I can imagine, and then you got this new job too."

She looked for him to smile but there was nothing. He seemed to still be waking up.

"Will you be home tonight?" she asked.

"Nowhere else I'd be."

"Okay, I'm going to come up with a plan at work then, and I'll give you a call." She said it as if it were a question.

He propped himself up on his elbows, seeming more engaged

now, trying to pull her back to bed. They still hadn't had sex, and she wanted to, now more than ever, but she was running late.

"Tonight," she said, kissing his forehead. "I promise, tonight."

When she got to work, her excitement diminished only a little at the thought that her parents might have spoken to Sybil. She told herself she didn't care if they did, and she believed it. She didn't have anything to be ashamed of; she was taking a chance on her family. Anyway, when she'd said those vows, she had meant them. In sickness and in health, and wasn't this a form of sickness? There were people like Sybil who believed his behavior was willful, but she'd seen him battle those cravings in the beginning. Sometimes it was all he could do to sit on his hands to keep them from shaking. She'd seen him stand up, head to the door, place his hand on the knob dozens of times, then force himself back to the sofa before finally acquiescing and slamming the door behind him. And now he had come so far.

Jackie's mama spoke in a normal bouncy voice, all, "Hey, baby, sleep okay? You look rested. How do you feel?"

Jackie hesitated before responding, but her mama just picked up her slack, answered her own questions, filled her in on the babies who were sick, and the mamas who'd be late.

"That Bradley boy has wet himself five times today. Five times and it's barely nine. I told his mama he's not ready but she doesn't get it. She doesn't get it. She said her daughter was potty trained at three. I said boys are different than girls and she accused me of being sexist." She shook her head. "These modern parents, I'll never understand them. And I don't want to," she added.

Jackie shook her head as if to say *me neither*. She set her purse in her cubby, looked through her sign-in sheet—all her kids had already arrived. They were still scattered throughout the room, a handful at the Play-Doh table, some at the art station, and a couple outside on the trampoline. For a moment she just watched them, suspended from the day's requirements, from the previous night's tension. Terry was satisfied; her mother still approved of her choices; and more than that, Jackie believed in her own decision. Normally she couldn't order a meal without questioning herself. Even deciding which movie to watch pained her; suddenly each future minute would feel too worthy to undermine with an imperfect choice. But now she was at peace; something close to surrender settled inside her, more fulfilling than surrender because she was certain of the outcome.

She called Terry during her break to tell him to meet her at City Park. She left the baby with her mama, then drove home to change. She picked over what to wear for too long before she decided on a red scarf, tight blue jeans, a black-and-white striped shirt, and tall boots. Her appetite had eased up since Terry's return, and she liked the way her shirt lay flat all the way to her waist even when she sat down. She wavered between red and pink lipstick. She didn't usually wear any on outings with T.C., but the red looked so good against the scarf and this was going out with her husband. How often had she spent time with an adult who wasn't her mama lately?

They had agreed to meet at the parking lot north of Big Lake. Terry was always early, but Jackie ran on time, and just like old times, when she got out of the car he was already there in his navy-blue down jacket, his hands in the pockets of the jeans she'd given him last Christmas. She marveled at the sight of him right where he was supposed to be, where she had been expecting him, and she couldn't imagine anything brighter, him waiting for her on the edge of the lake, beside an oak tree strung up with wind chimes ringing out a five-note scale.

"You look good," Jackie said. She was nervous and she looked down when she reached him.

"You too."

He didn't move his hands from his pockets, and she wondered if he was nervous too. It felt funny being here without the baby, like a first date with someone she'd spoken to only on the phone a few times, and even though those calls had been comfortable, the new context unnerved them.

He reached out suddenly and they hugged with just one arm; when their heads collided, they laughed.

"This is nice," he said, seeming more comfortable, looking around at the women hustling down the path with strollers, the water rippling in the breeze. "Real nice. What do you do here though?"

They laughed again.

"I normally come out with the baby," she said. "We walk a few loops around the water." She pointed to the lake, the ducks swimming along its shiny top. "Then find a bench and relax. We could do that now, if it's all right with you."

He nodded, and they started. They passed cyclists with babies behind their seats, picnickers sharing sliced oranges with their children, and Jackie felt comfortable enough to smile at them; most times she was alone at this park with T.C., flashing her wedding ring to whomever might be looking, as if it meant anything if there was no one beside her.

"My mama has the baby," she said, "all night if we want. I was thinking after this we could go to Dooky Chase's like old times." She reached for his hand. "Something special, you know.

"So tell me about it," she added before he could answer.

"About what?"

"The new job, what else?"

"Aww, it's not much." He was being humble, but she could tell he was proud. "Mostly sitting in a cubicle listening to people complain about their orders, but I like people, and it's a fresh start. I needed this, you know."

She nodded. "What about the coworkers?" she asked. "You like them?" She heard an edge of nervousness creep into her voice.

"The ones I met seem cool. I'm the only black, as usual."

"That's okay," she said. She was careful about what she said next; she didn't want to nag. "Maybe keep to yourself this time, anyway," she added after a while. "You have so many friends; you don't need new ones at work."

"You got that right." He squeezed her hand, pulled her closer. "You and T.C. are all I need," he said. Then, "You smell good. What's that?"

"Soap," she smiled.

"Oh, okay, you're getting real fancy, taking showers in the morning and whatnot."

"Anything for you." She winked at him.

He paused, then said, "Tell me something, if I jumped in the water, would you save me?" It was an old joke between them, started during their early nights at the Lakefront when he confessed to her that he couldn't swim.

"Hell, no." Jackie play-pushed him backward. "Not with my hair just permed."

He laughed. "What, girl? Didn't you tell me you and Sybil took swimming lessons back in the day? What'd you do with your hair back then?"

"Well, I didn't have a man to impress back then."

"Oh, is that right? And is there somebody now? That you're trying to impress?" He leaned in, studying her face, gazing at it as if he'd be questioned on the details of it and couldn't afford to forget.

She pulled him closer, shut her eyes, when she heard someone: "Look at the happy couple."

Jackie blinked, felt her husband pull away.

The white man in front of them looked familiar but Jackie couldn't put her finger on why.

Terry recognized him though. He pulled back from her more when he spoke. "Hey, Michael, what's going on, man? So good to see you."

Jackie could tell he was happy to see the man, but he was embarrassed about something too.

"Don't pay us any mind," Terry went on, "we're just horsing around. Don't get much time out without the baby," and that sentence came out like an engine dying; all the comfort and excite-ment that had been building inside them since they were teenagers seemed to dissolve right there at their feet.

Michael didn't know it though. He was all handshakes and shoulder pats. "You look so good, buddy. I'd heard you had gotten yourself together, but it's one thing to see it in person."

"Oh, thanks, man. Wouldn't have been able to do it without my family, let me tell you." Terry looked back at Jackie. He started to introduce her, but the man cut in.

"Anyway, you still keep up with Darren and Chase?"

"Nah, man, I haven't heard from them."

"Oh, okay, well, I'll have to tell them I ran into you. They're still over at the VA."

It hit Jackie then who the man was; he wasn't the one who had introduced Terry to the drugs, no, but a member of that same crew, and he could have been one of the ones who'd gotten high with Terry on coke those nights, then abandoned him as soon as he veered into crack. In her early research she had read about trig-gers, that addicts shouldn't go places where they'd taken drugs, that they shouldn't hang out with the people they used with, that seeing those same faces, or smelling the kitchen of the restaurant where they'd smoked in the bathroom might send them reeling back. She looked this man up and down, up and down. Maybe he was high now. Sybil had warned her people on cocaine had dilated pupils, that they wiped their noses a lot, that they couldn't stand still. This guy seemed normal though; he was over-the-top happy but maybe he was just glad to see his old friend okay.

"Have you found anything yet?" Michael went on. "I think hir-ing is starting to pick up, and if you want me to put a word in—"

Terry cut him off. "No, no, buddy. Don't worry about it. I have something now."

"Oh? What is it?"

Terry mumbled the name of the place, and Michael's face scrunched up in surprise.

"You're kidding. You can do better than that, Terry. You were the smartest one out of all of us."

"I don't know about all of that," Terry shrugged, but Jackie knew; everybody did; it was just a fact. She started to say something to that effect, but Terry kept talking.

"It's a process, buddy." His voice sounded strained all of a sudden, and Jackie cleared her throat.

"Oh, excuse me, Jackie, you remember Michael?"

She nodded.

"Of course, of course, the beautiful Jackie, and how's the baby?" Michael asked.

"Hungry," Jackie said, and they laughed. "He's twenty-five pounds now, not even one year old."

"Wow," Michael said, stretching the word out. "Wow. He'll be tall like his dad."

"Yeah," she smiled, "handsome like him too."

They all stood there for a while, awkward silence shifting between them.

"Well, all right, Terry, we're all getting together next week if you want to join," Michael said finally.

"Oh, that sounds good." Terry sounded surprised but lifted like a child with a Valentine in his locker when he was sure he'd be forgotten. Terry looked at Jackie while he answered. "I'll see what I can do," he said, and they said their good-byes.

Jackie felt relieved once the man was gone, but the interruption had ripped into their glee too, and she couldn't locate the exact space where it tore, or she'd try to put it together again.

Terry grabbed her hand, but they didn't walk far before they decided to turn around on the path and head back for the car. He said he was hungry all of a sudden, starving. They talked about what they would order, fried chicken and corn bread for her and red beans and rice for him.

She didn't ask him whether he would meet up with Michael or not. It was obvious he wouldn't. He hadn't said it that way because he was a people person; like her, he had trouble saying the word *no*. He'd come up with some excuse the day of and press on as if he had never even seen him though. She was proud of him for that, even before it happened.

Even still, a weight hung over them while they ate, and though she'd picked up new lingerie from Macy's and planned to put it to use that night, she turned over when he tried to touch her. He asked what was wrong, and she said nothing, she was just tired. But when he went to sleep, she lay on her back and stared at the ceiling for hours.

A couple of weeks later when Jackie got home, her answering machine was blinking. Her parents had called her four times. She'd just left them at work, and everything had been fine, but in the time it took her to drive back to Stately Grove, they must have talked to Sybil. Jackie wasn't surprised. She'd known this was coming. She'd expected to be angry when the day hit, but if anything, she felt relief.

She put off calling them back for the time it took to fix supper, set the table, bathe the baby, but she found her calmness grew thorns the longer she waited. Terry was working late, so she had to wait until the baby fell asleep before she returned the call. Of course today it took longer than normal, four stories instead of two, three songs instead of one. She normally waited ten minutes after his eyes closed to give him time to sink into a slumber that she couldn't rouse with footsteps or door creaks, but tonight she left as soon as his head fell back against the blanket, grabbed her cordless, stepped out on the balcony with the door ajar, and dialed the number.

Mama answered on the first ring.

Jackie couldn't catch it all; she heard Daddy's voice stream in too; they must have been on separate receivers, screaming over each other, barely decipherable. For every few sentences, she was able to catch one.

"What were you thinking? It's not just you anymore, Jackie Marie, you've got that baby to take care of too."

Then Aunt Ruby, who was probably sitting next to Mama: "The cat is out of the bag now."

"We're not trying to run your life but you're not doing a good job of it yourself."

"We know he loves you but he's an addict."

"He's not lying to you, he's lying to himself, and he doesn't even know it. That's what's so sad."

"You can't fix a man who doesn't want to be saved. You'll just wind up paying for his sins in the end."

And then Aunt Ruby: "A leopard damn sure can't change its spots."

"And you know it was wrong too, that's why you were trying to hide it. Sybil said if she hadn't gone over unannounced, you might have kept that secret till Christmas."

Aunt Ruby piped in again, "What is done in the dark will come to the light."

Jackie didn't say anything, just waited for the uproar to die down. Then she heard herself speak as if the voice was coming out of somebody else's body, slow as tar drying. "I love you, but this is my family now. Me, Terry, and T.C., we have to make our own decision about what's best for us."

Her daddy was hot on the heels of her explanation. "And who's going to be there when it all falls apart again, huh? Answer me that. You're ruining yourself, Jackie, lowering yourself beyond recognition, messing with him. You're throwing away everything your mother and I worked so hard for, and I can't spend my old age bailing you out."

For the rest of her life, Jackie wouldn't forget that comment. She and her daddy weren't as close as they had been, and she felt a pang in her chest whenever she saw him with Sybil, but most of that jealousy was mitigated by T.C. When she had the baby, she realized how much a parent loved a child, and she assumed her father's feelings for her were at least as sturdy. Because of that perspective, all this time she had also assumed that when he asked her how she was doing, when he drove her car to the lot for oil changes, moved her furniture, stopped by unannounced, and paid her light bill, that there was nothing else in the world he'd rather be doing. In reality though he'd been building up anger with every check he signed, every mile he drove, and the last thing she wanted was a favor laced in resentment. She waited for her mama to cut in with a word that might coat the ferocity of what had just been said, but there was only silence, a heavy resolve as though Jackie were the one who needed to explain, as if she would do anything differently if the circumstances tumbled into her lap again.

"Then don't, Daddy," she said, just as cool as rainwater, and she threw the phone across the cement. She heard it crack, saw the batteries tumble out.

"It wasn't the phone's fault," she heard her husband say. Terry was back, walking up the steps toward her.

"What?" Jackie asked, still angry and looking for some way to distill it.

"I said, it wasn't the phone's fault. Whoever got you so mad, that's who deserves to be thrown out. Now you gotta fork over thirty more bucks." Terry smiled, and Jackie felt herself sigh.

"Some people you can't just throw out," she said.

"Your parents." Terry had reached their floor now and leaned against the balcony beside her.

While she'd been talking to her folks, two police officers had pulled up across the street, cornered a young guy walking with his pants hanging past his drawls. She couldn't hear what they were asking him but she could see the young man shaking his head, heard him shout, "I ain't do nothing." He couldn't have been more than seventeen.

Jackie shook her head. "It's nothing," she said. And it was in the scheme of things. What mattered was Terry was here. He had been working at that pharmacy for a couple of weeks now. His passion for it seemed to be fading, but he'd get his first check next week, and pretty soon they'd be looking at places again; fingers crossed, they'd have enough for a down payment in the East. Still she couldn't shake the feeling of that call having emptied everything meaningful inside her; the filling she had managed to hold on to even when Terry left her seemed to be splayed out on the concrete just like that phone.

"Gotta be more than nothing," Terry said. He kept his eyes on the boy downstairs while he spoke. "Your parents found out I'm back, huh?"

Jackie nodded.

"Parents will be parents," he said. "They can't help worrying over you. I know with T.C., even when I was out there on the streets, I'd be thinking about him. Did he put something he found on the floor in his mouth? Is he going to grow up killing animals or worse 'cause his daddy's out there fiending for crack instead of reading him bedtime stories?" He shook his head.

Jackie hadn't heard him reference his life on the other side before and she felt a mix of curiosity and disgust.

The boy across the street was repeating himself now, his voice rising each time, "I ain't do nothing. But I ain't do nothing."

One of the officers gripped his arm and slammed him into the door of the police car. The boy didn't even wince, but Terry did. Still, he didn't take his eyes off him.

"Me too," Jackie said, trying to grasp his attention. Different concerns of course, but what mother didn't fear the worst for her child? When he was with her, when he wasn't, it didn't seem to make a difference. "But I'm a grown woman," she added. "That's the difference between me and my baby. At some point they have to accept that I have to take responsibility for my own choices in life, that I'm qualified to make my own decisions."

And that was the part where she stumbled, because she'd never been as judicious as her sister. Sybil said everything with a sense of certainty that obviated the presence of all doubt anywhere. Her failures seemed to only grant her more confidence. Tulane, for instance, was her dream school, but she didn't finish reading the rejection letter before she changed her tune, a shift so abrupt and thorough it swept out all evidence of any opinion preceding it. All of a sudden, everybody knew the best judges came out of Loyola. Tulane was all well and good if you wanted to teach, but when you looked at the best practicing lawyers in the city, most of them had studied at Loyola. Jackie didn't know if any of that were true or not, but more important, its veracity never would have crossed her mind.

"I'm a grown woman." Jackie repeated it to see if it would stick.

"I know," Terry said. He was nearly whispering. The police had cuffed the boy and were pushing his head into the back of their car.

"What do you think he did?" she asked, to change the subject.

Terry shrugged. The car's sirens cut on, twinkled down the block. "Maybe drugs. Maybe nothing. Hard to know sometimes.

"You did the right thing," he said once the car was out of sight, "hanging up. That's the only way to draw that line, to make them understand it's time to push back. Otherwise, they'll be riding your back for the rest of your life." He walked toward the front door of their apartment, but turned back toward her to speak. "Sometimes people have to see it to believe it. Sometimes you got to show them better than you can tell them."

She studied his face. He seemed spooked, maybe from the arrest downstairs. She wondered if anything like that had ever happened to him on the street. Who knew what he'd witnessed? He never talked about it, but he'd told her once that crack wasn't like alcohol, that he'd pay anything to be able to block some of his memories out, but that it wasn't that kind of drug.

"But everything is going all right otherwise?" she asked. His hand was on the doorknob now, but she wanted to keep him with her.

He nodded. "Everything's good. If you're good, and the baby's good, I'm good, girl."

Jackie smiled, but she wasn't satisfied; something in his demeanor was worrying her. "At work too, I mean?" she asked. He hadn't talked about it much. The first day, he'd been so excited to wake up with a purpose, but now it seemed he got out of bed later and later, and he was quiet more than buoyed up when he got back.

He turned back toward the house. "Umhmm," he grunted. "Same ol', same ol'."

"It's going to get better, baby," she said, not quite sure what the *it* she was referencing was. At that, he turned toward her again.

"Don't mind me, I'm just tired, baby, but everything's good." He stretched his smile out, reminding her of herself all those days before he came back.

"Well, that's good, baby," she said, and though she recognized her own fake smile in his, she let his words soothe her. "That's good," she repeated.

She walked toward him. He was still grinning, but she could see the defeat in his eyes.

T.C.

Summer 2010

T.C. decided it would be easier to clone than start from scratch. Then he realized this was too big of an operation to run from his mama's house, so once he bought the cuttings from his boy who also grew, they headed over to Tiger's. Tiger stayed in the Ninth Ward like T.C., in a house about the size of his, with the same rust-colored brick and postage stamp lawn out front. But unlike T.C.'s, Tiger's house wasn't done up with sofas from Aaron's, or salvaged baby pictures on the wall. No, the place looked as if it had been gutted in preparation for a remodel, but whoever was in charge stopped midway through, and the only thing that had been set down was an uncovered mattress and a TV in the last bedroom off the hall where Tiger planned to house the plants.

After Tiger gave him a tour of the space, T.C. stepped back out on the porch. There used to be a housing complex across the street, but now the townhouses were all fenced in, hollowed out, boarded up remains amid dead grass and neglected tires. Crackheads congregated in the unit diagonal from Tiger's; it was the first of the month, and they'd just received whatever check sustained them. All the houses were tagged with graffiti, but the house the addicts streamed in and out of was marked with fluorescent blue bubble letters and read: NOT A DUMP.

Tiger walked out on the porch all paranoid and shit.

"Get inside and lock the door, mothafucka. I don't know who tryna come in behind me."

"Man, ain't nobody trying to rob this shithole. You ain't got nothing to take."

T.C. regretted it as soon as it came out; he could see the shame spreading on Tiger's face.

Tiger was quiet for a few minutes. Then, "Don't come at me like that. At least it's mine. At least I ain't leeching offa my mama.

"It came with a sofa," he added, "but I sold it. Refrigerator too, but I don't need that shit. It's just me here, and my cousin, but he gone now."

T.C. let him talk, shook his head. "All right, all right, calm down. You right about that," he said. "You right about that," he repeated. He thought he could smell mold but how could that be? It had been so long; still there was no question that was it; he would never forget the smell that greeted him when he walked in his own house five years earlier. It was fainter here now, but there it was.

A few minutes later, Tiger started up again out of nowhere: "You know this is my grandmama's house," he whispered, "she came back after the storm, did her best to rebuild so I'd have some-where to stay, but . . ." He trailed off.

T.C. remembered the floors; half were hardwood and half were plywood.

"She took the rest of her money to Birmingham, said she's not gon' stand by and get her heart broken again. But this was all I had left."

"I'm sorry nigga," T.C. said. "I shouldn'ta said nothing. I didn't know."

"It's cool. No sad stories. In a few months I'm gon' fix this place up, knock everything down, start all over. I already got a crew. That Mexican mothafucka that used to play guard with us at Joe Brown, he's a foreman now. I ran into him on Bourbon Street and we already handled the logistics. I just need the dough."

T.C. smiled, and they dapped it off. "That's what's up," he said. "I'm glad I could help you out then."

They laughed like they did, low grunts caught in their throat, and they got in Tiger's car and drove to Home Depot for filters, fans, and lights.

T.C. was cutting it close with all the new purchases, but he wasn't going to ask Tiger to contribute, not after he saw his place. He checked his balance on the way out of the store. With the help from MawMaw he might have enough left to last him the two months it took the plants to flower, but he just wouldn't be able to eat out or anything like that. He supposed that wasn't a big deal: He stopped by MawMaw's every night to see her anyway, and she was happy to send him home with extra helpings of roast turkey, dressing, and gravy over rice.

That night at Tiger's place, they pushed their first cut branches into rock wool cubes, sealed them with plastic, and lined them up in a row under the grow lights.

When they were done, they stood and surveyed the scene.

"All right, all right, I see about you," Tiger said. "I wasn't sure, dawg, I wasn't sure. I thought they had scavenged you at that place, but you back just as ingenious as ever. Let's celebrate then, nigga."

They sat on the edge of the bare mattress. T.C. couldn't afford to buy weed, but Tiger pulled a bag out of his pocket, unwrapped a swisher, licked it, and rolled.

T.C. coughed up the first hit.

"Damn, nigga, you sound like a Mack Truck; you gon' be high as a mothafucka."

"I haven't lit up in a while."

"Why the hell not?"

"I'm trying to save, nigga. Who you think bought all these cuttings and lights and shit?"

Tiger put the tip of the blunt to his lips. "Well, that's all gon' be behind us in a minute, lil' bro. How long you said it take to flower, two months?"

"Yeah, but this is to sell nigga, not to smoke."

"I know, I know," Tiger said, "but how I'ma market it if I don't sample it first?" He passed the blunt back to T.C., a smile spreading across his face.

T.C. didn't say anything, just rolled his eyes and passed it between them for a while. This was his favorite part of smoking, the first fifteen minutes. After that, anything could happen, depending on the strain. He might pass out; he might get a ride home and gorge on MawMaw's homemade jelly cake; he might turn on a movie and try to drown out his certainty that any minute a horde of po-po would bust through Tiger's front door and send T.C. back to the place he swore he'd never see again. Now, though, he felt an ease in his heart, spreading out and touching everything that even crossed his mind. His problems showed up in different outfits, repositioned as opportunities. Alicia, for instance. He'd been wanting to call her since he came home, but he was afraid of what she would say, that she might try to lock him out of the baby's life, or her own. Now though, three hits deep, it seemed like if he could just get her on the line, he could explain himself from the most genuine angle. He didn't know exactly what the words were going to be, but the fact was, he loved that girl, and this baby was his chance to live again.

He reached for his phone.

"Who you calling, mothafucka?"

T.C. shrugged. "I don't know, I wasn't sure, but I was thinking about calling Licia."

"Aww, hell no, put that phone down." Tiger stood up as if he were going to wrestle it from T.C.'s hands.

"This ain't the time for that, bruh. You all loaded and shit."

"I ain't loaded."

"You ain't loaded, you been over there smiling that goofy-ass smile of yours for the last fifteen minutes, that's how I know you high."

"Anyway when that ever stopped me from doing something?" T.C. asked.

"Yeah, but you ain't smoked in a while. You liable to go and say something you can't unsay, you feel me?"

"Nah, bruh, I just want to tell her I love her, that I'm always going to be there for her."

"Yeah, and that sound all well and good right now, but she gon' be able to tell you high, bruh, and then how she gon' feel? You been out all this time, and you got to get out your mind before you call her?"

T.C. didn't say anything to that. It sounded too much like sense. After a while, he relit the blunt, inhaled but didn't cough, passed it back to Tiger.

"You hear that?" Tiger asked after he tapped it out.

"Hear what?"

"Them sirens."

T.C. didn't have to listen to know they were there, not directly but circling like he'd seen lions surround antelopes from all sides on the National Geographic Channel. Either way, he wasn't worried; surely it was for the crackhouse next door. It was the perfect place to grow in that sense; nobody would be bothering to look out for them. "Mothafucka, you trippin'. Don't get all paranoid on me now," he said.

"All right, you right, you right," Tiger said. Then, "T.C., that don't sound right, man."

"What don't sound right? Man, you killing my buzz."

"Better it's me than some nigga with a burner, mothafucka, or worse, po-po." He walked up to the window, peered through. "Come over here," he said.

T.C. walked over. There was nothing out there. The emptied houses were even eerier at night, like gaps in a mouth where teeth had been shattered.

"You see something?" Tiger asked.

T.C. looked out into the darkness, the empty fields of brown grass.

"Hell, no, I don't see nothing, mothafucka. Everybody's inside. I told you wasn't nobody out there. Now sit down."

T.C. turned on the TV, looking for a movie. *Friday* had just started, and Craig's mama was telling him she didn't feel comfortable loaning him money without a job.

"Here, watch this," T.C. said. "Calm your ass the hell down."

They watched until Big Worm pulled his ice cream truck up on screen, and Tiger said he was hungry.

"Don't nobody deliver over here but Domino's though. I could fuck up some Domino's right now."

T.C. didn't have any money, and he told him that.

"I got you," Tiger said.

"Stop fuckin' around."

"Nah, I'm serious; you always getting me."

By the time the movie was over, the pizza had arrived, and they huddled over the box in the dark. T.C. found himself feeling grateful.

"Thanks, nigga," he said.

"I already told you, don't worry about the pizza."

"Not for the pizza, bruh. For that stuff with Alicia. I would have said something stupid, something I couldn't unsay. You're right."

Tiger shrugged. "I just think it's rare what y'all have, that's all. I ain't never had nothing like it, but if I did, I wouldn't fuck around with it. I would treat it with respect, you feel me?"

Over the next few weeks, T.C. spent at least a few hours at Tiger's every day, feeding the plants, changing their water, testing the pH, applying the chemical adjuster. Meanwhile Tiger started his marketing campaign. T.C. told him the plants wouldn't finish flowering for at least a month, but he'd come in every day bragging about how perfect the middleman he'd found was going to be: "He got as much ambition as a NBA wife, nigga." Or how many people were begging him for T.C.'s Blueberry: "They know it's gon' be another month, but they still asking about it. That's the key, to have niggas waiting, hungry on the verge of an attack if they can't taste your bud so the first week that shit gon' be sold out from the sheer momentum."

One day, the door opened, and T.C. heard Alicia's voice behind Tiger's. "What the hell y'all got going on in here, Tiger? You can smell the gas from outside."

She stopped in her tracks when she saw T.C. though.

"I didn't expect you to be here," she said. "Tiger said he had something to show me. I wouldn't have come otherwise."

T.C. and Alicia both looked at their friend.

"What?" Tiger asked. "Y'all need to fix this mess, bruh. I'm tired of watching y'all both suffer."

T.C. hadn't realized he had been suffering. Of course Alicia was always on his mind, she was his life, but he hadn't known how very much he missed her until she walked in, his seed pressing on her belly so hard he thought there was a real chance she might deliver the child right there.

"What the hell y'all got going on in here?" she repeated.

He ignored the question, told himself to calm down. She didn't seem happy to see him, so he clipped his own joy out of habit; he wouldn't have it going out into territory it couldn't see its way out of.

He looked her up and down though. He couldn't help that. "You look good," he said.

"She big, huh, T?" Tiger shot in.

Alicia play-slapped him in his chest. "I ain't big, boy. I'm pregnant."

"That's what I meant," Tiger said.

"Then that's what you say next time," Alicia went on.

In all the squabble T.C. wasn't sure if Alicia would hear his compliment, so he repeated himself.

"You're beautiful," he lightweight whispered, and she looked up at him and smiled.

Once Tiger left, they went outside and sat on his stoop.

"I can't be in that house too long," Alicia said. "I'd wind up getting some contact high or some shit."

T.C. laughed. He had missed her candor. "I feel you."

"So when you got out?" she asked.

"A month ago."

She nodded. "I knew it was a month, I was just making conversation," she said.

"I was gonna come see you."

"Don't even start, T.C.," she shrugged, and waved her hand at him. "I've heard it all before and I don't have the energy for it, not today."

He didn't say anything to that. What was there to say? They watched kids jump Double Dutch across the street. T.C. didn't know where they could possibly be living.

Banana, banana, banana split,
What you got in arithmetic?
Banana, banana, banana for free,
What you got in geometry?

"How's your mama and them?" Alicia asked.

"My mama? Crazy as ever. You already know."

Alicia laughed. "I ran into her the other day at Castnet. She made the owner give me my sandwich for free, said her grandbaby was going to be eating it." Alicia shook her head, laughing.

"I didn't know she knew the owner like that."

"She doesn't, but I think they just didn't want to cross her."

Their laughter was so much a habit only part of them knew they were doing it.

"So how has it been? The pregnancy and all that?"

"Easy breezy. My mama was sick the whole first two trimesters with me, and you know she had a miscarriage between me and my sister."

T.C. shook his head.

"Yeah, so I was nervous you know, I was real nervous in the beginning, but now, I'm just ready to go."

"You due, what, in a week or two?"

"Boy, I got about four weeks left. I wish it was a week or two. Nah, lemme stop, I just want him to be healthy. Sometimes if they come too early, they gotta stay in NICU and shit."

"Aww, no, not our lil' dude." He put his hand around her shoulder out of habit, and she didn't move. "You thought about names already?"

She nodded, smiling. "I got a couple. Why, you wanna hear them?"

He shrugged. "Yeah."

"One is Malcolm Darrell, Darrell after Daryl, may he rest in peace." She made the sign of the cross.

T.C. could feel the emotion rushing to his face and he put his head down.

"And you know I just love Malcolm X."

"You still tryin' to be a Black Panther, huh?" he said, glad to change the mood.

"Boy, whatever," but she smiled. "The other one is Malik." She looked up at him to gauge his reaction. "I just like the name Malik." She shrugged. "Always have. What you think?"

"Those sound good," he said. "Those sound real good."

"You got a favorite?"

"Probably Malik," he said. "That just sound real cool to me, and unique. Malik Darrell. MD. Maybe he'll be a doctor or something like that."

"I didn't even think about that," she said, her face lighting up.

He nodded. "Yeah."

"Then Lewis of course."

He was too caught off guard to play it cool. He looked up at her with impossible gratitude. He had long since given up on having the last name, being locked up half his girl's pregnancy, and then he had gone and let the shame over that keep him from being there the rest of the time too. If it hadn't been for Tiger, who knew when he would have shown up? Kindergarten? High school graduation? But she was going to give him the name anyway.

"You serious, Licia? You really thinking about naming him Lewis?"

"It's your baby, ain't it?"

"Of course it's mine"—he sat up straight on the porch chair—"but I haven't done right by you. I know that. I'ma do better, but I let so much time pass; sometimes I worry it's too late."

Alicia sighed. "That's why you didn't call? You thought it was too late?"

He shrugged. "Something like that. I thought about calling all the time. I'd pick up the phone and actually dial the number. Then I'd imagine your mama in your ear telling you *that nigga ain't shit*, then imagine my kid hearing that over and over through the years. That's how it was for me, you know. I don't think my mama ever mentioned my daddy's name without following it with the word *mothafucka*, and I'd think about all that, and I'd put the phone right back on the hook, roll up. You know how that go." He was looking at those kids again now, anything to keep his eyes off her. The overgrown weeds were hugging their knees.

> *I know something,*
> *But I won't tell.*
> *Three lil' monkeys,*
> *in a peanut shell.*
> *One can read,*
> *And one can dance,*
> *And one got a hole*
> *in the seat of his pants!*

"I just thought you had moved on to somebody else, that you weren't thinking about me and old Malik," Alicia said.

He reached for her hand. "I could never stop thinking about you, Licia. You never have to think that."

"Well, you never have to think it's too late. No matter what happens with us, it's never too late for you to be part of his life, T.C. You hear me? That's your son." She moved his face so it was parallel to hers. He never wanted to kiss somebody more in his life, not fuck her, just kiss her, pour his whole heart into hers and have her pour the new merged contents back.

Instead he just nodded. They stared into each other's eyes for a while until the kids changed their song, and T.C. looked up.

> *Call the army, call the navy*
> *I heard Tashica gonna have a baby.*
> *Wrap it up in tissue paper,*
> *send it down the elevator*

"They over there ear hustling," T.C. joked.

Alicia shook her head, smiling.

"Anyway, what the hell y'all doing in here, nigga?" She gestured toward the house again. It smells like a high school bathroom. Better yet, it smells like the hallway to prison, that's what it smells like."

"Aww, please, you know it ain't nothing like that."

"I don't know a thing." She paused. "Now you doing good. Don't go fooling around with Tiger and get yourself back in trouble, T.C. I mean it. Malik needs you. We need you."

Tiger was right on both counts. T.C. had checked the buds just the other day, and they were cloudy as a glass of ice water. He chopped the branches off all twelve plants, trimmed the leaves so only the buds were left to dry. In another week or so, they'd be open for business.

Not only that, he and Licia were still kicking it together real strong. He'd worried that the momentum from a few weeks ago would whittle down, and she'd be back to going ham on him, worse than that, barely speaking to him, but no. Every morning first thing, he called her to check in, make sure the baby was still inside, see if she needed anything. He'd gone with her to buy that car seat too, and a pair of baby Jordans he thought his little man shouldn't be without. Then she'd invited him to the doctor's appointment last week, and he'd heard his baby's heartbeat, steady as the rhythm of God. Tears welled up in his eyes, and he didn't wipe them.

He was bagging up his first batch when he got the call from Licia's mama.

"You betta get over here to Ochsner, T.C. Labor's starting, and it's going quick."

He hung up the phone, then scrambled around the house looking for a suitcase among his mama's piles of shit. Once he found one as old as he was, he stuffed some sweats and a T-shirt inside. Licia had told him he could expect to stay up to a week sometimes depending on how the baby was delivered, and he stopped in the bathroom on his way out for his toothbrush, left a note for his mama, and hightailed it to the bus stop for the 94.

By the time he got to the fifth floor, there was an IV in Alicia's arm and something like a shower cap on her head. He was nervous to see her that way, but the nurse pulled him aside and reassured him: The baby was showing signs of distress, not moving as much as expected. Licia had done great carrying him, and he was big enough; it made sense to just pull him now.

T.C. nodded in silence, not sure how to formulate what he was really thinking. Finally he just said it. "Is she going to be all right?"

"She's going to be fine, sir." The nurse handed him some hospital scrubs and a cap, and he dressed, then sat outside waiting for anesthesiology to administer the spinal.

Then the same nurse came out and led him to the operating room. The doctors had already lined the curtain up at Licia's stomach. He hustled over to her. He kept looking around for her mama or her sister, but it was just the two of them there. He took her hand, let her squeeze his as hard as she wanted.

"Are you in any pain?"

She shook her head, biting her lip. "Just scared," she said.

"Can you feel this?" the doctor called out from the other side of the curtain. T.C. peeked back, watched as the doctor dug a scalpel into the bottom of Licia's belly. "Because we started."

Licia shook her head. She seemed to calm down after that, but T.C. tried to think of something to say, to take her mind off of the fact that she was getting sliced into.

"I know you wanted to do it the other way," he whispered.

"It's cool, however they can get him out healthy."

He was about to tell her not to worry, that the baby was going to be fine, that everything would be now, but a minute later, the doctor called out to them again.

"Baby here in a second, Daddy, if you want to see." He looked at Alicia to see if he could leave her. She nodded for him to go, her eyes wide and bright. He peeked behind the curtain again, and there he was, not anything like what T.C. was expecting amid the blood and goo, but he was his, long as a Lewis and red as one too, screaming like a banshee.

"You want to cut the cord, sir?"

"Sure." T.C. asked them if he was aiming the scissors in the right place three times before he snapped them shut. Then the nurses weighed the baby, wiped him down, wrapped him in a blanket, and handed him over. He was tinier than T.C. could have imagined. T.C. guessed he was expecting something the size of one of those newborns on TV, but Malik could fit in the palm of just one of his hands. He carried him to Alicia and she burst into tears before she even saw his face. She couldn't hold him because of the drugs, but T.C. held him out to her.

"Look at what we did," she said. "Let me see him. He's perfect, isn't he? Did they say he was perfect?"

"They said he was perfect."

"Can you believe it?"

T.C. shook his head. The baby's eyes were closed, and T.C. kissed his closed lids.

"This is your mama," he said. "And I'm your daddy, and we love you. We gon' always be here for you, you hear? No matter what."

T.C. walked out to the waiting room feeling even taller than normal. MawMaw, Mama, and Aunt Ruby had joined Licia's people in there. They seemed to be trying to distract themselves from waiting with an episode of *Judge Judy* but they jumped up when they saw him.

"Twenty-two inches." He pointed at himself, and they laughed. "Seven pounds, fifteen ounces."

Everybody shrieked.

"He gon' play ball like you, T.C.," Licia's mama said.

"That would be real cool," T.C. said. "Real cool."

•

He walked with his own family to the cafeteria, his mama talking nonstop while they waited on the elevator.

"Now that's what I'm talking about, boy, that baby is as fine as you were. Real fine, you hear me? Look just like you. When I get home I'm going to pull out your newborn picture, put them side by side, and you'll see. He got that same head shape, you got to mold it though so it flattens out, and that same nose, you got to squeeze it with your fingers, not so hard that it hurts him, you hear, but just to straighten it out. My baby, a daddy."

She paused; he could tell that whatever she was thinking was as amped-up as her speech. This was the woman who had started him on basketball, the one his friends wanted to holla at, the one he'd been so proud of those years she was around. She had come back.

"We got to exercise his legs 'cause big thighs run in our family, don't they, Mother?" T.C.'s mama went on, turning to MawMaw, who was holding her up as if she were the one who needed a cane. When MawMaw didn't respond, his mama kept on.

"I'm just so happy," she repeated. T.C. stood on the other side of her, and she squeezed his hand. "You're going to be a good daddy, none of that *here today, gone tomorrow* mess. You know how I know? Remember when Miss Patricia took her grandbaby in? T.C. used to go over there every day and just hold him. What kind of eleven-year-old boy got any interest in a baby? My son did. And this one's named after Daryl too. He's gon' be the light of your life."

When they reached the cafeteria, his mama went off for a doughnut, and he and MawMaw and Aunt Ruby picked a table and waited.

It was rare to be sitting in silence with Aunt Ruby there—she usually talked enough for the whole family—but it seemed as if they were all still in awe. He fumbled with the sugar packets on the table. After a while he asked them what they were thinking.

"Oh, nothing, just ruminating. Not every day you become a great-grandmother, is it?" MawMaw asked.

Aunt Ruby smiled. "No, it's not," she repeated. Then she paused, wringing her hands. "Times like these, I really miss our parents."

T.C. was surprised to hear her bring them up. They had died before he was born, and neither MawMaw nor his aunt mentioned them much. All he knew was that their father had been a doctor, the first black doctor in all of Louisiana or something like that, and that MawMaw and her mama hadn't been close when she was a girl, but something had happened along the way to change all that.

"You miss them too, MawMaw?" he asked.

"You never stop missing your parents, no matter how old you get." She paused. "No, I expect I'll take this grief to my grave. But I just know they would be so proud. Things have changed so much in this world. People don't do things in the same order they used to," she chuckled.

"Maybe they never did them in that order," Aunt Ruby cut in, laughing too.

"I guess not," MawMaw said, "but our parents, even though they were sticklers for the rules, I have to think they would be proud, despite themselves."

"They would," Aunt Ruby said, but it came out more like a question.

"I hope so," T.C. said, setting the sugar down.

He looked up. His mama had glided more than walked back with a bib for the baby she'd picked up in the gift shop.

GRANDMAMA'S BABY, it read in blue cursive letters. She sang the words aloud. Then she looked at T.C. with more tenderness than he remembered seeing even ten years ago when he'd been named high school player of the year. Nobody drafted kids straight out of high school then, so he chose LSU. Six months later he was home for spring break, playing pickup ball with Daryl, and he twisted his right knee, tore the ligament. His doctor told him to wait out the season, but Coach Domingue played him anyway.

Back then, he listened to everything Coach said, he was so happy to be wearing the same uniform Shaquille O'Neal had worn, but the second game of the season he fell again, fractured a bone in the same knee this time. LSU paid for the operation, but he was never the same after it, and when the school realized he changed, they did too. A few months later, Katrina hit and Daryl died, and T.C. was bottomed out.

He walked back to the elevator now though feeling like a different man than the one who had walked into the hospital a few hours earlier, as if he had been reacquainted with the boy he'd been, who'd held so much promise, but the promise wasn't specific to basketball or anything really, it was all encompassing, and there was no way he wouldn't be able to parlay it into something real. He didn't know what it would be, but it would have to be more than bagging groceries, selling weed even. No, he'd finish this last batch, then he'd start thinking about next steps.

He didn't go home for the next four nights. Alicia's people asked to relieve him, but there was nowhere else he wanted to be. He and Licia fell into a routine in that hospital room, taking turns waking up every two hours, watching old movies, and in a state of delirium, speaking the characters' names instead of each other's. Mostly, they just stared at the baby and imagined different versions of his future, reminisced on different aspects of their own lives that might apply to him, the height he'd get from his father.

"But now that I think about it, I don't want him to play ball. Too risky," T.C. said.

Or the intelligence he'd inherit from Licia, who was just a year from finishing nursing school.

"A doctor," she said. "Not a nurse, but a doctor."

At the root of it, they didn't care, not yet; the child they'd created had come out perfect, and it had plucked them both out of the realm of ordinary existence and elevated them to the level of gods.

The night before they were scheduled to leave, Aunt Sybil came to see them. She walked in in her fancy suit and sharp heels clanking against the linoleum. T.C. used to put on a collared shirt for her visits, but all he could think now was that her shoes would wake Alicia, who had finally fallen to sleep.

"I come bearing gifts." Aunt Sybil handed him a giant bag.

"Thanks," he pulled out the onesies, socks, and sailor suits. "We appreciate it."

He let her hold the baby, then when Licia stirred, they walked the portable bassinet up and down the hallway.

They talked about the delivery for a while, when he'd come back home; Aunt Sybil noted it was a good thing he could make it for the birth, said MawMaw was beside herself; Sybil hadn't seen her so happy ever since PawPaw died. When the pleasantries were over, she turned to him.

"I never had my own kids, and you know I hate telling grown people what to do, but the real reason I came out here is for you. It's always nice to see a new generation come in, but you've got to do right by him, T.C. He's too beautiful to let him down."

T.C. laughed the silly, nervous laugh Aunt Sybil had elicited from him his whole life.

"I know that, Aunt Sybil," he said. "Don't worry about me."

"I'm not just worried about you, son. I'm worried about that child. Well, I'm worried about the both of you. I want to see you do something productive with your life."

They turned the corner to walk back in the opposite direction.

"I wanted to run something by you, T.C. You know I closed my own practice and started working at a firm."

"Yeah, Mama told me the man got you."

"Yeah, well the man pays the bills, let me tell you. Nothing like a paycheck every two weeks." She laughed, a polite chuckle. "Anyway, they're looking for a mailboy. It's not much, but if you do all right there, you could rise up to paralegal. Then, if that seemed like a good fit, I have enough stowed away to pay for you to go to law school."

He laughed. "Law school? I barely made it out of the twelfth grade." He laughed again, but she cut him short.

"That's because your focus was off. Basketball is great as a hobby, but you can't rely on it. I told your mama that when you were a boy, but no, that made too much like sense. Anyway, here we are now, and I have an opportunity for you." She stopped walking, gripped his wrist. "Don't answer me now. I want you to think about it, really think about it, 'cause if you take it, I'm going to need your commitment. You know I'm just starting out at this place, T, and I'd be putting my neck out for you."

He nodded. "I know," he said. "I know."

Licia was up when they got back, and she and his aunt said quick hellos. T.C. walked Aunt Sybil out.

"I'll let you know in a week or so," he said before they hugged.

When he got back, Malik was more alert than T.C. had ever seen him.

"What she wanted?" Licia asked.

"To offer me some job."

"Hmph. Working for her?"

"Yeah. In her new office."

"That's funny, you always said you wished Sybil would give you the hookup."

"Yeah, I know. But the timing is off. I got some things I need to finish and then maybe—"

"Don't be stupid, T," Licia cut him off. "That's a once-in-a-lifetime opportunity, what she's proposing, and the timing is perfect. You know Sybil wasn't fucking with you after jail. But she came all the way out here to see the baby and offer you that job. That's something. I mean, maybe Malik worked out that miracle himself." She paused, cooing at the baby. "Don't mess it up by being prideful."

"I'm not being prideful." T.C. lifted the baby from Licia's arms. "I'm not being prideful," he repeated in a baby voice, making funny faces with his seed. "It's just a big deal," he said. "I gotta think about it first."

Alicia didn't respond; she just looked at him hamming it up with their child, and finally she laughed.

They were discharged the next morning. After T.C. dropped his baby off, he took Licia's car to Tiger's to check on his weed. He could see once he got inside that the bags were light, but he rooted through them anyway when he reached the mattress, trying to make sense of the deficit. He dialed Tiger up.

"What the fuck, nigga? Where my shit at?"

"Sold, mothafucka! I tried calling you, but you didn't answer."

"You know Licia had the baby."

"I heard, I heard congratulations were due, and I figured you'd be all camped out with her and lil' Malik, so I took it upon myself to put that lil' nigga I interviewed to work. He went out on Monday, and by Thursday a quarter of that shit was sold. I told you my marketing campaign was what's up. I was just on my way back to the house to reup."

"And give me my money."

"Right, and give you your money. I mean, I took a cut for myself like we discussed, but 75 percent is for you, nigga, and well earned. You did it."

"Well, I had help too, bruh," T.C. had calmed down some, knowing he was about to be paid. Shit, diapers were expensive, and as of this morning they were off Blue Cross's dollar.

"But you still coulda waited though, bruh," he added. "It's my shit. I like to label it, and I knock the prices up for some of the rare mixes," he added.

"Oh, I just took the liberty of knocking them all up. Sixty bucks an eighth."

"And people paid that much? Even for the OG?"

"Hell, yeah, I told you, leave the marketing to me. Anyway, you gon' be there in twenty? I'm on my way. I got some other things I want to discuss with you."

Tiger was manic when he arrived, scooping up the bags so fast T.C. couldn't keep track.

"Calm down, mothafucka. What's gotten into you?"

"Aw, nothing, bruh. I'm just amped, you know. My lil' nigga said they asking about more, and we gotta take advantage of all this momentum." He sat down on the edge of the mattress.

"That's actually what I want to talk with you about," Tiger went on. "I know you just had the baby and all that, but we got a market, a serious one. I'ma need you to go get some more of them cuttings tonight, start over, maybe double up. Two months from now is too long to have people waiting, T.C. I'm gon' be done with this batch in a few weeks max, and then how we gon' look, dry as fuck for the next two months? Nah, I'm thinking we could set it up so we always have some in rotation. Like halfway through the process, start on the next."

T.C. stood up from the mattress, his hands in front of him.

"Man, hell no. I told you when we started this it was just temporary, to get me on my feet. I got a kid now, bruh. I'm not messing with this stuff."

"That's why we got lil' Kevin on the street selling. Nobody's even gon' trace it back to you."

"Don't be stupid, the first thing that lil' nigga's gon do is tell on me when he get caught."

"You mean on me? He ain't never even met you. And I got you, bruh. Trust me."

"Till we beef out, then my name gon' be all over your mouth."

"What we gon' beef out over?"

T.C. sighed, shook his head. "Look, man, it's not that I don't trust you. I just don't trust the industry. I'm out after this. Go head, you and Kevin sell this lil' bit, and however long it takes, that's fine, but when it's over, it's over."

"What, Winn-Dixie calling for you?" Tiger started singing the theme song. *"Hey, by the way, While you're at the marketplace—"*

"Shut that shit up," T.C. cut him off. "Nah, as a matter of fact"—T.C. paused, not sure if he wanted to continue—"as a matter of fact, bruh, my auntie offered me a job."

"Who, that lawyer?"

"Yeah, she want me to start working by her firm."

Tiger bust out laughing. "What, you trying to be some lawyer now? Oh shit, now I know you crazy. They ain't gon' let you through the front doors of no law firm. If they do, *if* they do, they damn sure not gon' keep you the whole first day."

T.C.'s head was down, but he raised it before he spoke. "Well, maybe so, but I owe it to myself to try. I owe it to everybody, Licia, the baby, shit, my mama. She suffered enough over me."

Tiger didn't say anything to that, just started scooping up bags and piling them in his duffel bag.

T.C. studied him for a little while. "Actually, why don't you leave that with me?" he motioned for the weed.

"How I'm a sell it then, bruh?"

"You not gon' sell more than a few bags today. Most of the customer base already bought, and they gon' be straight for a couple weeks. Take a bag or two, then come back for the rest, but I don't want all that gas out on the street."

Tiger shrugged, fronting as if he didn't care, but T.C. could tell he was irritated.

"Have it your way," he said. He slipped the bags in his pocket and stood up. "I'll call you when it's time for more. Make sure you answer your phone, nigga." He walked toward the door.

"Ain't you forgetting something?" T.C. asked.

"What? Oh. My bad, mothafucka." Tiger handed him a rack and watched T.C. count it, his tongue dangling from his mouth while he flipped through the crisp dirty bills.

"It feel good, huh, nigga? It feel good, don't it?"

T.C. tried not to smile but couldn't help it.

"You say you owe it to your people to go work for the white man. I say you owe that baby some milk. And that will buy plenty of it." Tiger walked toward the door.

"I'll holla at you this evening," he went on. "Niggas stay talking shit early in the morning. You feelin yourself, you got the whole day ahead of you, but let's see what you sayin' tonight, the world weighing on your shoulder. Shit look different in the twilight, don't it?"

T.C. sat back down on the mattress and counted it all out again.

T.C. paid MawMaw back, not so fast she got concerned but in spurts that in a few weeks added up to it all. He bought his mama a pea coat. Winter would be here before he knew it, and he was tired of her leaving the house with that one missing button and the lining sticking out the back. She wasn't as excited as he expected.

"Where you get all that money from, boy? You started with Sybil already?"

He changed the subject. "Mama, the expression you're looking for is *thank you*."

"I just don't want to see you getting in trouble. Ain't no coat worth that much."

He reassured her, while she twirled around in the mirror. Then they sat and watched her stories together.

"Why you bother with this crap, Mama? Nothing has changed since I got locked up."

"Yeah, it's similar to life that way," she said, and he kept quiet after that 'cause that was the thing about his mama. She'd drop some knowledge sometimes that made you think. With his own baby around, he had stopped being so hard on her. Yeah, she still went ham on him sometimes, but she'd had a hard life, raised him all by herself really. He'd heard rumors from Aunt Sybil when she had too much wine that his daddy had been the love of his mama's life, that he was in and out the first year of T.C.'s life, but something happened after that, and he was just out. T.C. wanted to compensate for all the pain that man had caused her, make enough in life so she'd be comfortable. He knew that level of wealth wasn't going to come from dealing, but he was starting to seriously consider his auntie's offer. She had texted that he had another couple of weeks to decide, and it was all he thought about most days, to go or not to go. He knew it seemed like an obvious decision from the outside. A wide-open plain versus a dead-end hallway, but there was something holding him back from calling her and accepting, a knot in his chest that formed every time he imagined himself in that office, representing his auntie on any level, the certainty that he would find a way to fuck it all up.

Still he needed to do something; the baby was growing. One month already, and Malik had his daddy's same big lips, wide-open nostrils, thick nappy hair, and red skin. T.C. slept at Alicia's most nights. He didn't feel an obligation to, he just wanted to be there to see her wake up out of instinct right before the baby started crying, hear her coo with the baby though she must have been dog tired. She held Malik as though the inside of her elbow had been crafted to fit this specific child. And something about seeing her nurture his son made T.C. feel as if he was being nurtured, made him feel as if he would be nurtured for the rest of his life.

He didn't mean to start looking for rings, he just did it. The plaza used to be the place to go for all things ranging from Girbaud jeans to leather sofas. T.C.'s first job was at Spencer's, a gag gift store on the second floor, and he and his boys would meet at the food court every day after work, walk up and down the brown tiled floors, hit up the arcade, the ice cream shop, the Chick-fil-A. Sometimes if he had a little money, he'd go to the movies or buy a girl a record. Then crime spiked, stores closed, and a few years later, Katrina finished what white flight started. Now the only legitimate shopping center was in Metairie, so he borrowed his mama's car and headed over. His boy worked at a jewelry counter up in Macy's, a place T.C. couldn't afford to buy socks from ordinarily, but his friend hooked T.C. up with a discount when he bought his diamond earring, and T.C. was hoping for similar treatment today. He skimmed the rows and rows of rings. Some gold, some white gold, some round, some square, some sapphire, some emerald, some solitaire, some with two diamonds. It was overwhelming as fuck, as if the world were conspiring against him, as if maybe it were all a setup keeping the black family apart. His friend walked up then.

"Yo, T.C., what's up, I didn't know you was out." He was hyped at first, but he lowered his voice when the other customers turned to him.

"Yeah, bruh," T.C. talked low too, "It's been a few months. I had a baby boy and everything."

"For real? Lemme see pictures."

T.C. pulled out his phone and flipped through its memory.

"Damn, bruh, you ain't got to worry if that's your kid, huh?"

T.C. shook his head.

"You lucky like that. I'm still not sure with my second one. My first one, no question. His mama loyal like a mothafucka. But the second one don't really look like me. She dark for one."

"Her mama dark?"

"Hell, no, you know that's not my type. And you see I'm light as a mothafucka. So it don't compute, but what the hell?" He shrugged. "All this time, and I ain't had no test done, I might as well just accept it. What I'ma do, get her tested at her high school graduation?"

They both laughed and shook their heads.

"Anyway, what can I help you with, bruh?"

"Well, say, bruh, I was wondering if you could hook up a discount for a nigga."

"Hell yeah, anything for you, bruh, and then since we celebratin', you could get my employee discount too," he whispered that last part. "What you getting? Your lil' boy got his ear pierced yet?"

"Nah, he only a month."

"Getting close then. A lot of 'em getting pierced after their two-month shots now. You should see how many women bring their kids in right after that appointment, knock it all out in one day. It's easier then 'cause they ain't got no fear."

T.C. nodded. "Licia wouldn't go for that though," he said. "She could barely handle the vaccinations."

"Well, what you lookin' for then? Another earring for you? I got these studs just came in." He motioned for T.C. to follow him across the display.

"Nah, nah, that's not it." He didn't know why, but he felt embarrassed saying why he was really there.

"I'm lookin' for something for Licia."

"Aww, like a push present? White people be doing that, and shit, if it's good enough for them, it's damn sure good enough for you. Lemme show you the necklaces."

"Nah, bruh, I'm actually looking for a ring."

"Oh?" His friend stopped where he was and looked up at him as if T.C. said he was there for an ice cream cone.

"Like an engagement ring?"

"Yeah, an engagement ring." T.C. nodded, noticing he sounded defensive rather than happy. But he had been excited before he got there.

"Wow, wow, wow. That's cool, nigga. That's real cool. Wasn't expecting you to say it is all, but it's cool."

T.C. nodded again, his shame easing up.

"How much you willing to pay?"

T.C. wrote down the amount.

"Damn, nigga, that much?"

The funny thing was, he had paid half that for his earring, and the dude hadn't batted an eye.

His friend showed him what they had to offer at that price point. T.C. knew Licia liked gold, and there were four or five options like that. He fingered one he could see her wearing, a princess cut, his friend said, and with the discount he could afford half a karat. He was about to hand it over to be boxed up when he saw another one out of the corner of his eye. Gold too, but the diamond was a little bigger, and it was round. He held it up to the light.

"That's a little bit more though, bruh," his friend said.

"How much more?"

"Almost twice as much."

"Damn," T.C. said. "They sure don't make it easy on a nigga." He twirled it around the tip of his own pinky, imagining Licia's face when she pulled it out of the box. "It's real pretty though, and she deserve it," he said. Then he passed it over to his friend to wrap.

His friend seemed disappointed. "All right, all right, what size ring she wear?" he asked.

T.C. shrugged. "I don't know."

"You trying to marry her, and you don't know what size ring she wear? You sure she ain't just no Betsy friend, T.C.?"

"Yeah, man, we been together six years, and she got my seed."

"Shit, if I married every woman that had my seed, but nah, I'm not trying to talk you out of it. You doing the right thing, you damn sure doing the right thing."

T.C. nodded.

"Well look, let's assume she a 6.5. Most women a 6.5. We'll wrap this up, and if she don't fit it, bring her back to size it. I want to see this woman anyway, the woman who got T.C. to settle down."

"All right," T.C. said. Then, "Now look, that price you gave me, it's good, I mean that's what she deserve and all that, but I was wondering, y'all got like a layaway plan?"

His friend laughed. "Hell no, mothafucka, this ain't no Rent a Ring Express."

T.C. didn't smile.

"Look, what I could do is put it aside. We ain't supposed to do that, but I could do it this one time since you my boy and all that. You think you gon' be able to swing the money in the next few weeks?"

"Fa sho."

"All right then, come back then. I'll have it ready for you."

T.C. thought for a minute. He had enough to get the other one today. Maybe she'd be happier to have it sooner. No, a few weeks would fly by. He wanted her to have something she'd be proud to show off to her friends.

T.C.'s friend gave him the scoop while he bagged the ring up. Spud was running shit. Po-po was on the lookout for him though, and any minute he was going to get busted. T.C. just nodded. It wasn't anything he hadn't heard before, rather old shit Tiger had told him months ago when he first got out. This nigga didn't get around much. T.C. was glad to hear it though. Maybe nobody knew T.C. was the competition now, and if so, that was a damn good thing.

"You heard about Tiger?" His friend tied a ribbon on the box as if T.C. were just going to hand it to her. Even he knew you were supposed to get on your knees and shit.

"What about him?" T.C. asked, looking at his watch. He told Alicia he would meet her for the baby's one-month appointment today and he was running late.

"He started working for Spud when you caught yo lil' bid or whatever. He didn't sell all that nigga gas though, and now they beefed out, he owe him money. Spud been looking for him, said when he find him he gon' kill him. I heard Tiger don't even go to his old spots no more, that he be all the way out in Biloxi with some woman, but Spud think he here and he still looking."

"That don't even sound right, nigga. Who told you that?" T.C. heard his voice rise and told himself to calm down.

"This girl I used to mess with. Her brother-in-law used to talk to Spud's sister."

"Her brother-in-law used to talk to Spud's sister, come on now, man, that sound like a game of telephone right there. You sound like a lil' bitch passing around that half-wit information."

His friend looked around at the other customers, embarrassed now.

"Awright, awright, calm down. Don't get so upset," he whispered. "I'm just telling you what I heard. Maybe it's wrong." He shrugged. "Look, you still want me to put this aside?" he asked.

T.C. nodded.

"Then stay cool then, boy, awright, stay cool."

T.C. made it to the appointment on time. Malik was excelling. He could lift his head up for a few seconds when Licia held him upright; he even cooed a little bit when he saw his daddy walk into a room, but T.C. couldn't shake what he'd heard about Tiger. The only person he could talk about it with was Licia, but he hadn't told her he was hustling again yet. He'd wanted to, he didn't like keeping secrets from her especially now that they were doing so great, but she'd get the wrong idea. She would think it was forever; she would think he was jeopardizing their future when he was just weeks away from cementing it to their past. He tried to advise himself the way she might. Of course there would be the preliminary judgment.

What you fuckin with that stuff for T? You know the definition of insanity, doing the same thing over and over and expecting different results, right? He'd say she was right, and maybe she was, maybe she was. Then she'd look at him with her big brown eyes, really see him in the uncanny way she had of opening him up and reading him on the inside; she'd ask if he really thought Tiger would do that to him. T.C. would shake his head. He didn't, but what did he know? Tiger was no Daryl.

Why would Tiger fuck with Spud though? she'd want to know. *He's not stupid, he knows how crazy that nigga is about his money.* And T.C. would shrug. He had no idea, though it would explain why Tiger was so eager to get him started again, why he was so resistant to T.C. stopping even now. It would explain why he wanted a middleman, why he was so paranoid all the goddamn time, insisting he lock up the place, posting up at the window, hearing voices that weren't there.

That mothafucka played me, he might say to Licia. And she would tell him to calm down, he didn't know that for sure.

And he didn't. He didn't, and he learned in jail not to jump to conclusions, but damn sure he was going to ask Tiger straight up if he owed Spud money, if he had rigged all this, put T.C.'s life at risk for a little more pocket change. Either way, T.C. felt stupid, stupid and afraid all of a sudden as though he was closer to jail than he had been on his way out, standing in the parking lot with Tiger next to him. He texted his aunt right then and there. When she wrote back, her message full of exclamation points and emoji her interns must have taught her, he showed the phone to Licia. She reached over and kissed him on the cheek.

"I love you," she said.

"I love you too."

He would borrow Licia's car, confront Tiger tonight, see if he could make some sense out of the whole mess. Either way he had only a pound left. He could sell that himself if he needed to. He had done it before.

There was a black Grand Prix in front of Tiger's house but T.C. didn't pay it any mind. Probably one of the dealers for the crackhouses across the street. From the front porch, T.C. could have sworn he heard Tiger talking to somebody, somebody else's voice. Damn he was getting paranoid too. He stepped inside and closed the door behind him. He didn't walk two feet before he heard that voice again. He was sure someone else was in here now. He walked back to the front door, kept one hand on the doorknob while he listened. He could hear at least two different men talking. One of them was Tiger, that he knew. He couldn't tell what either man was saying, but it was obvious they were shouting.

He opened the door again. He didn't need to stick around for this, whatever it was. No, he'd catch Tiger later; anyway the conversation he was going to have with him was of a private nature. He felt a hand on his shoulder before he stepped out onto the porch.

"Whoa," the voice said. "Lemme holla at you for a second."

T.C. glanced behind him at the hand, fat puffy fingers squeezed through four gold rings. He didn't have a choice but to step backward inside. When he turned around, he saw Spud staring back at him. He told himself to calm down; it was probably like in jail when mothafuckas would start shit—most of the time they were just trying to front. Most of the time.

"Come on in," Spud repeated. "Make yourself at home." He was holding a duffel bag, and his Glock poked out of his waistband. "Don't mind that," he said, catching T.C.'s glance. "I was thinking about using it, but your friend is straightening some shit out for me, and"—he pulled his pants up and adjusted his shirt back over his belt—"so I don't think we're going to have any need for that. Are we, Tiger?" He was a big man and he walked wide-legged into Tiger's room.

T.C. followed him, listening to his own breathing accelerate as he walked, all the while debating turning around, sprinting out the front door, jumping into his car. He couldn't do that to Tiger though. And anyway, Spud just said everything had been straightened out.

Spud had reached the room by now, but T.C. dragged the walk along, listening to him talk.

"Your friend Tiger the type of nigga think he could get over on everybody, that's his problem. But that's my fault for not seeing it. See, a good middleman is content to just be moving your shit. They don't get big fanciful dreams in their head about turning out larger numbers doing it their own way. Tiger one of them niggas too smart for his own good," he chuckled, "but then again he not smart enough either. He sort of in between. 'Cause you didn't end up making more than I do, did you Tiger?"

T.C. had reached the bedroom by now. Tiger sat on the mattress. A huge dude knelt behind him holding a burner to his head. The man looked up when T.C. walked in. The first thing T.C. recognized was the color of his eyes, that unnatural sparkling green.

"Yo, Spud, I know that nigga," the green-eyed man jumped up. "I know that nigga," he repeated. "That's that mothafucka I told you was fuckin' with Natalia. I tried to slice him up when I caught him, you know I did, but bitch's mama came out with a 19 pointed in my face." The man looked up at Spud as if he were asking him for permission to finish the job now.

T.C. just stared at Tiger, whose head hung between his legs.

"You was fuckin with his bitch?" Spud walked up to T.C., rested his hand on the top of his own piece, but he was smirking.

T.C. shook his head.

"You calling me a liar, nigga?" The green-eyed man was in T.C.'s face now. "I remember your ass. How I'ma forget a giant-ass nigga like that? Mothafucka had to duck to get in here."

Spud cut his head back and laughed. "Yeah, I don't believe he confusing you with somebody else."

"Nah, it was me," T.C. started, "it was me, but I didn't know she had somebody, I swear I didn't, and since I found out, I never hit it." When he was done he felt as if he had been talking for hours, as if he had delivered the "I Have a Dream" speech, and he just hoped his message had come out clear, but he was worried that his nerves mixed his words up, clashing them together so they lost their individual meanings.

"You never hit it that day?"

"I never hit it that day," he lied.

The man seemed to be thinking about whether or not that was good enough consolation.

"You still with that girl?" Spud asked the green-eyed man.

"Aww, hell nah, we been beefed out. Plus she one of them bitches just lay there. I could rub myself off for all that. You know I can't get down like that."

"Like that bitch I used to fuck with in Metairie," Tiger cut in from the mattress.

The green-eyed man walked back over to Tiger, knocked the burner into his temple. "Shut the fuck up. Nobody talking to you, nigga."

Spud turned to T.C., reached inside his bag, and pulled out T.C.'s weed.

"Your boy was just showing me what a talented nigga you are. Real talented. I couldn't grow shit like this if I tried. Of course, considering the circumstances, it's mine now." He let out his deep belly laugh that seemed as if it might shake the whole house down.

"You lucky nigga, if you didn't have this—"

T.C. wondered if he should say thank you but decided against it, just gulped, kept one eye on the green-eyed man who still held the burner at Tiger's temple but who stared T.C. down.

"And why the fuck you even talking about some Betsy friend you don't even fuck with no mo'? She got your kid?" Spud was shouting at the green-eyed man now.

"Hell nah."

"Well, then, why you even mentioned her? You tryna get me caught up over some bitch in your rearview, didn't even have no good pussy. Come on, nigga."

The green-eyed man stood up and walked over to Spud. "That's it?" the green-eyed man asked.

"Yeah, that's it, for now." Spud smacked his friend in the back of his head as they walked to the door.

T.C. listened for the front door slamming, then the car's, but even once the sounds had registered, he couldn't find relief. He stayed in his spot, still staring at Tiger.

"Now, calm down, T.C., I didn't lie to you." Tiger stood. "I just thought it would be a win-win, see. Get you back in the game again, hook you up with some cash. You wasn't complaining when that money was coming in."

T.C. just shook his head. The scene had zapped him of his energy, and he wasn't going to waste any he had remaining on some bullshit.

"Look, he didn't even take all of it, see." Tiger was still talking. "I got a couple ounces in the back. We could sell that, make enough to buy some more seeds."

"Just give it to me," T.C. said.

When Tiger brought it out, T.C. stuffed it in his backpack and turned for the door.

Tiger followed him. "That's it then?"

T.C. nodded, put his hand on the knob. He was almost out when Tiger called for him again,

"T.C.?"

"What?" He turned to him from the doorway.

"I didn't have no other way to get the money. I didn't mean to fuck with your life. I just thought either way you was gon' hustle and if I helped you out, you'd bring a lil' bit more in. Look, you got your auntie and your grandma, and I ain't got nobody else, and I couldn't see a way out."

T.C. nodded. "I'll check with you later, dude," he said. Licia's beat-up old Camry seemed like Tiger's car the day he'd picked T.C. up from jail, and if he could just reach it, he might see his son again, his girl who was about to be his wife. He climbed in, reclined the seat, and just sat for a minute. Oddly he felt free. There wasn't much weed left, and he could just pawn the rest off on his old basketball heads. Tops, he'd be done in a week. He'd have enough in his pocket for the ring, bottomed out, but it would be right on time. He would start work the following Monday. That was when his real life would begin, the engagement, the wedding; maybe he and Licia would have another one. That's what people did, he knew. That encounter with the green-eyed mothafucka had him feeling out of place in his body still, but maybe it wasn't just the man; maybe it was the realization that his life was moving uphill, and he wasn't destined to plummet down the other side of it. He needed to take a minute to rest from the adrenaline of it all.

He turned the ignition on. Goddamnit, "Right Above It" again—Q93 played that song the hell out. Well, it was a good song to smoke to though, and if there was ever a time to smoke, it was now. He was tempted to go back inside and make amends with Tiger; after everything, he still loved to chill with him, hear the crazy shit that came out of his mouth. Nah, Tiger was bad news. T.C.'s mama had been right.

T.C. already had one rolled, and he pulled it out, flicked the lighter over its end, inhaled, closed his eyes. It was just his okay strain, OG Kush, more body than he liked, but he saved the heady shit for his customers these days. When he heard the siren, he wondered if he had mislabeled. That OG didn't usually fuck with his mind. The sound must have been in the song. If Tiger were in the car, he'd have them running around the Ninth Ward on a phantom high-speed chase. T.C. was glad he hadn't gone in to get him. He tapped the blunt out, turned the key in the ignition. He looked in his rearview before he drove off, and that's when he saw them. One police car had stopped, and one was in the process of rolling up behind it. The cop in the car behind him sat in the passenger seat just watching him; the other one had already stepped out. He heard the one who was walking call the stop in on his radio. T.C. looked at the weed he'd tapped out in an old coke can, thought about ingesting it, but there was at least an ounce in that bag right beside him. He hadn't broken any traffic laws, he was just sitting there, but when he rolled down the window they'd smell it on him, and that would be their cause to search his car. He could drive off, but that would just make things worse. On the other hand, he couldn't go back to that place, he wouldn't.

The cop tapped on the window. "Without reaching anywhere can you confirm that you have your license and registration on you?"

It was too late to leave the scene. They had the plate number and everything. He sat for a minute. One of his last games in high school, he'd been in a bind like this. There were only forty-five seconds left on the clock. His team was behind five points. The coach called a timeout, ordered the play where T.C. would flash open across the court, catch a pass from the point guard, then shoot a layup. T.C. wasn't nervous—it was impossible to win, so there was nothing to be nervous about. Still, as he waited for his forward to set a back screen, he felt himself floating above his body, looking down at himself posted up, then running, holding his hands out, catching the ball, and tossing it back up at the backboard. If making that shot had given him any hope, he lost it when he got fouled because he was terrible at foul shots. Always had been. But he made it, and then he stole the ball from the best point guard in the state, drove it right back down the court for a shot just outside the three-point line a millisecond before the game ended. He had never felt anything like that to this day.

The officer tapped again, this time with more force, and T.C. just waited for a miracle to kick in, for that magic that had lit up his heart on that basketball court to drive him away from there.

Evelyn

Winter 1945

Airing out her secret to her mama and sister had given her mind license to let its other private thoughts roam. Her doubt, it turned out, was almost as strong as her faith. In most ways she trusted Renard. When she thought about him a certain way, she could be sure he would muster the strength or nerve or whatever it took someone to do the right thing. But these were difficult circumstances, and when she thought about it that way, she'd remember how he'd collapsed when it was time for him to meet her father; and later, how when he told her he was going to war, everything she'd thought he was made of flew out of him, and she was left with a shell of a man. Not to mention, she'd never met anyone from his family. He could be of any constitution, and she'd have no idea. It was easy to pretend to be good when you were courting someone, and everything rode on their quick opinion of you, but when you had secured their love, and there was nothing left to fight for, it was the rare man who was in constant war with his own sense of himself.

Her mama tried to distract her with baby bonnets and receiving blankets.

"You had colic the first year, so you better expect the same from her."

"Mother, don't be so negative," Ruby would shout.

"I'm not saying it's destined; sometimes it skips a generation, but I just want you to be ready in case."

Mama had opinions about how long Evelyn should stay in the bathtub, how much pork she could eat, what her relentless heartburn meant. Mama sewed a season's worth of baby clothes and knitted booties; she bought beef broth from the outdoor market and mixed it in Evelyn's grits; she forbade her from attending Miss Georgia's son's funeral although Evelyn wouldn't have considered it anyway—she barely left the house save for the walks her mama mandated in the evenings. Most of the time, Evelyn just succumbed to Mama's whims without a word. The one thing they agreed on with enthusiasm was that Evelyn was carrying a girl.

"I had a dream," her mama announced one morning. "The girl was a beautiful shade of brown, one I hoped would show up in one of my own children, but—" she shook her head. "A head full of hair, that's why your indigestion has been paining you so. She was a perfect angel, just as beautiful as you were when you were born."

Evelyn, for one of the first few times since her confession, felt her own joy pulsing inside her.

"I thought it was a girl, too," she said.

"No thought about it," her mama repeated. "Women make themselves sick to have a boy first, but the truth is," and she lowered her voice to a whisper, "when I'm old and feeble, Brother will be off with his wife and his new family. You and Ruby will be the ones to see after me." She shrugged. "Sons are nice in the beginning, a boy who might never leave you, but once they hit fifteen, it's the girls you can count on."

It was like her parents were one body, and her mama had usurped all the happiness there was between them. Mama confirmed that she relayed the information to her father, but otherwise Evelyn wouldn't have known he knew. Just as he didn't look in her direction before, he didn't now. He stopped talking to her and touching her too, but the piece she missed most was the looking. They had shared so much through glances, apologetic eye gestures when Mama made a negative comment, or shining eyes when a shared joke between them cemented their love. Often when she heard him creaking through the house, she longed to go to him, apologize, assure him that she had made a mistake, but she could rectify it. All wasn't lost. Maybe he would echo the same sentiments back to her, but he didn't linger inside long, and before he'd leave, she'd lose her nerve.

On one of the few days she didn't make it out to the mailbox with Brother, Brother came back in with a letter. It was only the third one she'd received from Renard, the one before it stating more of the same as the first, a little less upbeat but only in tone, and when Evelyn thought back on the words that she memorized, she actually couldn't find any that made a difference.

She brought this one back to her room, her heart racing from walking faster than she had in weeks. She sat on the bed, fingering the envelope for a long while, holding the actual paper up to her nose and searching for a scent that she could link to Renard. There was none. Finally she splayed the paper out. Three pages, all in blue careful ink, his handwriting better than her own. She skimmed the letter first, drifting again to the last page, but she couldn't find anything that her mind could grasp.

Finally she started at the beginning.

Dear Evelyn,
I am coming home. I can scarcely believe it. I'm afraid to.
But I've been granted a convenience of the government dis-
charge and I'll be back on the 21st of January. I have missed

*you more than I can say, and every day that gets closer to
reuniting me with you is one I want to toss away, throw
back at God, say "here take it." I didn't want to scare you,
but it has not been as great as I've let on. Still it's over
now. And in a few short weeks, we can be together and put
it all behind us.*

She felt a tightening in the bottom of her stomach. She'd been
having early contractions all week, but Mama said not to worry, it
didn't mean it was time. She didn't cry out or even grimace. She sat
down and rubbed her belly.

Ruby walked in and called out to her, but when Evelyn didn't
respond, Ruby ripped the note out of her hand. She didn't need to
read the whole thing to grasp the gist.

"Oh," she said, dropping the letter, then peeling down her slip
and unzipping her girdle on one side. "Well, that's good then."
Ruby forgot to smile though. "That's real good. Mama will be real
pleased. Daddy too, if he'd admit it. You'll have your little family,
sister." She paused. "I'm happy for you."

She went on talking, her words pouring out like an avalanche.

"I'm not having any children. I thought I might with Andrew
when I first met him, but what if he got called off again? Then
what? I'd be by myself taking care of something he had half the
mind to make. I don't think so. Wouldn't be me.

"Don't even make me mention what it does to your body. Have
you ever looked at Mama's stomach when she takes off her nightgown? Woo, I wouldn't want to be Daddy or even a fly in the room.
So many stretch marks sliding across that belly you'd think it was
a railroad station. No, ma'am, not me. Mama's an old lady, Daddy's
probably not even interested in that anymore, but I'm young, I've
got to maintain what the good Lord has given me."

She rubbed her hands over her body and let out a sharp laugh.

"Anyway, all children do is tie you down. Maybe I might travel
the world the way you used to say you would. No chance of that hap-

pening anymore. Maybe I'll take the money Mama and Daddy saved, go off to Boston University. They might accept me. They might."

She collapsed on the bed.

"And then Renard said it hasn't been all good. Well, he's probably not half the man he was when he left anyway. Maybe that's why I haven't heard from Andrew." She sighed. "That's my point though. You can't trust these men. Not you, not me. Sometimes I think they're the weaker sex really: They're just more prone to unnatural changes that distort their perspective and leave you all alone. Don't think just 'cause he's coming back you're home free. Did he write about the baby at all? Did he say he would have it?"

Evelyn shook her head, without answering. A few weeks ago, on Mama's urging, Evelyn had promised to notify him that she was expecting. She and Mama had decided he deserved to know, that he might fight harder knowing he had life on the other side. And Evelyn had written the words out and everything, but when it was time to seal the envelope and walk it up to the mailman's truck, she dragged for a long time. She didn't know why then. Now she wondered if she suspected that the fear of being a father would drive him out further from her, or worse, make him feel he had nothing to lose.

"He's the kind of man who would own what's his," she said to Ruby now.

"Maybe that's the kind of man he was, but war changes people." Ruby looked at her, her eyes narrowed in a sliver of rage.

Then Ruby burst into tears. She put her head down.

"Don't cry now, Ruby." Evelyn started to stand up to comfort her, but it took too long in her compromised state. By the time Evelyn reached her, Ruby had stopped.

"I'm fine," she said. "Nobody will ever say Ruby cried over a man, a no-count one at that." Ruby looked down again. "It seems like everything and everybody is being taken from me, and you're getting added to the list."

"Oh, no, Ruby." Evelyn embraced her. She didn't know where

this burst of love had sprung from, but she wondered if it was from her daughter, still a promise in her belly, or the vow Renard had made to return.

"It's true. You know it's true. You're getting Renard back, and I got"—she opened her hands over a ball of air, then collapsed them—"nothing. I got nothing."

"You got me," Evelyn said.

"Yeah, right. As soon as that baby comes, and Renard gets here, you're going to be out so fast it'll make your head spin."

"Oh, Ruby, who knows if he'll even have me when he comes back?"

"He'll have you." Ruby nodded. "He'll be more pleased when he sees you like this. Trust me. Everything always works out for you."

Evelyn had wavered until that second, but her sister's words rooted her faith. There were only so many times Ruby said anything kind, and she'd never lie just to save face. No, maybe it was true. Maybe Evelyn could relax into it: Renard was coming back. Renard was coming back. Not only that, but he'd be more excited to see she was expecting. It was going to work out.

Evelyn rubbed her sister's back. "We're sisters, Ruby. I'm never going to desert you." She didn't know how many times she repeated that, but at some point, she looked down, and her sister had fallen asleep.

Jackie

Winter 1987

Jackie had called in sick the last few workdays to avoid seeing her parents, but she'd had the weekend to calm down, plus she was running out of paid leave. She had decided the night before that she would head in this morning, and she woke up early, got dressed in her knee-length blue dress with lace at the top, spent some time on her makeup—etched the eyeliner over her lashes just so—let Terry drive her all the way to the front door instead of dropping her a block from the school. There were no more secrets after all.

Her mama was composed as ever, and they discussed the status of the school day with polite nods while Jackie folded her kids' just-in-case clothes, washed the paint off their smocks, hung them to dry. It didn't take long before Mama started really talking though and Jackie felt trapped inside what she might say.

"We didn't want to upset you the other night, Jackie Marie."

"No?" Jackie was far less concerned about her parents' opinion after talking to Terry, and she could tell that came across in her plain expression; her mother looked at her as if she didn't recognize the woman who had spoken.

"No," she said. "Of course not. You're not just my daughter, you're my friend, and I would never want to cause you pain."

That softened Jackie to her. Her mother *was* her friend, her best friend since Terry had gone, and Jackie had shut everyone else out. Mama walked over and stood next to her, and Jackie leaned onto her shoulder.

"I know, Mama," she said, sighing. "But you have to let me make my own decisions."

Mama nodded. "I'm working on it," she said. "I'm working on it," she repeated. Jackie looked at her hands as she spoke, noticed the veins that had started to pop, sharp tubes like the inside of a spider web. When had that happened?

"I talked to your daddy," Mama went on, "and he's coming around. I'm making it so that he'll come around. I just want to ask you before we move on any further with this—are you sure this time?"

Jackie paused before she answered. The question was so antithetical to her new method of survival; the only way she had maintained her peace these last few months was by embracing the fact that she would never be sure. And who was sure about anything? Were they sure Daddy wouldn't walk outside in a few minutes and get toppled over by an eighteen-wheeler? That Mama wouldn't go in for her next mammogram and walk out with a death sentence? Who of them could pretend to be sure?"

"I just want to be certain," her mama repeated. "Because it's not just you, it's that baby." She clutched her heart.

"It's been good for him to have a father," Jackie said, trying to dodge the question.

"Now it is, but— Never mind, I didn't even want to get into this, Jackie." Her mother stepped back from her and Jackie's head wobbled from the shift. "You were right to say it's your decision, and as your parents, we just need to stand by you. I just want to be as clear as I can, are you as sure as you can be?"

Jackie didn't speak for a while, then when the last paintbrush had been cleaned, she looked up. She nodded.

"More sure than I've ever been of anything in my life, Mama," she said, and her mama grimaced as if that wasn't the right answer.

Terry fell back in with her family after that though, as though Jackie saying she was sure had made it so. It started with him picking the baby up from Mama's one night because Jackie had to stay late at work. When Jackie got home that evening, he still wasn't back, and when she saw his car pull into the parking lot a few minutes later, she ran down the stairs to meet him. It had to be a good sign that he'd stayed so long, and she wanted to hear the details of the visit, unwind them, spin them out. Before all this he was just as entwined in their family unit as she was. Sometimes she'd drive up her parents' carport, and she'd see his car out in front. She'd walk in and he'd be watching the Saints game on her mama's sofa, clutching a bowl of gumbo in his lap. She had missed that familiarity as much as she had missed him, and she begged him to tell her it was back.

"We just talked," he said, settling his white jacket on the arm of the sofa.

"Yes, I get that you talked," she teased, "but talked about what? You were gone three hours."

"Was I? Time flies when you're having fun, I guess," he chuckled, knowing he was leading her on, and Jackie slapped him with a pillow.

"If you don't tell me everything they said and then everything you said back—" she threatened, smiling.

He rolled his eyes at her, sat down at the kitchen table. "You know your parents, baby. You know what they said better than I do. They drilled me at first of course. Wanting to know what my plans were for you and the baby."

"What did you say?" She sat down next to him.

"I'm getting to that, Jackie. I said it was to make you happy, to make up for any wrongs I've done.'" He smiled at her then. "That was good, right?"

She nodded, trying not to laugh.

"They asked me about work, if I didn't think it was too soon to go back, if I really thought I was in a position to handle that level of responsibility. 'Now be honest with yourself, son'"—he was mimicking her daddy now—"'every man has his weaknesses, but the important thing is to be honest about what they are.'"

Jackie laughed. "That sounds like my daddy."

"He talked more than your mom did," Terry went on. "She just listened, looking halfway like she felt bad for me."

·"And that's my mama," Jackie added.

"I answered them best I could."

"That went on for three hours?"

"No, indeed. I couldn't have handled it. After a little while, we just watched the Cosby show, laughed over that fool Cliff. Your mama wanted me to eat before I left.

"What'd she cook?"

"Red beans and rice."

Jackie nodded. It was a Monday.

"How do you feel?" she asked finally.

He sighed, a long exhale. "Good," he said. "Really good actually. Like all the missing pieces are back in place. I didn't want to admit it to myself, but I was worried they weren't going to take me back."

"They loved you. You were a son to them."

"They loved me, but I hurt you. I wouldn't blame them if they couldn't get over it."

"They're good people."

"They are." He paused for a few minutes. "And I'm going to do right by them."

She pulled him to her then. "You are," she said. "You are," she repeated. She kissed him for a long time the way they would kiss when all they had were ten minutes in her daddy's Lincoln before curfew. She straddled him, and he groaned. She dipped her body down to feel him beneath her. She clutched him to her as tight as she could, and the heat of the embrace poured over her, reached through her and back out again, radiating between them both as if they were one unit. Soon their clothes were off and it felt so much like before that she let herself believe no time had passed. When they were done, he wanted to talk. He'd missed her so much, he'd needed that more than she could imagine, he never wanted to be without her a day in his life. She'd grunt here and there. Though she felt the same way he did, she just lay still, afraid to speak or move for fear she'd unsettle this new feeling.

It was more of the same after that. Jackie and Terry dropped by her mother's as much as they could, sometimes to leave the baby so they could catch a movie at the Plaza or grab a bite at Praline Connection, but often they'd just sit on her mama's sofa and talk about city politics, stuff their faces with jelly cake. Her parents always asked Terry about work, and he'd say it was fine and change the subject. He still ironed his white jacket and whistled on his way out the front door, usually some Prince song they'd listened to the night before while making love. Those days, she'd go to work whistling herself, feeling as if the world were organized in her favor, the way she'd grown up thinking it would be.

Sure, she thought he seemed despondent some nights. He wouldn't say much to her or the baby. Rather, he'd just stare at the TV screen as if he were engrossed in some show, but he wouldn't always laugh when a joke was told, and he'd fall asleep in that position, sometimes without changing from his work clothes.

She told herself he was just tired. After all, he got up at 5 a.m. every day, watched her while she nursed the baby, then when she was done, he'd shower first, start breakfast, and, sure, she did it too, but he wasn't used to it. Surely it would take some time to adjust.

He seemed to perk up when it came time to schedule T.C.'s first birthday party, and at the first sign of his excitement, she did too. The morning of, she woke up at 4 a.m. to cut finger sandwiches and break off the crusts; she made homemade ice cream and pasta salad; she cut grapes in half and baked a three-layer chocolate cake. She wasn't good at frosting, so she stood over Terry's shoulder as he etched roses along the circle's border, then drew in scribbled white icing, HAPPY BIRTHDAY T.C.!

They'd arranged to have it at the Fly, the piece of Audubon Park behind the zoo, and on the way they stopped at Castnet for fresh crawfish to boil. By the time they had set up the propane cooker, people started arriving, people that she hadn't seen in months, not since Terry had gone and come. While she cut potatoes and onions to add to the boil, her girlfriends caught her up on who was hitting the clubs at night, who had stepped out with her boss, who had lost twenty pounds on that new three-day diet, and by the way, what was Jackie doing because she'd dropped that baby weight like it was hot. Everybody was so happy to see Terry. They must have heard talk about his absence, but they were polite enough not to ask questions, and Jackie didn't even worry about rumors springing up, because in this new world she had accessed, it didn't merely feel as if the rumors weren't relevant, it felt as if the circumstances that had led to them had never taken place. Halfway into the party, once the crawfish had been dumped onto the newspaper and people were licking their fingers and asking what spices she'd added to the pot, Jackie realized her face cramped from smiling so hard.

After the cake was cut, her daddy beckoned her over for a family picture. And even seeing her sister didn't cut into her joy. The two women talked briefly. Sybil tried to take the baby, but he cried to stay with his mother, and Jackie squeezed Terry's hand as they lined up together to smile for the camera. While he was gone there had been so many occasions that called for pictures like these, and she'd been alone. Those instances had fomented her gratitude now.

When they were done, Jackie waved the Polaroid in the air, waiting for the faces to coalesce. Then she really studied it. It was a great picture of her, her skin glowed, she had lost weight, and she'd treated herself to a hair appointment the night before. Terry looked even more groomed than the day he'd come back: He had grown a goatee, he was going to the gym again, and his skin had smoothed out where there had been light splotches before. Then there was Sybil. Jackie's sister stood between Mama and Daddy in the same position she'd occupied when they were still children. She wasn't smiling, but she wasn't angry either, only sad, if Jackie was reading it right. And Jackie felt a sharp pity for her, but not something she wanted to do anything about, like the emotion you'd feel for a beggar on the street.

Terry strode up to her as they were packing up.

"It went all right, huh?"

"Better than all right."

"People loved that cake. I mean, I think it was the frosting that did it, the way those roses were coiled on the top just so."

They laughed.

"Some of the boys want to go out from here."

"Where to?" Jackie asked. She had hoped the comfort of the day would extend itself tonight, that they would go home, settle into a movie, and fall asleep together.

"Just to a quick dinner, I won't be out long." He yawned. "I'm tired from today as it is." He paused. "It was so good to see people though," he went on, "and I just want to see it through."

She nodded. She understood that. She felt as if she'd stepped back into their old life, and back then if Terry had said he wanted to go out, she would have just nodded, not even asked where he was headed.

"Of course," she said now, smiling, puckering her lips for a kiss. "Have fun." She watched him walk away. Aunt Ruby approached her from behind and rubbed her back.

"You did the right thing, baby," she said.

Letting him go? Jackie almost asked, but Aunt Ruby kept talking.

"You got to live your own life. Bad or good, it's got to be yours."

•

Jackie didn't mean to stay up. It just happened, watching the old numbers fold into new ones on her digital clock. When Terry came back, it was 3:42. He stopped in the kitchen for water, tip-toed down the hall, undressed in the bathroom, then tried to slink into the bed.

"Where were you?" she asked with more edge than she knew was there, and she thought she saw him jump.

"I'm so sorry, baby," he started. "One thing led to another, the wait was too long at one place, so we went to a different one."

"The food didn't come out till after midnight?"

"Well, then we ran into my buddy from the VA. You remember Michael from the other day?"

"The one who got you started on those drugs," she said. She knew it wasn't him but she wanted to make her point.

He just breezed past it. "He wanted to take me out for a drink."

She paused before she spoke, taking in the full meaning of what he'd just told her.

"You can't be in a bar, Terry," she said finally, trying to contain her voice so she wouldn't wake the baby.

"No, no, not technically, and I told him that, I told him that a bunch of times, but I did all right, Jackie. I didn't have a sip. They asked me and they asked me."

"And that's my point!" She was screaming now. "Today was a good day. We celebrated your only child's first birthday, but sup-pose you go back next time and things aren't going so well, you think your will is going to be as tough?"

"I'm not in the habit of frequenting bars, baby. You know that." He reached out to nuzzle her cheek, and she pushed back on instinct.

"I don't know anything, Terry. Things have changed now." She paused. She sat up in bed, wringing her hands out as if they were dish towels.

"What's changed, baby? Nothing's changed. We celebrated the baby's birthday, I went out for dinner, and now I'm home. Every-thing is the same as it was."

She shook her head.

"What, baby? Name me one thing that's changed." His voice was coming out hot now, not angry but animated, as if he were arguing a case for a jury.

"Shh." She nodded at the baby. "Look," she said, "I just know that you made me some promises, and now they're starting to break."

He sighed. His conviction seemed to wilt at the sound of the word *promises*. He sat down, put his head in his hands.

"You're right," he whispered so low Jackie had to ask him to repeat it.

"What's that?"

"You're right," he said. "I'm sorry, baby, you're right, you're right. I let you down."

"You let yourself down."

"I let us both down," he said, and he reached for her hand, but she held it back. "But I just choked. I said no a few times, but they kept asking."

"Michael knows your situation and kept asking? What kind of friend is that?"

"Not everybody understands, Jackie."

"Well, then you need to be the one to explain it to them. It's your life, after all. Their lives aren't going to be affected in the least if you go back to using." It was the first time she had referenced the threat out loud, the one that kept her up some nights, the one that was gripping her now.

"What was I going to say, Jackie?" He was getting worked up again. "That I couldn't handle it? That I didn't know if I had the strength? I spent all that time working with those guys trying to feel like I was as good, and what was I gonna do? Admit that they had me whooped?"

She didn't say anything to that. She understood him, and she felt for him too, but it was almost as though it didn't matter.

"Michael's tried cocaine, you know," he went on. "He had some on him tonight, but he never fell into it, and what does that say about me? That I couldn't resist? What could I say that wouldn't make me look weak?"

You could have said you're human, Terry, she wanted to say, but she kept quiet. She didn't see the use in going on. He tried to cuddle her and she refused him. Then he turned from her fast to face the wall as if she had been the one to break her word. A part of her wanted to console him, but she didn't know the answer to the question. What did it say about him that he didn't know whether he could trust himself? What did it say about her that she was hanging on to a man who was barely upright himself? She found no relief in the fact that he'd gone in and fared well this time. Instead it made her more wary, as if the fact that the temptation still lived inside him necessitated its coming out, its unfurling into something hard and mobile, something that would carry him away.

Terry woke up the next morning even more apologetic than the night before. He swore it all off, drinking, that group of friends, and Jackie let on that she believed him. They settled back into their routine, but she stopped being able to sleep altogether. They'd moved T.C. back to his bassinet, and sometimes she'd walk over to him, stare at him with tears in her eyes. She didn't know why she felt so certain tragedy lurked in his future. Everything was fine now, and she tried to remind herself of that. She'd grip the edge of the bassinet and wipe her eyes, but the early grief wouldn't budge.

She'd wake up late and frazzled and barely make it to school before group playtime was over. One morning during circle time she realized she'd left the assessments she'd need for the parent-teacher conferences in her kitchen. She told Mama to feed T.C. a bottle and she hustled back home during her lunch hour. She remembered where the pages were; she'd been reviewing them as her pasta boiled and when it was done, she'd stacked them in a pile on the counter. She had only an hour before her kids woke up, so she'd run into her apartment, grab them, and be on her way. She was rushing so hard she didn't notice the front door to her place was unlocked, and she wouldn't have noticed that the television was on either if she hadn't seen Terry sitting directly in front of it. His white jacket with his name tag, LEWIS, PHARMACIST inscribed on it, lay crumpled on the carpet beneath him.

He started talking as though he'd been expecting her.

"I lost my job," he said, but his words came out fast and frenetic, as if he were telling a good joke and if she just listened a little while longer, he would get to the punch line.

"What?" The word came out flat though. Jackie wasn't as angry as she was resigned, as though the doubt she had been warding off had won the final battle and could now take residence in her heart.

"They have a pool of company cars. On the days I didn't drop you at work, I'd borrow them, take them for a spin during lunch, just to get out of the office more than anything. I wasn't used to sitting in a cubicle all day. I had more interactions with the patients at the VA. That made it more fulfilling. This was just clocking in more than anything, and I'm not complaining, it felt good to hand you a check every two weeks, it felt . . . normal, but also not normal at the same time."

"So, what?" Jackie asked. She sat down across from him and sighed. "They found out you were taking their property?"

He shook his head, sighed. "No, not at first. I'd take the car out to Bourbon Street, park if I could. I'd even see some people I used to score with. I didn't speak or anything like that. I didn't even get out of my car. I felt stronger somehow for being able to stay inside it. I felt like I was locking in my sobriety, if you will, and it helped me to face the rest of the day. I'd get so caught up in being there, in the rush of knowing I could be there without using, I'd lose track of time, get back to the office ten, twenty minutes late."

"So, what, they got rid of you for being a few minutes late, Terry?" Jackie asked as if she was bored by the story, and in a way she was. She already knew the ending.

"Nah." He waved her question away. "Nah. It wasn't that. Most times they didn't even notice."

"Then what happened, Terry?"

He shook his head.

She heard her voice rising. "Goddamnit, Terry, what happened?"

"I took the car again a few days ago. It was after we had that argument, and I was on edge. I'd been at the bar the night before and you were right, I never should have gone there, it was like it unlocked something in me, woke a part of me up that I would have sworn was dead."

Jackie couldn't bear to hear the rest. She sat there, she listened to half the words he said, smatterings of phrases, like *my friend from the VA, not Michael, but the one I was closest to,* and *I didn't expect to see him on Bourbon Street, that's not where he used to go, and I was so surprised I just got out of the car. I didn't even lock it.*

She sat forward, but she didn't let it seep inside her. Instead she thought about the time, that she had ten minutes before she'd need to leave to make it back to the nursery, that she still didn't know how she was going to tell the Bradley mother that she might want to have her son tested for speech delay.

"When I caught up with him, he was so happy to see me, he just passed me a pipe. I didn't even have a chance to say *hello, how are you,* and it was in my hand. I hadn't held one in months, but it all came rushing back, that buzzing in my ears that I'd get right after a hit, that sense of being outside myself in the best way possible; even the paranoia, I could sense it would come too, but I wasn't afraid."

Jackie stood. "I've heard enough of this bullshit."

But he followed her, gripped her wrist. "Let me finish, Jackie. I didn't do it. I held it, I put it up to my lips, I closed my eyes, and I imagined how good it would feel to just let go, not even for the high itself, but so I could stop fearing another relapse. I was so close to just walking back out to the other side."

"You expect me to believe you didn't smoke it?" She was shaking her head, trying to reach the door, but he caught her, held her in place.

"I didn't, Jackie, I swear I didn't, I turned around, and I headed back for the car. But."

"But what, Terry? But what?" she repeated.

"But it wasn't there. I thought maybe I had forgotten where I parked exactly and I retraced my steps for an hour, but it wasn't there. Finally I called the police, waited for them to arrive and take a statement, then I took the bus back to the office. When I didn't show up with the car, I had to hand them the police report. They saw where I'd been, knew I didn't have any business in the French Quarter, and fired me on the spot. I got a call just now when I got home. The car is back, no damage to it either, but they don't care. They can't trust me anymore, they say. It wasn't a good fit."

They were still standing in the hallway now, her back arched and pressed against him, his hands around her chest. She stood up, wiggled him off of her, sat down again. She figured she had five more minutes. She would get back to those babies on time. After everything he'd taken from her, he wouldn't take that. He walked to the sofa opposite her and sat too. Then he folded his hands on his lap, bent his head into them and began to weep. She watched him for a while before she got up, then she walked over and rubbed his back with the palm of her hand, up and down, up and down, the way she'd seen her mother rub her father's so many times over the years. Mama had told her once that Daddy had wanted to be a doctor like Jackie's grandfather, that he never got over the fact that he didn't make it happen. *No matter how much success your father grabs, he'll never feel like a man, not all the way,* she had said. And that was the way Jackie felt about Terry now, as if the blank look in his eye at this moment preceded this firing, as if he'd lost a part of himself when he started those drugs and it wasn't a part he could simply restore again.

She shook that thought out of her head.

She told herself to focus on the now.

"I'm sorry, baby," she said every few minutes. "We'll get through this," she'd repeat, but the words came out flat because she wasn't sure she meant them.

She sat with him a little while longer, as long as she could before the clock struck twelve. If she didn't get back, she'd be late. She apologized over and over for going, and when she got back to work she called to check in. He said he was fine, but all the while she painted with the babies, pushed them in the hammock and read them *The Berenstain Bears' New Baby*, she could only conjure his face, that blank wall of defeat when he'd looked up to watch her leave, that seemed as if it were in the middle of crumbling.

Jackie usually felt nervous before the parent-teacher conferences. It was only her second one; she still hadn't caught up on the jargon, and once she'd led a conference for five full minutes before she realized she was referencing the wrong child. It wasn't only that, the parents could be cruel. Last time she'd had to tell a mother her son lacked impulse control, and the woman had filed a complaint against Jackie, said without the proper certification Jackie wasn't in a position to judge a bathing suit contest.

Now Jackie wished one of these people would, but they were all sweetness and light this evening, praising Jackie for the strides their children had made. "He says *please* and *thank you* now every single time," or "She hasn't had an accident in weeks." And Jackie would have carried those compliments with her through the rest of the year, but the words just streamed over her head today. The one thing she needed to be successful at had failed and there was nothing she could do to right it.

As if the day hadn't dragged on enough, her sister tiptoed into the nursery as the last conference was ending. She snuck into the kitchen, trying to fix a plate without disturbing the meetings, inching the drawers open so they wouldn't creak, setting the plates down on towels so they wouldn't clatter. Jackie just ignored her, and when the last parent had gone, she packed her bag, grabbed the baby who'd fallen asleep in Mama's arms, and headed for the door.

Her sister ran over to her, her heels clacking, and gripped her by the wrist.

"I came over to see you," she said.

"It's not a good time, Sybil."

"Oh." Her sister stepped back. "I'm sorry," she said. "I know you must be tired with the baby and all that. I was just thinking about you this week, since the party and everything, and"—she paused—"I wanted to apologize about everything with Terry."

Jackie wasn't too far gone to grasp the enormity of her sister apologizing. Even with everything that had happened that day, she wanted to spread the moment out. "What with Terry?" she asked.

Sybil shook her head, sighed. "Everything," she said. "I saw you with him the other day, I saw the baby, and it's obvious that he's trying, it's obvious that you're happy. After everything you've been through, you deserve that. The baby deserves a proper family."

"Oh," Jackie said, too stunned to think of much else to say. "Well, thank you," she stammered finally. "That means a lot to me." She started for the door, then turned back. It wasn't more of her sister she was wanting, it was that Sybil always possessed such good judgment and maybe her perspective here was something Jackie could inhabit too.

"How can you tell?" she asked. "That it's real this time?"

Her sister was halfway across the floor near the railroad table Daddy had just built for the toddler classrooms, but she stepped back again.

"Just watching you at the party," she repeated, shrugging with her head down, seeming uncomfortable in this new role. "For one, he looks great; he looks *clean*," she stressed. "I don't know, Jackie, I was telling Mama, it seems different this time. Some of my clients are lifetime junkies but a few come out of it. They hit bottom and they tell me they're never going back. Something about the way they say it, the steel in their eyes, makes me believe it. That's how I felt about Terry the other day." She paused. "I think you made the right decision."

Jackie didn't trust herself to speak, so she nodded and turned away. Her sister reached out and rubbed the baby's head, then she kissed Jackie on the cheek. Jackie smiled, but she also felt as though she might sob, and she turned fast for the door so her sister couldn't see her face.

Sybil stopped her again before she reached her car. "Jackie," she called out. "I had a rough day. Maybe I can come back with you, spend some time with the baby, apologize to Terry. I was going to call, but I think I need to say it face-to-face."

Jackie didn't have the energy to decline, and once she was in the car she was glad for the company. Sybil talked the whole way home. She had secured the Taco Bell contract, finally, but now they were trying to give her the runaround on the terms they'd agreed on, the 20 percent of the settlements they had offered had dwindled down to 15. It didn't matter; she was going to fight them until they came back around, because at the end of the day she didn't need that job. She'd made plenty enough on her own.

Jackie just nodded and smiled, delivered of a lot of *Umhmm*s and *I know that's right*s. She thought about what Sybil had said back at the nursery, and she repeated the words to herself. Sybil wasn't the type to say something she didn't mean, and what was it Daddy had always encouraged her to ask herself? *What would her sister do?* Here, she'd said she'd do exactly what Jackie had done. That was cause for a celebration, but for some reason Jackie couldn't manipulate her heart into matching that tone.

She wasn't expecting Terry to be home when she walked in. Any other day he would have been, but she felt somewhere inside her today would be different, and because she couldn't anticipate how long the difference would drag on, how she would respond to it, she was grateful Sybil was beside her. She bathed the baby, really washed between the folds on his neck where milk tended to gather, greased his entire body with Vaseline. He had more hair now, and she'd taken to playing with it at night, giving it the attention she would if he were a daughter, combing her fingers through the curls until he cried. Then she latched him on her breast. People had started to ask how long she would nurse him, but she couldn't imagine stopping, as if the gulf of emotion that had been building in her over this last year would break forth once she was finished, force itself out of her body in powerful heaves, and she didn't know what form that would take. When it was midnight and Terry still hadn't come back, Jackie asked Sybil to stay over, and without asking why, Sybil obliged. Jackie placed the baby in the bed beside her, just like old times, and she caught herself watching the clock throughout the night. 2:49; 4:28; 6:42. Still nothing. She woke up to her alarm sounding, and he hadn't come back. He wouldn't.

She dressed the baby as if she were going to work though she knew she'd never make it a full minute there today. Still she just needed to keep her mind busy, her body distracted. She didn't bother dressing herself, or brushing her teeth or washing her face, just walked to the living room where Sybil was sleeping on the couch, a night scarf still tied at the back of her head.

Sybil sat up in the bed like she slept on sofas every night. "Hey, girl."

"Hey," Jackie said back. "I was going to make some coffee. You want something?"

"The same," Sybil said.

In the kitchen, Jackie realized she hadn't done the dishes the night before and she didn't bother to start them now, just poured water into the pot. She knew it was only a matter of time before her clothes were spewed on the sofa, and old food was stacked on TV trays again.

Sybil didn't ask where Terry was, and for the rest of her life Jackie would be grateful for that, that she didn't make her spell it out. Sybil only took the baby from her, held him up to her own shoulder, and chanted in a baby voice Jackie couldn't have imagined coming from a more unlikely source, "Mama's not feeling well but she'll be back, she'll be back, oh yes, she'll be back."

Jackie didn't bother to correct her, to point out that something about this time felt permanent, felt as if she'd been driven down to the bottom of a hole and wasn't capable of feeling her way out of it because it wasn't just about missing him this time, or missing out on the family she had banked on. It was about knowing that whatever pain had driven him out had managed to touch her too, and she didn't have crack to deliver her from it.

She didn't correct Sybil though; she just poured her coffee, sat down on the sofa and stared ahead at the TV screen. She flipped it on. *The Price Is Right* had just started; someone was betting on a two-seater sofa, a nice leather one Jackie knew she could dress up with pillows and throws from Macy's, but the woman on the show was betting too much, $999 when a sofa that size, nice as it was, wouldn't go for more than $500. Jackie wanted to intercede, cry out, *Don't set your sights too high, girl, it won't hold*, but she just sat in silence. If she was listening, she would have heard the sirens building in the distance, then leveling off, meeting their target, but as it was, her mind was as focused as a tide breaking, ready to crash. On what, she didn't know.

T.C.

Winter 2011

Going back, when T.C. thought about it, was just like getting out, anticlimactic. His aunt had whittled the sentence down to three years, but he didn't think about it like that. He just thought about who he needed to be nice to to get an old TV and what CO might let him play ball a half hour longer. The second time was easier in that way. He didn't have to learn the system. He knew most of the people in there either from his last stint or just from the street. Some he had been close with at home, and they weren't happy to see him, as much as they were comforted by a familiar face.

He told his mama he didn't want visitors. Not yet, he said, though the truth was, not ever, and he planned to drag her along until that became clear. That was the thing about people on the outside. They thought it cheered him up to see their faces, but it just reminded him too much of freedom when everybody knew it was better to adjust to the kind of freedom available on the inside. For instance, he didn't have a roommate this time, and that was something; he could also go out to the yard whenever he pleased.

It was those small victories he wanted to bask in, those small victories that kept him afloat so when his mama came, he stayed in his cell as long as he could. The CO had to ask for him a third time before he stood up, and even then he dragged more than walked to the waiting area.

He didn't understand it, but she looked better than he'd ever seen her. Made up, thinner, joyful. He wanted to ask if she had come to the right place. She pulled him to her in a tight embrace.

"Hey, my baby," she exclaimed. "You look good. You look real good. They treatin' you all right in there? I sent brownies. Did you get 'em? Made 'em from scratch, and MawMaw is going to send a cake, she wanted me to make sure and tell you that."

"Is everything okay, Ma?" he couldn't help but ask.

"Oh, everything's good, real good."

They sat while she finished answering him.

"I started volunteering as an aide for Miss Patricia. You know she lost her hearing, and I'm helping her through that. She's got so much grace, this woman, it's really given me some perspective. What do I have to complain about? I have my health. I have my family. And this." She waved her hand at T.C. and shrugged. "Well"—she paused—"anyway, have you seen any good shows lately? I know they let you watch television, right?"

T.C. nodded, told her he had been watching Modern Family. "It's good," he said, "I laugh at some of the jokes, and that Sofia Vergara, man, if I had a woman like that—" He stopped because he was talking to his mother.

"Well, I'd say Alicia is a good girl, a real good girl," his mama said. "She brings the baby by every Saturday for me to keep him all by myself while she's at work. She doesn't want to cut his hair, but I don't hold that against her because she doesn't have to bring him by, I know she doesn't."

This was the part T.C. hadn't wanted, the reason he'd told his mama not to come, and the reason he wanted to crawl under the steel bed in his cell when visiting hours approached.

"How's he doing?" he asked, because he couldn't not ask at this point and because he wanted to know, but he was afraid of what he would do with the information, how it would haunt him once his mother was gone, and it was just him and those four walls and all the time in the world to consider what might have been.

"Oh, he's good, real good, baby. Saying some words. *Mama* and—" She stopped. "I think I've even heard him say *MawMaw* once or twice. I want to bring him by, son. Alicia doesn't want to come herself, and that's her business, but she said I could bring Malik, and I want to. Maybe next time, for your birthday?"

"No, Mama, hell no," he shouted so she wouldn't bring it up again. "I can't have my son seeing me like this, thinking it's all right to go to jail."

"Oh, he's not going to even know what jail is." His mama lowered her voice as if she had been the one screaming. "He's a baby."

"Yeah, but that stuff sticks with lil' kids, and if he keeps coming, in a couple years, he'll be old enough to remember. I don't want him to ever think of me like that."

His mama just nodded. "I understand," she said. "I understand." She took her time saying the rest. "I just thought it would be good for him to see you. The thing is, I want him to know his father. Children don't need their parents to be perfect, they just need them to be there, they get so much from that, and I just, well, I always wished I had pushed your relationship with your father more. He wasn't perfect, but he was your father, and that was something. I just don't want to see Malik go through what you did."

Time was called on the session, and T.C. told her he would think about it, call her next week. But the thing was, there wasn't anything to think about. It was one thing to be in there, to know that he had gone back out of his own stupidity—that ate at him enough. But to see his best thing, the person he'd let down most thoroughly, witness what a fuckup he'd become, well that would have broken him, and he didn't think he'd be able to recover.

He told his mama as much when he called her on Saturday. "I just can't do it, Mama," he said. "It's only three years. I'll start fresh with him when I see him then."

"I understand," she repeated. "Say, Alicia's over here, just dropping him off. She wants to talk with you."

"Okay." His heartbeat was going. He hadn't had the nerve to call her since going in, and he thought that was a good thing. She deserved better than him, better than what he'd done, and what it had made out of all of them.

"Hey, T.C.," she said. She sounded all right too.

"Hey, Licia."

They didn't talk for a while; there was just something about the air between them, and when he went a long time without experiencing it, it commanded awe just to behold it.

"I don't know what to say," he said finally. "I'm so sorry, but I know that's not good enough."

"I know," she said. "I know." She sighed.

"You deserve better than this. You deserve better than me," he added.

"I know that too," she said. She paused. "And I'm going to get it. But our son, now that's a different story. Miss Jackie said you don't want to see him?" She paused, waiting for T.C. to answer, but he didn't know what to say.

Finally, he muttered, "I just don't want him to see me like that, Licia."

"Oh, I get it, I do, but don't do that, T.C. I mean, I hear what you're saying, but think about it, think about him, think about everything you went through not having a daddy."

"I didn't need that bastard."

"Oh? Well, I'm not saying he was a great man, but if he could have gotten it together for you and made you part of his life, I can't see how that would have been a bad thing. Maybe I deserve better, but there's no better our child could do than his own daddy."

She paused again. "Can you at least think about it for me, T.C.?"

He nodded before he spoke, he was too choked up. Then he croaked out a hacked-up *yes*.

"Good. Well, I gotta get going, but you doing all right?"

"Yeah, I'm all right, you know it's all relative."

She laughed. "Well, I'm glad. Miss Jackie says you look good. I hope you feeling that way too. I'm going to put her back on, okay?"

"All right. Alicia, you take care."

But she had already passed the phone.

He could hear Malik crying in the background, and his mama said she needed to tend to him. T.C. set the phone down, imagined seeing his son in the waiting area down the hall, staring across from him, or maybe T.C. would have a chance to hold him.

As the day approached, he got excited, dapping off every inmate he passed, retelling the birth story, bragging about how alert the baby had been even at a few months, how he had the same nose and eyes as his daddy, how he was already saying words, *Mama* and *MawMaw*.

Then a couple days before the visit, T.C.'s mood shifted without his consent. The thing was, he'd never thought he was good enough to father someone as perfect as his son, and then he'd gone and proven that by getting himself locked up. Now he had a constant, gnawing reminder of his own inadequacy, and that pain threatened to eat him alive. He almost called his mother to cancel the visit, but he remembered Licia, Licia who had been so patient and forgiving, who had asked only this one thing of him, who had thought it would be good for their child, and maybe she was right.

He gave one of the inmates his brownies so he'd twist his locks the morning of the visit. T.C. was glad for the activity. It plucked him out of the dread that would have consumed him; it distracted him from the image of his son lying against his jail clothes.

"What's the matter, Lewis? People are usually happy to go see their family," the white CO said as they walked.

"I am," he said. "Just nervous, that's all." He tried to smile but it didn't come out right.

When he got to the door, he saw his mother. She was leaning over to wipe Malik's mouth where he'd drooled. T.C. could still just back out, and she wouldn't even know he had seen them, but he wouldn't have his son thinking he'd been abandoned.

He walked over. She stood up to hug him, then when he sat down, she plopped Malik in his lap. The baby didn't cry the way T.C. expected him to.

"He goes to everybody, huh?" T.C. asked.

"Not really," she smiled. "But he's going to you."

T.C. didn't know what to say to him. Before, when he was on the outside, he'd just talk in baby talk, lift him up to the sky until he squealed, but he felt funny doing that here, now, unfit somehow.

His mama just talked like she did, and he used that time to examine his son. The baby seemed to be doing the same back.

Aunt Ruby had a new friend, a man in his fifties, and Mama had heard Aunt Ruby say she'd never known love until now. Maw-Maw wasn't looking good. Mama was thinking about bringing her up next time she came, if she was doing better. It would have been too much this time, with the baby too.

"Oh, but she did send you one of her jelly cakes. For your birthday. You should get it any day now. Make sure you call her and tell her you enjoyed it."

Malik started to fuss, and Jackie stood. "I got his bottle right here. They only let me bring in two." She handed it to T.C., and he popped the cap off and pushed the nipple into the baby's mouth. Malik leaned back as he rested, let his head fall into the crook of T.C.'s elbow. T.C. smoothed his palm over his son's thick eyebrows, marveled at his eyelashes, how much the baby looked like him, yet he was his own distinct being. T.C. bent down and kissed him.

When the baby finished eating, T.C. lifted him to his shoulder and burped him.

"Like riding a bicycle huh? You never forget," his mama asked.

T.C. laughed. "Naw, I guess not." T.C. kept him propped up there on his shoulder for a while, rubbing his back.

"Well, I need to get him back by four. That's when his mama gets off work," she said.

"Okay." T.C. sat the baby on his knees again. "Daddy will see you next time, lil' man. Daddy was so happy to see you. Daddy loves you, okay?" He handed him off, gripped his mama to him.

"Thanks, Ma," he said, "for everything."

Walking back to his cell was as hard as he feared it would be. As euphoric as he'd felt holding his son, the feeling had been dug out when he gave him back, compounded by his fear that bringing Malik to this hellhole even for a visit had somehow bound the kid to the place. No, he told himself. This life wasn't acceptable for his seed, and T.C. would do whatever he needed to do to ensure that.

He ducked into his cell, lay down on his bed, remembering the way his son had looked up at him, with so much innocence and trust. Malik didn't know who his daddy was yet. And T.C. supposed he didn't know who he was yet either. In his son's eyes he saw so many possibilities. Maybe Malik would know him to be a warrior, someone who turned the odds on their head. Maybe he would see him as just a good man, and, yeah, he'd made some mistakes, but he loved his family, he was there for his son. For a second, T.C. could see himself through the same lens. He bathed in that vision, let it wash over him, closed his eyes. The longer he dwelled inside it, the more he could imagine it being real.

Evelyn

Winter 1945

Seven months in, Evelyn wore a big coat, but she still thought Renard might walk right past her. She'd been at the station longer than she expected. The train was late pulling in, and she'd had to wait for the white passengers to disembark before she saw Renard hustle out of the baggage car and down the steps. When she caught sight of him, she called his name, softly at first, then when he didn't hear her, she stretched her voice past the point she was most comfortable. He turned toward her from where he'd already advanced near the station lobby, in his crisp and fitted uniform and his hat that made him seem like a different man altogether.

She forced herself to look at his eyes; his eyes were what would tell her how he really perceived her, thirty pounds heavier, breathing hard, leaning back and wobbling, with the weight of his child inside her. When she caught them, she thought she caught a glimpse of his soul too, that it was that which pressed his eyes against his sockets so hard it seemed as if they might break through.

He ran over to her. She didn't have time to move herself. When he reached her, she collapsed into his chest, clung to the sandy pocket flap on his uniform shirt. There was an assortment of smells, some from the station, some from his coat, some from him, all congregating to hide his main one, the smell she had been carrying in her mind of him. She burrowed her head through his clothes now that he was in front of her, searching for it, but it wouldn't be found.

"What's the matter with you, girl?" he asked, looking down at her shaking her head back and forth like a dog in a hole.

"I can't smell you."

"What?" He was smiling, but he moved his head a touch away from her.

"Different countries got different smells, baby," he said laughing.

"But you're not a different country. You're just yourself."

"Yeah, I'm still myself." He raised her head up as close to his as it would stretch and kissed her. He pressed her into him, then pushed her back.

"What's this?" he asked, eyeing her middle, putting the context together but not so certain he didn't need an explanation.

She just stared at him, objective and resolute. This was the moment when she would learn if her daddy had been right.

"You remember what we did last time you were here?" she asked.

"Do I remember? It's all I could think about back there." Then a smile spread slowly on his face.

"You serious, baby?" He opened her coat wider and squealed. "Baby, you serious?" he repeated. He tried to spin her around but stopped himself, then patted her belly with the flat palm of his hand.

He jumped up on the station platform. "Yes!" he shouted. People turned their heads, but he only repeated it. "Yes."

Evelyn still couldn't let herself believe his reaction.

"You mean it?" she asked. "You're happy? You're not upset?"

"Not upset? Baby this is what I always wanted, what I'd go to bed dreaming about since I was a boy, and for the woman to be carrying it to be you, well, that's more than I could have dreamed, that's more than I could have imagined deserving."

He marched her straight to her father's house with her hand cupped in his. When Mama said her daddy was out tending to a breached baby, Renard just waited, devoured every dish Mama offered, drank her tea, nibbled on her petit fours.

"I know you must be hungry being away all this time," Mama said. "What was the food like over there?"

"Slop," he said, "nothing like this."

She smiled. "Well, you're home now."

When her father came in, he didn't seem to sink at the sight of them; if anything, he just seemed resigned.

He changed clothes and washed his hands before he walked back out to the table.

Renard stood to greet him, and when he sat back down, Evelyn gripped her man's hands under the table. She could feel them shaking, and she expected his voice to shake too the way it did in those early days, but it came out like steel.

"I know you must be disappointed. You've done so well for yourself, and you expected your daughter to uphold the standard you set."

Her daddy didn't say anything, only nodded, but he kept his eyes on Renard's, and that was more than she'd seen him do in the last few months.

"Then we go and embarrass you further with this." He pointed to Evelyn's stomach.

"Don't go calling my baby an embarrassment," Mama snapped.

"It's not the baby, it's us, it's me, and I admit that. I admit that I might be disappointing. I've always wanted to be like you. From the day I was born I wanted to be a doctor. Unlucky goal for a Negro, but I wanted to sew people up, fix the problems that were wrong in their bodies, in their lives, and I still intend to do that. I do. My father was a janitor, and my schooling hasn't come easy to me. I work two jobs, and I still get help, but I'm not trying to complain. I'm trying to explain to you that I'm the type of man who will do anything to accomplish his goal."

Then he turned to Evelyn in front of Mama and Daddy, bent his left knee until it touched the floor. "I love you, Evelyn; one of the things I love most about you is that you're such a proud woman. It pains me that you had to walk around in this condition, and I haven't been able to do anything to help you. I vow to you, I vow to you, sir, ma'am"—he turned to her parents then—"I will never diminish that pride again." He leaned back into Evelyn, lifted her hand.

"If you will have me, Evelyn, I would be honored to be your husband, to serve you for the rest of your life, to spend the rest of my own life ensuring that you never feel shame."

Evelyn didn't allow herself to speak, not with her father there whose disdain she could sense from where she sat. Her tears started anyway, the heft of all those years of girlhood dreaming, these last months of yearning, culminating now on the verge of release.

Still she didn't say a word. She thought if she said the word *yes* in her father's presence it would doom her life and everything it yielded to a gloomy, stunted fate, so she clipped her great rush of emotion, and she nodded instead, wrapped her arms around Renard, and exhaled into his neck.

That was enough for Mama, who yelped, dabbing her eyes, but her father just sat looking at Renard as though he wanted to slap him but didn't have the energy.

Evelyn's father turned to her finally, gave a look of sad surrender, and said, "Okay." Then he stood, shook Renard's hand, picked up the sandwich Evelyn's mama had packed for his next round, and left the table.

When her father was gone, Evelyn let out a squeal she thought Miss Georgia might be privy to across the street. She let her tears stream out hard and fast, and when Renard stood up and spun Mama around, she cocked her head back and laughed and laughed.

When they were done celebrating, Renard asked Evelyn if he could take her to his own people's house to show her off, and she said nothing would make her happier. They rode the bus all the way to Amelia Street. She had never been to this part of town, and she was alarmed by the dust on the road, the narrow brown double houses, their old crumbling wood. Dozens of people crowded into them, standing on upper-level stoops looking down. Shoeless little boys danced outside to beats they made from pans and tin cans. Mules pulling garbage trucks passed with their pungent stench.

"It doesn't usually smell like this," Renard said.

"I know," she said, as if she hadn't been wondering the same.

There seemed to be as many people in Renard's daddy's house as there were in her own family's for a holiday, and everyone was overjoyed to see Renard in one piece. They said they had heard about her. They said she was too pretty for Renard. They kept lifting his uniform pants and tapping his legs to make sure they were real. They offered him liquor, they rubbed her belly, they said the baby was a boy, had to be because of how her round belly pointed out. They said Evelyn and Renard could both come and live with them if they needed. They said they'd watch the baby while the newlyweds were in school, and Evelyn couldn't remember being so happy.

That night when Evelyn and Renard walked back home, Renard pulled the picture he'd been keeping above his nightstand out of his pocket. It had one crease in it from where he'd folded it to fit his wallet but otherwise looked the same as it did when she'd given it to him at the train station nearly a year earlier.

"Seems like it was just yesterday that I gave it to you."

"Not to me," he said.

Evelyn wasn't ready to part from him when they reached her house, so they sat on the porch like they always had. They didn't talk for a while; she just held on to his jacket, and he rubbed her stomach with the fervor of a man who had to make up for lost time.

"Why didn't you write me about the baby?" he asked finally. "It might have given me more to look forward to."

Evelyn shrugged. "I didn't want to scare you off. I didn't know what your reaction would be, and I was scared I guess, scared you wouldn't have us."

Renard shook his head. "You know me better than that."

"Of course I do. I should have said something, but don't you see I was frightened? And war changes people. It sounds like it wasn't so bad for you, but I've heard terrible stories of people coming back fractions of themselves."

He nodded. "I understand. It doesn't matter. At least I know now. At least I can be with you now." He paused. "I didn't know what to expect going, and I certainly can't complain. I got to see another part of the world, and I'm back safe. But, well"—his stammer returned on both words, and Evelyn clutched his hand—"I didn't tell you about the worst of it."

She shook her head.

"We were stationed in a small town outside of Paris. There was a white unit next door, and they came by from time to time, shot off the word *nigger*, but otherwise kept to themselves. At first it wasn't much different than home really. The whites got their food on plates, while we got tin trays. We were served one meal, but whites had seconds. Whites lived in rooms with shiny floors and washing machines, and we had concrete and potbellied stoves."

"But like I said, that was nothing. I was used to that and would have been grateful to tolerate it. Only it didn't take long for it to escalate. One night there was a party and we were preparing to go; see, the French people had invited us, trying to show their appreciation toward us black servicemen. So they made up the passes for us, and I put them on the commanding officer's desk. When he saw them, he shook his head, tore them up, said there weren't going to be any Negro girls at that party and he didn't want his niggers dancing with any white women. I didn't want to go anyway," Renard pinched Evelyn's side. "Wasn't any dance partner I was seeking overseas, but some of my buddies, they went just to spite him. They were arrested that night."

"Then the next night, the white unit got drunk, walked over, tried to start trouble, throwing bottles at us, swinging ropes around our heads. I ignored it, but one of our men fired three shots in the air. I don't know where he got the pistol, but he told them we were all armed, and I've never seen white boys run as fast as they did then." Renard seemed as if he wanted to laugh but couldn't allow himself the levity.

"They didn't take too kindly to that treatment. They came back again the next night. There were more of them than there were us, and they all had guns. They beat the hell out of us, Evelyn. All of us, even the ones who didn't say a word. The French were so nice, so welcoming. You'd talk to them and forget you were Negro, but the other American soldiers beat us like they wanted to see us dead."

Evelyn was clutching his whole body now. "I'm so sorry," she said. "I'm so sorry," she repeated. "I didn't know. I'm so sorry. You didn't deserve that."

"No," he said with more authority than she'd ever heard come from him. "I reckon I didn't."

His demeanor changed after he told that story. His eyes darkened, he let go of her hand.

They stayed out there on the swing for a while, but neither said another word.

The next morning, Mama knocked on her door bright and early to discuss wedding preparations. Ruby sulked—she'd been testy since she got the news—but she followed Mama around with a notepad making lists of all they'd need.

"Of course we can't do it as big as we always imagined because of the, um, circumstances, but I still want you to celebrate. I think you deserve a celebration."

Mama sent fabric over to Miss Georgia's for the gowns, an off-white variation for Evelyn and a pink one for Ruby; Ruby went to the market for sugar and flour; Daddy bought ties, Brother raided the garden for flowers, and if Evelyn didn't know better, she would have sworn it was the same family from a year ago, preparing for Renard and Andrew to come over for dinner.

The night before the big day, Daddy called Evelyn and Renard to the table.

"I want to talk to you, son," he said. He seemed to stand straighter, and some of the light seemed to have reentered his eyes.

"Evelyn's mama and I have been talking, and we want to make things easier on you all. That's why I worked so hard, so my daughter would be able to sail through this life as much as a Negro woman can, and I reckon you deserve a little ease too; maybe you can finish school."

Mama slid her a key. "It's nothing," she said, "nothing, just a two-bedroom old shotgun house down the block where Miss Georgia's son used to live, but I thought it would be a perfect starter house for you two. Then, when Renard gets on his feet, well, you can have your dream house then."

After her father had retired to bed and Renard had gone home, Evelyn sat with Mama.

"What do you think it was?" Evelyn asked.

"What do I think what was, baby?"

"What do you think changed Daddy's mind?"

"Oh." She sat for a little while just thinking. "Hard to say with that man," she said finally. "Maybe it was the way Renard addressed him like a man first thing when he got back, or maybe he could see his family slipping away from him and this was his last chance to salvage it. I overheard Ruby talking to him the other day, so maybe that worked too. Maybe it was a combination of all those things. Lord knows it wasn't me. When it comes down to it, he loves you, Evie, and he just wants you to be happy."

Evelyn walked back into her bedroom. Ruby was lying down but not asleep. Evelyn sat on the edge of her sister's bed.

"Mama told me you talked to Daddy," Evelyn said.

Ruby shrugged. "He needs to realize how much he's hurting us, how much he's hurting you."

Evelyn pulled her up in a tight embrace. "Thank you, sister."

Her sister held her back for the first time Evelyn could remember. "Evelyn, it's the least I could do."

It was a simple wedding. Evelyn's gown wasn't what she imagined it would be, as it needed to accommodate the bump in her belly, but by the time Mama had unhooked the curlers and tightened the girdle, and Ruby had made up her face and positioned her crown, Evelyn couldn't stop looking at herself in the mirror. From a certain angle, she wouldn't have even known she was pregnant.

Still, it was a house ceremony instead of the lavish church affairs they were accustomed to, and they didn't invite many people, just Uncle Franklin and Aunt Katherine, Miss Georgia since she'd made the gowns. Mama made everything look nice the way she always did: Petunias and pansies hung from the stairwell, rose petals danced on the floor of the foyer, and the table was spread with the cake in the center, gorgeous, white swirls of frosting on top.

When it was time for Evelyn to walk down the foyer, her daddy met her at the doorway to her bedroom. His eyes lit up when he saw her, and she started to cry.

"You look beautiful," he said.

She had been so angry at him, so disappointed that he couldn't make room in his heart for her love. But today was different. And maybe it wasn't just him who had changed. Maybe it was thinking on having a child herself. She had hopes for her already. There was no question in her mind that the girl would be a doctor. By then, there might be other lady doctors, maybe even Negro lady ones. Wouldn't that be something? She understood now that was what her daddy had dreamed for her. He had a good life: Most Negro men they knew tipped their hats at him on the way to church; everybody called him sir, but she knew he'd wanted more for Evelyn, could hear it in the charged way he'd asked her what she was studying when she'd pore over her books at night.

"Oh, but, Daddy, is my makeup smeared from crying?" she asked.

"No, no, absolutely not." He shook his head. "You look beautiful," he repeated.

He gripped her hand as if he were the one who was nervous, and they walked on together.

She passed Mama, who dabbed at tears in her eyes with her embroidered handkerchief, and Ruby who beamed as if it were her own wedding day, but Evelyn couldn't quite trust it. She felt it was all too good to be true, everything she'd imagined coalescing in one solid reality, and she didn't know if she deserved it. Still, she told herself to make room for it anyway, to assume it should all be hers, to hold her hands out and embrace it.

Her father dropped her off with Renard.

"Take care of her," he said in a soft admonition, and Renard nodded.

All of a sudden, she wanted to reach backward, cling to the man who had been her most sturdy guide, but he was already joining Mama in the hallway, and she was left afloat with her man, yes, with her unborn child too, but weren't they all virtual strangers when she compared them to her family? What if she had mischosen? What if her father was right?

As if her daddy's consent triggered her own mistrust, she found herself staring at the leg of Renard's hem, which was still uneven if she looked closely, though it seemed someone had tried to mend it the night before.

And the hem began to represent the uncertainty of their new life, the question of whether Todd's would hire him back, if there would be enough money coming in for them both to return to school, what she'd do with a baby strapped to her breast.

"Renard and Evelyn, have you come here freely and without reservation to give yourselves to each other in marriage?"

Then Renard slid the ring on her finger, which was nothing like Mama's, but his eyes were so hopeful, so impossibly hopeful, his smile wide enough to wrap them both inside it.

And so when it was her turn to speak, she said *I do* because, her nerves aside, standing across from Renard on this day was everything she'd ever wanted. She let herself be swept up in his arms, though as big as she had become, it was uncomfortable to be held. The pressure of the ceremony behind her, she could feel the joy surging inside her. The sun streamed in through the glass panes on her front door and slanted across Renard's face, and she kissed the spots where the light landed as he carried her down the foyer. When he set her down, alone in her bedroom for the first time together, she squealed despite the people on the other side of the door listening because it was still so early in the morning, and their lives lay out uncharted before them, and the voice of ambivalence that had taunted her a minute before had gone.

Acknowledgments

I am eternally grateful to my parents, my first fans. You never stopped believing in me, and you never stopped convincing me to believe in myself. Daddy, you encouraged me to dream, and you made it possible for me to make my vision a reality. Mom, my creativity comes from you, and so does my courage.

Kathryn and Roy, you always made me feel like I was one of your own. Carlton and Betsy, your love and support mean the world to me.

The following books greatly influenced me and the writing of *A Kind of Freedom: Black Life in Old New Orleans* by Keith Weldon Medley; *Creole: The History and Legacy of Louisiana's Free People of Color*, edited by Sybil Kein; and *Witness to Change: From Jim Crow to Political Empowerment* by Sybil Haydel Morial.

To my editor, Jack Shoemaker—thank you for shepherding this book with such passion and care. I owe so much to Jane Vandenburgh who treated me like an author before I was one. To my agent, Michael Carlisle, thank you for your unwavering dedication.

To my early readers: Jennifer Levitt and Johanna Thomas, the world would be a better place if everyone had friends like you. Jessica Redditt, Megan Nicholson, Pat Connelly, Nancy Lai, Chloe Pinkerton, Cary Fortin, Iris Tate: I know it is awkward work reading an unfinished manuscript, and I appreciate you for doing it anyway. Kerry Radcliffe and Kathryn Goldberg, your feedback was indispensable. Joseph V. Blouin, Joseph M. Blouin, Zara Blouin, and Raymond Williams, thank you for spending hours with me sharing stories about the city you love. Nubia Solomon, you help me do life.

Special thanks to my village: Josie Wilkerson, Debhora Singleton, Patsy Wilkerson, Felthus Wilkerson Jr., Kevin Williams, Bruce Williams, Oran Williams, Cynthia Williams, Felicia Johnson, Buck Johnson, Roy Williams Smith III, Joseph Sexton, and Abbye Simkowitz. Florence Wilkerson, Felthus Wilkerson, and Audrey Chapital Williams—I know you are celebrating too.

Nina, Carter and Miles, you are my greatest blessings.

And my Chuckie, without you none of this would be possible. You were a tireless editor and supporter, and your faith was tireless too.